A Place Without A Postcard

Written and Illustrated by Christopher Crockett

Edited by Justin Nordstrom
Cover Design: Christopher Crockett
Author Photo: Sam Otero

Library of Congress Cataloging-In-Publications Data

Crockett, Christopher
A Place Without A Postcard / Christopher Crockett
ISBN 979-8-9855502-5-2
Library of Congress Control Number: 2023901900
First Edition
1.Mystery with Cats 2.Suspense 3.Fiction – Cats - Mystery

Dedicated to my parents
Ron and Jimmie

A Note from The Author…
This is a cat novel, but probably not the one you were expecting. For this story, all of the characters are cats. Anthropomorphic walking, talking cats who wear clothes and drive cars, go to work and have dreams of better lives. Their world is a mirror to our own, with only a few minor differences such as name changes and somewhat ambiguous geography to mask my relative ignorance of the setting. The only major difference is the complete lack of glorified apes, replaced with beings evolved from superior life forms.

VIOLET WINTERHAVEN

JOE ANTONOV

LIZZIE CAHILL

BLACKIE LAWLER

CONSTANTINO GANDINI

As I walked on a Monday morning near the end of November, the air was cool and crisp. A few thin and wispy clouds traced their way across a quiet sunny sky. The sidewalk bustled with cats on their way to work, while cars plied the crowded streets. Such was a normal weekday in New Amsterdam. Everyone had somewhere to be.

I arrived at my building and took one last look around as I pulled the door and walked inside. I was, as usual, alone. The lobby, dusty and quiet, had been constructed with a desk for an attendant, but one had not been present since well before I located my office here. The walls were dull, the carpets old and in places, threadbare. Still, the older building was in good order and the rent reasonable, so I was satisfied. I walked to the grand staircase at the side of the old lobby and climbed until I reached the second floor, then walked down the hall past closed doors of wood and glass, some with painted titles, others bare. A series of hanging lights illuminated the hall. These, combined with the light shining through the frosted glass in the doors made the hallway surprisingly bright. I could hear a typewriter click-clacking away as I walked by, the fingers that worked it owned by a modestly successful journalist I had only met in passing. From somewhere ahead of me, a soft news broadcast filtered through. I reached my suite and opened the door, then walked inside and hung my hat on the stand. The lights were already on.

"Good morning, Max," the voice at the desk behind me said. As usual, Violet had arrived before me. Since hiring her, she made a point to always arrive early. "I went ahead and filed the Shaw case since you closed it out a couple of days ago. I don't think he got the result he wanted, and I don't think he's coming back."

I nodded once in agreement. Mr. Shaw had hired me to gather some information about his fiancée, but in doing so I uncovered some rather questionable secrets about him as well. When I asked him about his past to gain some insight as to his present situation, he had stormed out of my office and skipped town. No one had seen him since. My policy has long been payment up front, and in this case, it had proven to be a smart decision.

Violet continued. "We don't have any appointments today. Actually, we don't have anything for the rest of the week either. The pre-December slowdown has officially begun. If you like I can keep organizing some of your older files or clean out some of the redundancies in the cabinets."

After giving her some brief instructions, I thought to myself how odd it really was that she should even be here. It wasn't the first time I had thought this. Violet Winterhaven came from one of New Amsterdam's wealthiest families and was smart enough that she could excel at anything she set her mind to. But instead of sharing drinks with captains of industry, she worked for me in a moderately run-down building in a working-class neighborhood. She was always cheerful and helpful, but the mystery remained. When I had asked her why she chose to work here, she just laughed and said that she enjoyed figuring out a mystery. Though my instincts told me that this answer was only the tip of a deeper iceberg, I had never pressed the issue further. Perhaps in time she would reveal herself and her motivations, perhaps not, but the truth was that she was very good at what she did and I had no desire to talk her into leaving for something better.

Outside my office, the percolator, that working man's holiest of holies, had worked its divine magic and I poured a cup of glorious, caffeinated elixir. Not for the first time, I thought that whoever invented the glorious machine should be showered with reward in this life, and in at least a few others as well. With my mug now full, I took a few steps into my office and lightly tossed the newspapers I was carrying onto the desk, from which a thin cloud emanated. I chuckled to myself; I didn't trust the building's custodians not to snoop around, so my office was perpetually veiled in a thin layer of dust. I removed my coat, a dull black trench with a button missing from the sleeve and a couple of obvious scars from use and crude homemade repair. I liked this coat, even though Violet sometimes chided me to find a new one. I liked to repair that which could still work, even if this often left it a little wanting for looks. Two wooden hangers graced a faded brass stand, and after slipping the trench on one, I removed my suit jacket and hung it on the other. At least Violet couldn't fuss about wrinkles. Lastly, I took off my fedora, giving my ears a chance to breathe, then placed it on a projecting hook on the stand.

I took a seat at my desk, leaned back into the old burgundy leather and closed my eyes. Then I stretched, took in a deep breath, twitched my whiskers and rested my arms on the chair's sides with paws just overhanging the edge of the rests. This was part of my morning ritual. The chair was something of a relic, hand made in Turin many years ago if one went by the hand-written cloth tag sewn underneath. It was very comfortable and had obviously been crafted by furniture artisans who knew what they were doing. The building's landlord had been emptying out one of the vacant suites and asked me if I'd be interested. Five dollars exchanged hands and the old chair was mine. After applying a little conditioner to the leather and performing some spot-sanding and staining to the base, the chair looked surprisingly good. It had taken station behind my desk forthwith and had been there ever since. I always sat and took a few deep breaths to clear my head, remaining motionless and silent for a minute or two before moving on to the work of the day.

When I opened my eyes, I saw Violet looking at me through the wall with an amused smirk. My office was unusual in that the upper two-thirds of the inner walls were glass. Fifty or sixty-odd years before the architect had designed the interior offices this way to allow more natural light into the interiors of the suites, and originally, they had been frosted for privacy. In my office, three of the panes were replaced with clear glass, with the rest missing

3

entirely. Although rods graced the tops of the windows, they had remained entirely bereft of curtains since my arrival. My office door remained open, allowing Violet and I to move and converse freely throughout the suite.

With a shake of her head and a slight smile, Violet turned back to the important work of painting her claws a deep shade of crimson, which she had informed me was fall's hottest color. I took a sip of my morning coffee and picked up the top paper, scanned the headlines and read the first few paragraphs of the stories. There had been a shooting in Little Italy, thought to be perpetrated by ne'er-do-well ruffians or small-time street gangs. The police had their hands full as violent crime had been undergoing a renaissance of sorts since the end of the War. In this latest shooting, two cats had been gunned down in an alley by a lone shooter with a machine gun. Possibly a Thompson, witnesses said, but they were too busy scattering for cover when the shooting started to get a good look. No one really knew anything, and the gunman escaped in a waiting car, the best description of which was 'Black'. The police were asking for any good citizen with knowledge to step forward. Fat chance of that. Ordinary felines had learned a long time ago that keeping one's head down and minding one's own business was an excellent way to remain safely above-ground.

Most of the rest of the paper was minor stories. A fishing boat tied at its berth caught fire below decks and burned to the waterline. No injuries were reported, but the boat was estimated to be a total loss. Three bar patrons in Haarlem were arrested after a fight had spilled outside, and when an officer tried to break it up, he received a broken nose for his trouble. The perps were admitted to the hospital with various bodily injuries after his partner introduced them to his nightstick. Two cars had opted for the same real estate and collided in a busy intersection in Queens, tying up traffic for a little while. The Giants had scored a come-from-behind 28-14 win against the Boston Yanks by scoring three touchdowns and conversions in the second quarter and another in the third after going down 0-14 in the first. It was just another day in the big city I called home.

When I arrived at page six, I saw a small story, tucked neatly under the fold, that got my attention. I called out. "Violet, did you read where there may be another tuna shortage soon? Apparently, those in the know are predicting it based on existing supplies. This is, what, the third or fourth time in two years?"

Violet came in the office and sat on the sofa to the right of my desk. "I think it's more than that, Max," she said. "Regardless, these shortages are really a problem. What's really scaring me is that this one is predicted to hit home in a week or two, right when the cold really sets in. The prices are going to spike when people are already spending more on heating fuel, and some people won't be able to afford it. As it is, some cats are just getting by, and if they can't afford heat or food, they'll be in bad shape. It will affect other fish too. If people don't have access to tuna, then other fish will start to rise in price and become scarce too, like those wretched things you eat out of those insipid little tins."

I gave her a wry smile and pulled out a tin of sardines from my desk. "You mean these, right?" I said as she rolled her eyes and wrinkled her nose. I put the tin back with a couple of its closest friends and shut the drawer, then leaned forward and placed my arms on the desk. "Violet, I've been thinking about these shortages and how they keep happening. They keep happening every four months or so, like a recurring pattern. I don't think these shortages are natural. Someone is causing them. I'm convinced of it, and I can't be the only one who thinks this. Every time the shortages have gone away for a few months or so, they come right back and push the prices sky high all over again. The experts are questioning if it's depleted stocks while the fishermen say it's not.

I've heard some things that make me question if these so-called experts are on the take, because the captains are all saying the

5

same thing, that the fish stocks are healthy and the catches are good. It's strange though, the captains and the fishermen aren't saying this out loud, only to people they trust. The only reason I've even heard anything is because Russian Joe told me. He wouldn't divulge his sources, but I'm sure it's the fishing captains. He has some friends out in the fleet. Something is going on and not much is being done about it. I'm beginning to think that this something may warrant a look to see if certain things are all above board. I don't know what it is, but something is definitely wrong here."

Violet and I spent the next few hours brainstorming our approach to the tuna shortage. Work had been slowing down recently with the oncoming holidays and with nothing on our docket, we bounced ideas off each other. We decided early on that I should take a walk later to Russian Joe's Bar to see if the ex-seaman bartender might have anything to help us. Beyond that, we decided that too many variables might throw a wrench into any fixed plans and settled on a wait-and-see approach. It didn't seem like a particularly inspired start and by lunch I had sent Violet home for the day.

Now alone, I gazed around the office. Aside from the two desks, a few filing cabinets and an old wardrobe, it was sparse. A picture hung near Violet's desk, a generic print for clients to ignore, and of course the percolator outside my office. Two well-used chairs sat inside the front door, while two more sat forlornly in front of my desk. Aside from my Italian leather chair, the only other concession to comfort was an old pinstriped green sofa to the right of my desk. From years of experience, I knew that I could lay on it and gaze out the windows to the adjacent buildings and the sky above. Overall, the office was worn and mostly bare yet comfortable, a place in which I could relax when I needed to. This allowed my mind to unwind and wander, this to allow the information, evidence and clues to my cases swim unhindered through the recesses of my consciousness, there to mingle and collide. In this way, I was able to connect seemingly unrelated bits of information into workable theories, often without conscious thought.

These seemingly random connections often sparked the elusive lynchpin clue which allowed me to tie everything together and solve whatever inscrutable mystery lay before me.

Having spent the past few hours trying to pound square pegs into round holes with Violet, my mind was spent. I suspected that a few other shapes, triangles and pentagons, perhaps even an errant parallelogram, had obstructed our attempts at peg-pounding, but the end result was that I needed to clear my mind for a while. I thought that time spent studying the insides of my eyelids would surely do some good, especially as I was to meet with Russian Joe Antonov later that evening. If nothing else, a nice catnap would recharge my increasingly depleted inner batteries. I unbuttoned my vest and hung it over my jacket, then walked to the closer window and opened it slightly. The late November chill mixed with the baseboard heat to create a space neither too warm nor too cold, but cool and crisp. It was the perfect environment for one of my favorite things: sleep. From the bottom drawer of the file cabinet, I retrieved an old green Army blanket and walked over to the couch. After removing my shoes, I flipped my legs onto the sofa and covered myself with the blanket. As my head rested against the old pillow, I closed my eyes and felt at peace as my paws gently kneaded at the olive cover. Within minutes, I had fallen into the blissful unconsciousness of undisturbed sleep.

2

When I opened my eyes, the hazy diffused sunlight of midday had transitioned into the waning light of a fading sunset. The short nap I had anticipated had somehow grown into several hours. This sofa had that effect more often than I cared to admit. My office was cooler but not yet cold, and as I sat up and stretched, I took in this quiet corner of the world. In the rapidly dimming light streaming through the windows, the office took on the appearance of an old photograph, worn around the edges and somewhat yellowed in appearance. Violet enjoyed teasing me about it, claiming the aura of my office, if such a plain and nondescript enclosure could possess an aura, was so bleak and dry that only the olive was missing. I, however, found it comfortable, a working space devoid of excess personal touch. In truth, it lacked personal touches entirely. I chuckled to myself, inwardly laughing at my overactive imagination that supplied all the personal touches internally, where no one else could see them.

I stood and closed the window, retrieved my vest, then sat down on the old sofa. As I laced my shoes and buttoned my vest, I casually wondered what, if anything, I might learn regarding the impending tuna shortage. I quickly folded the old blanket and placed it back in the cabinet, then grabbed my jacket and coat. I took my hat from the rack, then closed and locked the door. I took the stairs and left out the front of the building, nodding to the nonexistent attendant before walking out the door. The air was chilly and somewhat damp, a portent of rainy weather, but my destination lay only a few blocks away. The streets hummed with end of day traffic, while the sidewalks held cats heading home after a day at work. No one paid much attention to me, lost as I was in my thoughts, and the short walk would prove brisk and uneventful.

As I made my way, I passed through one of the working-class neighborhoods that made up this part of New Amsterdam. Mixed use buildings, two or three stories tall, businesses at ground level and residential apartments above, lined both sides of the streets. Cars sat motionless by the curbs, though most cats generally walked, took the subways or paid for a ride. Like the block where my office was situated, the streets were quiet, though a few cats were still out, finishing up business for the day. Beneath one streetlight, three teenage kittens swapped exaggerated stories and laughed among themselves, paying me little mind as I walked by. Some cars, not many, plied the streets, mostly pre-war designs with only a few new models in their midst. Apartment flats housed regular toms and queens making their way in the world.

After the War, things had been a bit difficult with so many young and able cats coming back from across the water, but the jobs soon came and with them, a bit of prosperity and a sense of optimism. But previous tuna shortages had already put a strain on families city wide, and with this one predicted as the worst shortage yet, the financial strain could well push a lot of these cats into a freefall. I wasn't always a particularly brave person, and by 'wasn't always' I meant seldom. I preferred to work in the background, putting pieces together to form a picture for others to act upon. As of yet, it seemed, no one was actively trying to find a solution to these shortages. Tonight marked the beginning of my quest to unravel this mystery and bring the tuna shortages to a halt. I inhaled deeply, letting the neighborhood smells come to rest in my nose, feeling shivers of excitement in my muscles. Little did I know that tonight would set in motion events that would soon move well beyond me and come to the edge of spiraling out of control.

After walking a few blocks, I turned a corner and walked a block down an intersecting street. As I came to the next corner, Russian Joe's Milk Bar lay diagonally across the intersection. Though set in a corner lot, the outside of the establishment wasn't particularly attention-grabbing, or even interesting. It appeared as what it was, just another neighborhood bar, one of many throughout

New Amsterdam. The interior was equally plain, with heavy, dated furnishings on a worn hardwood floor, livened only by four exquisite nautical paintings which seemed both oddly out of place yet right at home. The lighting was a comfortable dim in which conversations seemed more private, and the clientele mostly comprised the local gentry, regulars who came for a drink or two and familiar conversation. Though usually a quiet lot, sometimes they could get rowdy if something inappropriate were said. But occasionally, people from all over would patronize the bar, people who often had secrets to share, secrets that could be had over a cold glass of milk for a song. Such activity made the bar interesting, for a surprising amount of information passed through this nondescript place. This was why I came that night, to see if anything about the shortages had come through, for behind the bar stood the cat I was hoping to see.

As I walked inside, I saw him. Iosef Dmitrievich Antonov stood behind the bar, drying glasses in his large paws. He was a Russian-born farmer turned ocean-faring citizen of the world and erstwhile milk connoisseur, among other things. Though he kept the demeanor of a quiet and modest man, he was far more than whom he appeared on the surface. And if one knew what to look for, one soon found that the big blue-gray cat with the notch in his ear and the deliberate movements of later middle age was a veritable gold mine of useful information. His gold eyes blazed bright, reflecting both the intelligence of a lifetime spent on the sea and the shrewd intellect of someone who could put together the myriad pieces of information he heard into a coherent picture of the world. It was Joe whom I came to see, to sip a cold glass of milk and listen as he told a tale of his adventurous youth, sometimes of his time in the Merchant Marines, sometimes as a citizen trader, occasionally as an immigrant to a bustling city where he would come to make his way. Every tale was different, exotic and evocative, every story woven like a fine tapestry, but in the end, Joe had an uncanny way to turn life into parable, and to make his own experiences hold the answer to the vexing question posed in the first place.

The interior was familiarly dim, the shadows seeming to conceal the murmurs of the evening clientele. No matter the hour, the Milk Bar always looked the same, cozy, dark and slightly run down in a comfortable sort of way. Joe would open the place at four and work the bar from then until closing, whenever that would be that night, pouring his milk and engaging in conversation. His large frame could usually be found behind the bar, pouring drinks, drying glasses and engaging in healthy conversation. He saw me and waved, then moved to his taps to pour me a milk. No one ever came into Russian Joe's and didn't have a milk. Very few ever left after drinking just one. Joe and I had our routine. He'd see me in the evening and knew I was probably on a case. A light milk to sip over some useful conversation that might help in solving a case. Sometimes I was certain that Joe had more information than he was sharing, but he was a valuable source and a good friend, so I let it slide.

"How are you today, Max?" The big Russian Blue spoke with a trace of a Ural accent as he set a milk before me, offering his large right paw for a shake. "Is the beautiful Miss Violet keeping you in line or has she come to her senses and moved on to better things?"

I smiled; having met Violet numerous times, Joe's friendly affinity for the young heiress was apparent. "I don't know why she keeps coming back, Joe, but as of a few hours ago she was still holding down the front desk, keeping her claws sharp and freshly painted." Her continued presence was a question that vexed both of us, and one we had pondered together on more than one occasion. But today I needed his help, so I got to it.

"Joe, I read that another tuna shortage may be coming. If it's made the papers, my guess is that the threat is real. But the thing is, the more I think about these tuna shortages, the more I think there's something that's just not right about these repeated occurrences. I think that something must be going on behind the scenes. It's the

11

timing that's been bothering me; every time one shortage happens things gets tight because the prices go up, and it takes a few months for it all to settle back to normal. But every time the market is about back to normal, another shortage happens, one after the other. These shortages aren't happening in any other cities like Boston, Philly or DC, just New Amsterdam. Seems like it's being manipulated here somehow, and if that's true, someone's making money hand over paw off these things. Violet and I talked about this today, and we think that because business is slow right now, we're going to look into it."

"I've been thinking the same thing, Max," said Joe, his twinkling eyes shining bright. "I sailed on a merchant steamer called the *Calico Lady* just after the Great War. She was a beauty, an elegant freighter that sailed across the Pacific, calling in at ports all over. We were making our way from Port Moresby to Hong Kong with a cargo of exotic lumbers, but when we put to port and took leave of the ship, we quickly realized that something was amiss. The local fare there is rice, they use it in almost everything, but on this particular visit there was scarcely any to be found. What it meant for us was that we were spending several times what we normally would just to feed ourselves, but for the local populace, particularly the poor, it was proving a struggle just to survive. Those cats were hungry, real hungry, and they were almost delirious with anger. The situation had almost reached a critical phase, with gangs of starving locals attacking any foreigner they saw. Made for a short and real unpleasant stay. We found out later that a local crime syndicate was hoarding and storing rice in order to drive up the prices, and when the prices hit a certain amount, they would start releasing rice back into the marketplace in small quantities, then when the prices dropped a certain amount, they would just cut off the supply and drive them back up again. Made me glad to be on the open water heading for anywhere but there."

Joe slowly blinked and fixed his gold eyes on me. "I wonder

if the same thing's happening here. Thankfully, the fish I serve don't make up more than just a small portion of the overall fare to keep this place afloat, but tuna makes up the biggest part of that, and I've had to raise the tuna prices just to break even when I restock. I had hoped that someone out there in this cold, cold city would take it into their hearts and figure out what is going on."

"It's funny you mention that, Joe." I took a drink from the cold glass of milk that I had not quite forgotten. "I was thinking of heading down to the docks, maybe talk to a boat captain or two to see if they knew any reason why the prices have gone up. The problem is, most of those cats won't talk to me, either because I'm a landlubber or they think I smack too close to the law, or maybe both. Either way, if I'm *cattus non gratus*, I won't have an easy start of it. But if I can get someone to talk, he or she could help point me in the right direction."

Joe put his hand to his chin and looked at the ceiling for a minute. "I can give you the names of two captains I know. They can be a little rough around the edges, so when you go to talk to them, carry your hat in your hand, metaphorically at least but physically probably wouldn't hurt too. I'll tell them you're coming and will vouch for you. And lastly, bring your sea legs, Max. You might need them." With that, Joe bid me adieu to tend to his herd of thirsty barflies.

As I sat, I thought about the coming day, meeting with the sea captains. Meeting with this superstitious and occasionally surly lot was definitely not my idea of a good time. Nor was the thought of heading out to the deep blue sea on a boat. Like most cats, I maintain a healthy respect, if not an outright fear, of boats and water. The thought of plying the seas seemed not only unnatural, but completely foolhardy. Yet if I were to get a foothold on this case, talking to them and taking to the high seas like some misplaced buccaneer might well be the price I had to pay.

I lingered at the bar for a little while, engaging in small talk with a graphic artist and a tow truck driver. In the back of my mind, though, I was thinking about what Russian Joe had said. In hypothesizing that the tuna shortages were deliberate and that someone was profiting off the price hikes, his thinking mirrored my own suspicions. In correlating the present situation to something that he had encountered before; he made the certainty of it that much more likely in my own mind. A mystery was afoot, and Violet and I had tasked ourselves with solving it. I was certain that the first piece of this mystery lay at the docks, among the boats and the tough captains who ran them. After our exchange, Joe had given me the names of two captains of his acquaintance, and he gifted me some crucial information to give to each when I spoke to them that would let them know that I was who I said I was.

I ordered another working day milk and made sure to leave a bit extra on the final tab before I left. Joe had taken the liberty of calling me a taxi, as between the *leche* and the thoughts in my head, I was beginning to feel a bit tipsy. By the time I stepped out the door, the hour was getting late. While I had found a couple hours sanctuary from the day, thick and ominous clouds had settled over the buildings, their ethereal forms dimly reflected in the glow of the streetlights. A cold north wind had begun to blow, lonely and balefully from higher latitudes. I pulled the collar on my trench coat up and cinched the belt around my waist, and within a few minutes the yellow car arrived to take me home. As I sat down on the back seat, relishing the dim as the dome light went off, I knew that tomorrow would prove an interesting day. What I didn't know was whether it would be a good interesting or the kind of interesting I might rather forget.

14

3

I awoke the next day on the sofa in my apartment after an uneventful night's sleep. Though my mind fruitlessly clung to the fragments of a dream, the memory of it was already fading, and within a couple of minutes it had passed from memory altogether. The radio was playing Count Basie, which meant I had fallen asleep listening to it. Sometimes when my mind would ponder the day's events, the music would keep me grounded, the radio dial's yellow backlit glow providing a warm light on which to focus on dark and clouded nights. I stood and stretched, then walked over and turned the volume up slightly, letting the jazz wash over me like a river of sound.

I walked to the kitchen nook of my apartment and pulled down a pan, then retrieved two eggs from the small refrigerator. After two cracks and a few minutes on the stove, a pair of fried eggs awaited me. Though it wasn't an elegant breakfast, it would do for what might prove a long and frustrating day ahead. After washing and replacing my culinary supplies, I walked into my bedroom and opened the armoire to select my clothes for the day. I took a moment to marvel at the piece; built during the waning years of the French Rococo style, it was large, heavy and intricately carved. It was a thing of beauty, made by hand for the elites of Parisian society, yet incongruously filling space in a modest apartment flat, sharing it with plebian ware and a base commoner. I had spent a small fortune to purchase it, and that was after the seller reduced the price because I had done some work for him. It was as out of place here as an exotic parrot in the Scandinavian fjords, but I liked nice things. It also held my suits, from which I picked one to wear.

Once dressed, I called for a taxi, donned my coat, gloves and hat and stepped out the door into the hallway, and from there to the staircase and out into the lobby. As I made my way out the front door, I took a glance at the morning sky. The heavy clouds from the night before remained, dull gray and low in the chilly air, still with the ominous portent of rain that had yet to fall. Their swollen appearance meant that such precipitation was only a matter of time. I suppressed an involuntary shiver and pulled my overcoat tighter about me. I would not be heading to the office this morning, but rather to the docks to meet with the contacts Joe had recommended. I thought to myself that sea captains could sometimes be a salty bunch, distrustful of outsiders and occasionally physically hostile. I hoped that Joe had already contacted them, as a private detective showing up and asking questions might not be particularly welcome. A minute later, I spied a yellow Plymouth rounding the corner before coming to a stop. I opened the door and sat inside and tried to lose myself in my thoughts as the car took me to the harbor.

The cab ride was uneventful, and after a quiet ride, I arrived at the waterfront. Ships of all sizes sat anchored, some offloading cargo recently arrived, others taking on merchandise bound for distant ports of call. The docks were a steady hive of activity, busy round the clock. As I walked slowly toward the fishing fleet, I remembered previous visits. Today's faces were different, but the expressions they wore remained the same. Their looks were etched with grim lines carved by years of hard living mixed with the fatalistic acceptance that their nine lives could end at any moment, often violently and sometimes with no physical remains for the survivors to mourn. The sea remained almost as hostile as the mountains of the moon, and in some ways just as remote. It took a special breed of cat to sail its waters, and an even more elite type to fall in love with the nautical way of life. Most of the gazes that I encountered were of those whose veins ran with salt water, and though they were a curiosity even in the city proper, these sea cats kept community here in the docks and out on the open ocean. They lived by their own code, wrote their own rules, and took no interference from outsiders. I felt distinctly out of place and knew that diligence was a must, lest trouble come to find me in short order.

Russian Joe had guided me toward two fishing captains with whom he had conducted business through the years and who, he assured me, could be of use to my investigation if I could convince them to speak to me. This convincing had constituted the main purpose of my visit to the Milk Bar. Joe's own background as a seafaring crewmember and commander still resonated here with the people who knew him and sailed with him during his younger days. I had hoped that he might offer me something with which I could convince them to open their world to me for the good of New Amsterdam.

In addition to two names, I was given a single fact about each captain with which to prove the validity of my character by the company I kept. True to form, Joe never just gave anything away; if I were to gain the trust of his contacts, I would have to earn it. It was nothing personal, and I never took it as such, for with Joe any potential rewards must first be earned. He had lived an often-difficult life, but one full of tales and experiences that made him the stuff of legend. He could be a hard man to come to terms with at times, and seldom tolerated rudeness or ignorance. Because of this, among other things, he had earned my admiration. As for any facts I might glean from this outing, I suspected they might prove a bounty and was grateful for the old mariner for his assistance. These facts turned out to be extremely useful, for the information gained became the first tangible proof that something bigger was afoot.

I found my first contact on his boat, and the welcome I received proved every bit as cold as I had been told to expect. Russian Joe had warned me that Captain John Ryder did not suffer fools lightly, nor did he take kindly to outsiders poking into his business. I dared not lie to the cat as I was already intruding on his turf, and I made sure to be polite and very careful.

"Captain Ryder, my name is Max Persian and I'm a private detective. I'm investigating the tuna shortages to see what might be causing them. A mutual acquaintance gave me your name and I was hoping to speak to you to learn more about the fishing out of New Amsterdam." I stood on the dock beside his boat, and slowly removed my fedora in what I hoped would be seen as a gesture of humility and respect.

On the stern of his boat, wearing a waterproof coat, pants, boots and topped with a yellow Sou'wester fishing hat, Captain Ryder eyed me warily. "I don't usually have much to say to outsiders. Normally, Persian, I'd tell you to take a walk, but since you say a 'mutual acquaintance' sent you to me, I'd like to know why. Then you'll have to give me a reason to trust you. It had better be good." He placed his thick paws on the railing, claws slightly out, and leaned his stocky frame toward me. He then said, coldly, "So, impress me."

I took a breath, knowing that the next few seconds would determine whether I could gain his trust. All I could do was press on. "I'm a friend of Joe Antonov. His milk bar is a few blocks from my office, and I go there whenever I need something to drink or to discuss some information. Yesterday I told him I was hoping to talk to some fishing captains, and since he had a background on the water, I was hoping he could help." I paused. "He gave me your name, not much else, but gave me a piece of information to prove I knew him. Something very few people would know."

I took a breath and continued. "The name of your boat is the *Lady Messina*, but most people don't know the origin of the name. It relates to your early career, from when you worked a Mediterranean freighter hauling oranges from Sicily to Marseilles in the spring. In your second year while docked in Messina, you met a lady named Helena de Cericho. She was the daughter of one of the local grove owners, and in short order you became infatuated with her. When the freighter departed, you chose to stay behind with her, ready to give up the sea to be with her. You were engaged, but before you could marry, she perished in a fire. When you recovered your wits about you, you boarded the first ship you found, another freighter, bound

18

for the Black Sea to offload machine parts and take on iron ore in Sevastopol. You kept to yourself, miserable and angry, but one of the other sailors took you under his wing anyway. That sailor was Joe Antonov, and because of him you stayed on the sea. When you settled down, you followed Joe to New Amsterdam and bought this boat with your earnings. You named her *Lady Messina* to honor Miss Helena."

As I finished, I could see Captain Ryder's dark amber eyes, blazing, hard and unforgiving. His claws were fully protracted now, biting into the wooden railing, and his posture was taut and stiff, as if readying himself to leap down to tear me in half. But then I saw him tilt his head back slightly, close his eyes and relax his posture. He took a single deep breath and brought his eyes back to look at me. This time the blazing anger was gone, replaced with what I can only surmise was the memory of eternal sorrow. Though the large cat no longer looked like he would rip my arms off at the shoulders, he still outsized me by a good margin and had the strong physique of someone who worked hard, every day, to make a living. I wasn't sure what he would do next, but then he offered his paw to me, telling me to climb aboard, that he had something he wanted to show and tell me. I took Captain Ryder's paw, stepped across the low rail and onto the deck, hopefully to discover my first clue.

"Welcome aboard the *Lady Messina*, Mister Persian." I noticed the change in how he addressed me right away and countered with a change of my own.

"Please call me Max. I've never been entirely comfortable with being called 'Mister'. I guess I've never really embraced formalities."

He nodded. "In that case, call me Turk. It's been my *nom de guerre* since I was young. Since before I ever met Helena. She never liked the nickname, always called me John, but pronounced it almost as two syllables, *Gi-an*. It was beautiful how she said it, like the name was something special. It became very special to me." He closed his amber eyes again, lowering his head. "When she died, I abandoned the name John; I just wanted to be alone in the world and I never wanted to hear that name again. Now the name belongs only to her. It's something that only she can have, something that I gave freely to her and her alone, in life and forever in death." He shook his head slowly, as if weighed down with sorrow. "There are very few felines left in my world who know that, Max. I thought my little secret would die with Joe, but now I've revealed it to you too." He shrugged sadly. "Perhaps you have an honest face."

He opened his eyes and fixed them on my own. "The history that Joe told you was correct in every respect except for one. Helena was my second love. My first was the sea. I had wanted to sail across its blue waters since I was small. I had set out on a few ships before, and when I met her, I had a couple of years' experience on the large ships. I loved the sea, loved life on the water. And yet for Helena I would have given the open seas up, without hesitation. I could have lived in Messina with her and watched the ships come in, wondering where they came from and where they were going, maybe talking to the crews who kept them plying the seas. I would have happily left the water for a life with her. But when she died, I had nothing left, nothing but the blue ocean to return to. Her family was always very kind to me, always accepted me for the sea cat I was. They asked me to stay and work in the family business, that they loved me as a son and that I could be a great help in negotiating with the ship captains. In a different life I would have stayed, but with Helena gone I knew there wasn't enough for me in Messina anymore. All I could do was bid her family goodbye and go back to the sea. I didn't even look back at them as I left, it was too painful because I kept seeing her in each of their faces. All I wanted was to walk away, far away and just vanish like a ghost. So, I went to the only other place I knew. I walked to the harbor and talked my way onto the first ship I saw, an aging Ukrainian freighter that needed a few more for the crew."

"Her name was the *Kazanova* and she was bound for the

Black Sea. After stops in Sevastopol and Odessa, we turned westward and headed back toward Italy. I expected to disembark once we arrived in Genoa and just walk away and disappear into the European landscape, but it didn't work that way. Joe Antonov was a senior crewman, and he took a curious interest in me, this angry young cat who wanted nothing save to walk into oblivion. He got through the layers I'd put up, the anger and the rage, and he made me see that I still had my first love. He gave me back the sea, the first love I thought lost, and, in the process, became the best friend I could ever have. That history he told you is how I know you know him. There are certain details only he knows, and now that you know some of them, I would appreciate that you keep them between us. Joe wouldn't have revealed them to you if he didn't completely trust you. So, I will trust you too."

Turk closed his eyes and shook his head. "There's nothing like the ramblings of a sea cat to bore a man to tears, eh?" I chose not to respond while Turk hopped to the dock and proceeded to the stern line, untying it from the dock before heading forward to the bow line. "To really understand what is happening, we need to go out there." He pointed to the dull gray skies and smiled. "There won't be bad weather for a little while yet. The sea is calling, Max, and with it, secrets!" As he untied the bow line and climbed back aboard, he noticed my concern. "It's better if we go where we can speak alone, Max. You'd never know it by looking, but the boats, they all have ears."

As the diesel caught and settled into a low idle, Turk motioned me into the wheelhouse, which sat on the deck toward the front of the boat. Though open toward the stern, the enclosure blocked the wind as we got underway. Turk turned the wheel to port, and the boat responded, soon pointing toward the mouth of the harbor. His demeanor had changed; his paws rested lightly on the wheel and he easily, instinctively shifted slightly every time the boat pitched in the minor waves, while the hardness in his face had given way to an expression of serenity and calm. His eyes, blazing bright as he looked toward the horizon, were no longer piercing and accusing, but rather keen to gaze into the distance, both observing and anticipating what lay in the waters ahead. And in that moment, I thought I might be starting to understand his meaning, his pathos, when he had spoken of the sea as his first love.

As we exited the harbor, Turk opened the throttle further and the *Lady Messina* picked up speed. The water grew rougher and as the boat pitched more, I held on to the bar affixed to the left of the instruments. To his credit, Turk swayed a little but never gripped the wheel any harder than he would a newborn kitten. I had to admire him, for this place was his element, while to me the water was something to be respected, even feared. We had ridden in near-silence for almost half an hour as the diesel engine's oppressive monotone precluded conversation, the drone broken only by Turk's occasional observation of wildlife and weather. As we glided out to sea, I watched as the land grew further and further until it had almost disappeared in the distance. Turk throttled the engine down to an idle, giving us some slight movement but reducing the noise to something approaching a civilized level.

My curiosity finally got the better of me and I asked him why he loved the ocean so strongly. He smiled mischievously, lifted his hat and said, "Maybe it's this!" Above his salty white face and amber eyes stood two bright orange ears, bridged by a small patch of orange on the top of his head. Along with a ringed orange tail poking out from under his coat, those ears told a story. His nickname was no accident of chance, for he was an example of that ancient breed that emerged in eastern Anatolia countless centuries before: the Turkish Van.

Turk laughed softly as he saw the spark of understanding flash in my eyes. "The legends say we emerged from the water fully formed by the Goddess of the Lake. Lake Van. From whence we came and to wherever we voyage, the lake, the water, that will always remain the home to which we Vans long to return. The lake gave us life, gave us some essence of the Goddess herself, and for this reason we long for her timeless dwelling, the eternal water." Turk smiled at me, a twinkle in his eyes. "I don't know if I believe in old wives' tales, but most Vans have a strong affinity for water. I can still remember when I first saw the ocean.

"I was just a small whelp of a kitten then, Mom and Dad took me down to the coast for the day, and when I saw the water, I was transfixed. I knew then that whatever I did, however I earned a living, it would be tied to the ocean somehow. We're a breed apart, Max; most other cats won't tolerate water as we do, and of those who do, only a special few can stand to be far from land for very long. Everyone knows that a Turkish Van is a cat born for water, born for hull and sail and ready to take on the high seas."

We were well offshore, out on the water yet still within sight of now-hazy land; I realized that this was a courtesy for me, as he could no doubt sense my mild unease. As he cut the engine the boat rocked gently on the dark water, turned a dull gray by the oppressive clouds. The stern faced back toward shore, and though I remained in the wheelhouse, Turk walked out onto the deck of the softly swaying boat. A steady breeze, chilled and laden with the smells of the deep, blew across the water. I was glad for my overcoat and gloves. But even with the cloud cover, the daylight compounded with the reflections off the waves proved surprisingly bright. Even under his hat, Turk's eyes were partially closed, his pupils drawn into slits. My own hat would have been nice, but the nautical winds would have made quick work in offering it to Poseidon. I was quite fond of that hat, so it remained clenched in my left paw. No other boats were near, so Turk and I sat alone on the waves, far enough out for a private conversation.

"You'd never guess how well sound carries over still water," Turk said, "and I don't trust many of the other captains to keep what they hear to themselves. They already saw you, watched you from the moment you entered the harbor, and they saw me take you out. By now the word has spread to every one of them and they are all wondering what you're up to. But at least our words will stay between us. So, what is it you're working toward and how can this aging sea cat be of help?"

I told him about my initial suspicions with the tuna shortages, how I wanted to see if the shortages were caused by a lack of fish or, as I believed, something else. And if it wasn't something natural, then my best guess was that someone was manipulating the supply to drive up the prices. I was hoping that something he had seen or heard might be of help. Turk listened intently, then took a minute to pace the deck in thought before offering up a reply.

"Now I don't fish tuna myself. Tuna is a deeper water fish and found further offshore than I like to venture on a boat this small." He smirked coyly. "Even we Vans reach the point where we like to stay a bit closer to shore. Besides, this boat isn't really equipped for tuna; they're sizable and heavier than they look, and even if I could catch them easily, I lack the space in the hold to store enough of 'em. Those bigger boats you saw when you walked in, those are part of the tuna fleet. Sometimes I cross paths with the tuna captains and we say a few friendly hellos. Usual chit chat, talking about nothing while waiting for a milk."

Turk paused, then turned to look at me, his eyes bright with thought. He pointed a finger skyward, remembering something he thought might be of use. "A few nights ago, I was in the harbor, doing a bit of maintenance. I took a break at sundown and walked to the bar just outside the harbor, you would have passed it when you came in, and ordered a skim milk. A couple of the tuna captains were there, both locals that I've known in passing for years. They were in a real good mood, talking about how they were getting record hauls this year, but when I asked them how much they were pulling they just laughed and said that the hauls were the same but the pay was better. Really playing it up. I thought they were just tipsy on milk

24

and catnip, but something else a little later got me thinking too.

"I got back to the boat and finished up my repairs, then gathered up my tools and turned off the wheelhouse light. I was sitting on the stern, alone in the dark, just taking a few minutes to admire the harbor; it's pretty at night, with the lights and the boats and the sound of the water lapping against the pilings and the boat hulls. As I was sitting there, I could hear two cats talking about a tuna shipment, talking about paying off the captains and the trucks. I looked and saw that they were over by one of the tuna boats, talking to each other in normal voices, voices I didn't recognize. Even though they were some distance away, I could hear them clear as day; the night was quiet and the water almost still, and the sound carried a lot further than they realized."

"When I first saw them, I thought they might have come with a truck, but a closer look showed that they weren't any delivery drivers I'd ever seen. For one thing they were wearing suits and coats, like you, only their suits looked more expensive, even from that distance. They were definitely landies and something about them made me think they were up to something."

"I got a pretty good look at them because they were standing under one of the lights on the dock. One of them was black, solid black I think; he was the quieter one, while the other was a brown tabby, like you. Both of 'em were big, and something about their mannerisms told me to just stay on the boat until they were gone. They only stayed a few minutes more, then they left. I don't know what they were doing, but at that point I had to get some sleep before heading out in the morning, and by morning it didn't matter to me so much."

Turk then glared at me, hard. "I'm only telling you this because you're a friend of Joe's and when he contacted me, he told me I could trust you. But those guys make me nervous, and I'm not usually the type of cat to scare easily. I hope you can use what I've told you, but I'd appreciate if you didn't do anything to send those two back my direction. At least not before I can hop a freighter bound for New Zealand. Or better still, Antarctica." He paused briefly, eyes softening as a large paw came to a brief rest on my shoulder. "Watch yourself, Max. You seem like one of the good ones, and I'd hate to read about you in past tense."

With that, Turk and I stepped into the wheelhouse, started the engine, and steered the *Lady Messina* to shore. I was grateful that the boat started moving again, as the rolling and pitching on the waves while floating on the current was making me ill. Once in motion, my stomach stopped performing somersaults and I was able to process what he had told me.

It was a quiet ride, each of us in our own thoughts as the boat motored on. As I stood in the wheelhouse watching the land grow nearer, I pondered what the seafaring cat next to me had said, that the boats were pulling the same sized hauls they had pulled for years and that someone was paying top dollar for the tuna and paying trucks to transport them. No doubt Turk was thinking about the two strangers in the nice suits; that they could instill fear into someone like him was something in itself. He was a few years older than me, but a lifetime of labor had given the cat solid ropes of muscle, rugged and strong. For them to have intimidated a cat who could likely break me to pieces without ruffling his fur meant that they were two tough characters, indeed. His nervousness now trickled down to me, and I made a mental note to exercise caution from that moment forward. As for Turk, I wasn't sure but he might prefer I walk off his boat, off his dock and never come back. With what I would come to learn, I wouldn't blame him at all.

When we arrived at the dock, Turk expertly placed the *Lady Messina* in her slip, then tossed the ropes and stepped to the dock. I followed him off and watched as he wound the ropes securely around the cleats. We said our goodbyes, avoiding a shake in case anyone untoward was watching us. As I looked Turk in the eyes one last time, I nodded slightly, while the right side of his mouth raised slightly. He had not only proven an excellent source of information but had also proven to be an honest cat I very much liked. I turned and walked along the dock without a backward glance, hoping that in a calmer future, our paths would cross again.

I put my fedora atop my head. In the short time, I had come to like the tough captain, and I regretted that my job might preclude any future contact. Unfortunately, such occurrences went with the territory. Mine was a life of few friends and long periods of loneliness, and I sometimes wondered why I stayed with it. There were easier ways to make a living, to be sure, but the few rewards that this job might give were ones of satisfaction and personal accomplishment. Plus, though I kept few friends, the ones I kept were of a high quality, ones who could be counted on when help was needed. Perhaps Turk Ryder might become one of those friends later on, but for now I felt it best to take what he had offered and leave him be.

I didn't know at that moment, but my second contact soon found me. While preoccupied in my thoughts, I walked right into and knocked over a petite Oriental cat who looked to be part Siamese, sending her sprawling and upending the contents of her arms. As I leaned over and put a paw out to help her up, she hissed loudly and glared with ice blue eyes, then said in a soft whisper, "Pick up some of my things and follow me. I might have some information for you, but we need to be fast." I did as she instructed, taking a couple of heavy coils of rope under each arm. She led, quickly, and I followed behind. I'd learned that in this business sometimes things often happened quickly and to be ready to change tack at a moment's notice. This appeared to be one of those times. We quickly came to her boat, similar in size to Turk's and painted orange and black. The name on the hull read *Inferno*.

She set her items on the dock and climbed over the side and onto the rear deck. As I stopped next to the boat, she took the ropes from me and said, "Hand me those things, one at a time. Not too

27

quickly either or I won't have time to talk. I saw you on Turk's boat, which means that the other captains and crews saw you too. You're a landie and you look like a cop, and that's gonna make some cats nervous. I know why you're here, what you're looking for; Joe sent a message to me this morning and asked that I tell you anything I know. I'm not sure what Turk told you on that pleasure cruise, but there's been some odd stuff going on.

"Up in the restaurant, we get to know the truck drivers, they're all Union guys so we see the same ones, but lately they're all different. I don't know any of them. These new guys, they're real quiet, real stiff, and if we try to talk to them, they get unpleasant and menacing. And the trucks, they're all rentals, every last one. Trailers too. It's weird, a lot of the regular drivers have their own trucks and they run those Sail Fin Transport trailers, the ones with the blue marlin on the side. All these new trailers are unmarked. And there's always at least one suit around, sometimes two, always watching what's going on. Big guys too."

As I handed her the last bundle of rope from the pile, she said, "There's something going on here, and I don't know what it is, but I don't like it. I hope it's related to whatever you're working on, because someone needs to get to the bottom of this." She crossed her arms and rested her elbows on the wide railing, looking through me with piercing intelligence in her eyes. "You're Max. I'm Aurora Kowalski, Lady and Captain of the *Inferno*. If I find out anything more about those trucks or the tuna boats, I'll let you know. Now scram before any more of those floating gossip queens see us talking!"

I thanked Aurora quickly, then turned back and walked once again toward the entrance. Though the chill of morning had transitioned into a cool midday, the harbor, like the city at large, remained cloaked beneath threatening clouds. As I passed by the harbor restaurant I glanced inside. The clock on the wall showed the time as eleven forty; I had spent almost three hours here, much of it on Turk's boat. My thoughts were alive with ideas and scenarios, and I decided not to return to the office; the paperwork could wait until tomorrow. I could sit by myself at home just as easily as I could sit at work and the boss wouldn't care at all. Yes, sometimes it was good to be the boss.

As I left the harbor, I spotted the phone booth across the street I had seen when I arrived. After crossing, I put in some change and dialed for a cab. After ten minutes or so, a yellow Ford pulled to the curb and I climbed in. As I started to give the driver a destination, I noticed a black Cadillac sedan drive by and turn into the harbor, pulling to a stop by the restaurant. I told him to wait a moment; the luxury car seemed a bit out of place here and I wanted to see who might have come here in it. As I watched from a distance, two doors opened and a pair of cats in expensive suits emerged, one with stripes, one solid black. As I gave my address to the cabbie and he quietly pulled away, I knew why both captains were nervous. They had very good reason to be.

4

When I saw who had emerged from the car, I knew immediately that the stakes had just gotten a lot higher, and that I had left the harbor at an opportune time. I also had a very good idea as to who was behind the change in the trucking personnel. Someone who had his paws in a lot of different pies. Someone who held influence in City Hall. Someone who would not hesitate to cross any line to ensure he got what he wanted. That someone's name was Constantino Gandini, and he ran the city's criminal underworld. The two cats in the black sedan were his top henchmen, Blackie Lawler and Rufus Segovia. The three formed the core of the most powerful criminal syndicate in New Amsterdam, and they were characters that no one wanted to cross.

I had never met Constantino or his higher ups, but I knew full well who they were and the business they did. Anyone in my line of work would. From his beginnings as an immigrant pauper, he had steadily built himself into the leading crime boss of New Amsterdam and was both ruthless as a syndicate boss and cunning as a businessman. He always kept both eyes peeled for any new opportunity and oversaw the numerous interests in which he held a share. He liked to style himself as a legitimate businessman, clothed in fine suits, owning expensive cars, and with a well-crafted public image that saw him move among high society with practiced ease. His appearance was well suited for public life; a cat of average height with a somewhat pronounced muzzle capped with a pinkish nose. He was blessed with a naturally radiant smile that he used to his every advantage, while his short, cream-colored fur, always immaculately brushed and trimmed, draped over a strong though somewhat heavyset build. His golden-green eyes shined brightly, reflecting the sharp intelligence that lay within.

In his tailored suits, fine coats and expensive Italian shoes, Constantino cut an impressive figure. As a member of New

Amsterdam's *nouveau riche* and someone who frequented some, but not all, of the most happening parties, he liked to cultivate the image of a self-made multi-millionaire. To most, Constantino embodied the classic rags-to-riches story of someone who had, through sheer determination, guts, and hard work, pulled himself out of meager circumstances and made himself into someone far better. It was a beguiling story, and one which had served him well, but while some parts of it rang true, other parts were at best exaggerations, with the rest consisting of authentic fabrications and outright lies.

Very few people knew where Constantino really came from and how he arrived at his present status in life. Out of curiosity, I had looked into his background some years before and found that while a lot of the details were long missing, a general outline of his life could be constructed with what was available. He had been born Simoné Constantino Muratore di Accettura somewhere in the south of Italy. While this indicated some past origin in a small southern town called Accettura, the name had been long divorced from its source. The records I had managed to find failed to agree as to where exactly Constantino had been born; while some sources named Brindisi, others placed his point of origin somewhere in Calabria or even Sicily, but none knew for sure.

One of three kittens, his family emigrated to Boston when he was ten or eleven and had settled in Portland, Maine by 1915. His father had worked the docks loading and unloading cargo but was killed soon after the family arrived in Portland, leaving his mother to raise the destitute family alone. No good records existed that clearly told what life was like for him, but Simoné, as he was then known, went to school into the tenth grade and dropped out before graduating. As for his mother, odds are that she took whatever odd jobs she could to raise her children as best she could. His two siblings, a brother and a sister, graduated high school and went on to respectable careers, but Simoné followed a different, darker path.

After leaving school, Simoné disappeared for several years,

with no extant records giving any indication of his deeds or even living arrangements. Some accounts indicated that he worked menial jobs along the Maine coast as far as Eastport and possibly into Canada, while others seemed to hint that he drifted south along the New England highways taking odd jobs for cash whether the work was legal or not. Though I suspected the truth was closer to the latter, nothing concrete had ever surfaced during this period of his life that told where he lived or what he did.

He showed up in New Amsterdam sometime in 1926 or '27, now going by his middle name Constantino, which he apparently felt was more imperious and suitable for his lifestyle than Simoné; his last name, Muratore, had also fallen from his favor, replaced with the enigmatic Gandini. No longer the impoverished urchin, he had discovered the means to a lifestyle more worldly-wise and worthier of his lofty ambitions. The poor immigrants' child had grown into a tough and vicious mafia enforcer, working low level jobs within New Amsterdam's established Carpelli syndicate. His was a violent underworld of crime, leverage and deceit, and he had found his true calling. His raw intellect, coupled with an innate gift for organized crime which served to focus his ruthless and violet nature, saw Constantino steadily move up the ranks until he was a top general of Don Giovanni Carpelli himself.

From his earliest arrival Constantino proved an ambitious and clever study, willing to take risks in search of a bigger reward and never satisfied with the status quo. Though his personality could be described as audacious, even bombastic, he also boasted an uncanny ability to manipulate the cats around him, persuading them to follow his command. In only a few short years Constantino increasingly assumed a primary leadership role within the Carpelli syndicate as Don Giovanni grew increasingly frail with age. His Italian roots ensured Constantino's elevation to a Made Cat, putting him in line for leadership of the entire syndicate, and as his power grew, he began to consolidate power by placing his own lieutenants in positions of power.

When the childless Patriarch passed away in his sleep, his will stated that control of the syndicate would fall upon Constantino Gandini, his strongest lieutenant. He took to the role of a Don with a fury, purging those within the organization who had defied him and replacing them with his supporters. It was rumored among the low-level cats that Constantino was not Don Carpelli's first or even second choice. Furthermore, it was said that Constantino had only chosen to lead because the Don believed that had he not, Constantino would likely have launched a bloody civil war against the organization that would have weakened the syndicate.

His ambitions realized, Constantino set about strengthening the family and marginalizing all competition. The smart syndicates allied themselves with Constantino, but more often they chose to defy the large cream cat and ended up succumbing to his henchmen in pitched street battles held in the trucking yards, warehouses and docks. Now the head of the most powerful crime syndicate in New Amsterdam, and possibly the eastern seaboard, Constantino was the undisputed boss, the cat in charge, The Don. He was on top, and even in city hall, hapless politicians and their lackeys started to say the same thing: Constantino runs this town.

It was tempting, particularly in the beginning, to view Constantino Gandini as a flash in the pan, just the latest claimant to power whose time had come and whose time would soon go. He dressed to the nines, lots of flash and glitter, with expensive suits, handmade Italian loafers, expensive watches and fine jewelry on his fingers. He often affected a cane in hand when in public, more to look like some Old-World gentleman. He cut a rakish figure on the social scene, added with his flamboyant personality, the Don was a highly visible figure among high society. But this was the public Constantino Gandini, the side that schmoozed with the mayor and opened soup kitchens in the poor districts. The side that wanted to appear as a respectable businessman to the world. Beneath this façade, hidden from public view, lurked the real cat. He knew that to keep a litany of thieves loyal to him he needed to keep them distracted and pay them well, or at least better than his rivals. He devised and adhered to a personal code of ethics, standards to apply to any given situation that brought consistency to the organization. But most of all, Constantino knew to appoint the right people for the right job and to make sure they stayed happy to keep them from turning against him. And upon his ascension to the lofty heights of power, Constantino knew that he must appoint a loyal second to help carry out his orders and serve as a faithful general to him at this, the pinnacle of his power. Constantino knew this could potentially prove the most important decision of his career, for he knew he must choose carefully. And choose carefully he did, for after years within the syndicate, Constantino knew just who to appoint.

When Constantino arrived in New Amsterdam and hired out his services to the Carpelli syndicate, he met another young low-level player with whom he forged a close friendship. The two couldn't have been less alike in almost every respect. The cat's name was Darwin Lawler, and when he and Constantino met, it was as if the stars aligned with regard to their lives. Everything about them seemed completely opposed, even their appearances; Constantino was an average-sized cream-white cat with an average build and short hair, while Darwin was both physically large and a longhair, with thick, coal-black fur that made him look even larger than he already was. That fur gave Darwin the *nom de guerre* of Blackie, a name which suited him well; for all of his imposing size and physical strength, he never felt that Darwin was a suitable name for a gangster. Where Constantino's personality was gregarious and outgoing, Blackie kept quiet and maintained a lower profile. Constantino's ambitions sometimes led him to unrealistic expectations from himself, his cats, and his criminal empire, but Blackie's more cautious nature and darkly realistic worldview served to keep Constantino's unrealistic ambitions at bay. Even their style of dress differed, with Blackie's conservative black and gray suits a far cry from Constantino's stylish pinstriped affairs.

The only adornment Blackie allowed himself was a battered pocket watch on an old and tarnished chain, kept in his vest pocket. No one knew where that particular piece came from, but its importance to Blackie became the stuff of legend when another gangster tore it out of his vest, taunting him with it like a schoolyard bully. For a moment Blackie only stood, watching his adversary with a bored gaze, as if he had hardly noticed this transgression. But then he attacked his feckless tormenter with impossibly quick and savage ferocity, beating him severely and without mercy. Almost as soon as it began the fight was over, leaving Blackie's unfortunate opponent with several broken bones and bleeding from his ears, unconscious and in need of serious medical attention. After calmly retrieving his watch, Blackie stood and eyed his rivals with quiet contempt, then turned his back on them and walked away, unafraid of any sudden reprisal. He had not uttered a single word during the entire episode, and no one had ever touched his watch again. Through their years together, Constantino came to rely on Blackie as an essential partner in his dealings, and together they rose to the top, Constantino the public and vocal life of the party, and Blackie his quieter behind the scenes counterpart.

It was Blackie who brought the third member of the inner circle to Constantino's attention. As Constantino began to solidify his grip on power, a young tough cat named Rufus Segovia was quickly making a name for himself in the organization as a dependable if somewhat heavy-handed enforcer who always finished the job. A common brown tabby with thick black stripes, piercing gold eyes and a naturally stocky, powerful build, he certainly looked the part, but his shrewd, if somewhat unpredictable manner coupled with a somewhat unconventional approach to his work quickly set him apart from the rank and file. His ability to finish the job no matter the circumstances had drawn the attention of then mid-level boss Blackie Lawler, who quickly promoted him to be his personal enforcer. Rufus never gave any reasons for regret, and the two made a formidable pair in the streets.

Rufus did have a couple of idiosyncrasies, however, ones kept hidden from the world. The first was that Rufus was rumored to be terrified of thunder. Some said that his fear was rooted in his youth and that if storm formed while on the job, it took a tremendous force of will for him to remain calm and effective in his duties. Rufus was also rumored to possess a high sensitivity to catnip, more than most other cats, and if exposed to it in even small amounts his judgement would falter. Another rumor stated that he brandished a quick and extremely violent temper that sometimes got the better of his judgement leading to unnecessarily savage endings for those unlucky enough to have provoked him. But perhaps the most unusual rumor, repeated just enough to seem credible, pertained to Rufus' supposed fear of the dark.

Though most cats see well in low light conditions, it was said that Rufus realized early on that his night vision was limited at best, which presented problems for someone in his profession. Over the years he had learned how to partially compensate for this by training himself to utilize his excellent hearing and his sensitive whiskers to function in situations in which he couldn't see. His limited night vision embarrassed him, and he took great pains to hide it from everyone, though Blackie had supposedly deduced it through observation.

Blackie Lawler never revealed Rufus' secret to anyone in the syndicate, or in general, and because of Rufus' exemplary record, Blackie chose to work around his junior's limitations. This as much as anything cemented Rufus' loyalty to his boss, who continued to employ his unique services and move him up in the organization. Blackie convinced Constantino of the unique value of Rufus' unconventional techniques and his ability to best utilize them in any situation, and that Rufus, though young, was an obvious choice to join Constantino and Blackie as a junior boss in running the now-renamed Gandini Syndicate. The three cats now ran the most powerful crime operation in New Amsterdam, and the city's criminal underworld was theirs for the taking.

5

As I rode home from the harbor, my thoughts had wandered again in the quiet taxi. Though I said nothing as I headed back to my flat in the ever-present city traffic, my mind was a tempest of ideas. The fishing boat captains had given me a great deal to work with, clues that began to form a rough picture of the greater whole. The trick would be figuring out the intricacies of how it all fit together. It seemed certain that someone was renting trucks for the express purpose of transporting the tuna catches to some undisclosed location, presumably to be processed and stored away. It almost seemed too simple a plan, but more often than not a simple and straightforward plan worked far more effectively than something large and complex. I had once heard this theory summarized as something called Occam's Razor, where the simplest and most obvious solution to a given problem was usually the correct one. Though I doubted he ever dabbled in detective work, Occam knew what he was talking about, and his simple theorem had served me well through the years. But questions remained. Who stood to profit from these repeated tuna shortages? Why was tuna the item of choice instead of another dish? How exactly were the tuna being used to gouge prices? Were they being salted and stored somewhere, and if so, where? Why were gangsters taking fish catches? And, perhaps most importantly, what had I gotten myself into?

As the cab turned onto familiar streets, I shook myself out of my reverie. The driver stopped in front of my apartment building, pulling close to the sidewalk as he found a rare vacant place. After I paid the fare and exited, I looked at the scene before me. In the mid-afternoon light, the street was somewhat busy but went along at a casual bustle. A few children played on the sidewalks, their mothers taking a break outside to catch up on neighborhood gossip and laugh among themselves. These would be some of the people hit hard if another shortage came to pass, ordinary working cats just trying to make a living and get by. I looked up; the thick clouds above already cast an ominous pallor over the city as if signaling that darker times were once again to come, and like ancient Cassandra, the mythical soothsayer who could accurately predict the future though no one believed her, I felt like I was the only one who could see it coming.

I stood for a few more moments and turned to the main entrance. Once safely ensconced in my apartment, I shed my overcoat and hat, then removed my gloves and set them on the small dining table pushed against the wall. After removing my jacket and vest, I walked to the radio and turned it on. As the tubes warmed, the sounds of jazz and big band filled the air.

I walked to my sofa, another old and somewhat worn beast that could complement its counterpart in my office, sat down and leaned back, then kicked my shoes off and kicked my feet upon the cushions. Now sideways, I reclined into the armrest, tilted my head back and closed my eyes as my churning thoughts mixed with the horns and strings of the bands which filled my apartment with sound. I took a deep breath, then slowly exhaled, the tension and stress leaving me as my form seemed to melt into the soft comfort of the couch.

After several hours, some milk and a couple of sardine tins, I turned off the radio. Outside the windows, the sky had shifted to dark, while the clouds, now reflecting the light of the city, remained low and heavy. The thoughts I had juggled inside my head had played themselves out, and with little chance of any further breakthroughs I decided to turn in early. As I removed the last of my suit, I decided that I would treat myself to a long and restful sleep. To that end, I pulled down the covers on my seldom-used bed and climbed inside. With my head on the pillow, I could see the building across the street and a hint of sky above. My brain tried to form a coherent thought, but before it could surface, the veil of sleep descended, postponing all thoughts until the following day.

6

Morning greeted me with the oppressively heavy cover of a steel gray dawn. The dark day paralleled the darkness of my mood; I had dreamed I was alone in a boat out on the ocean, battered by storms and nearly swamped by waves. I managed to beach the craft on an island and for whatever reason Violet was there, as were her two sisters Iris and Daisy. The tempest raged on, and as we set to find shelter, two armed stiffs came out of the underbrush. What happened next was a confusing scene of misguided affection and fickle emotion. I didn't know how it ended as I abruptly woke, breathing heavily and dazed from the transition to reality. The experience was disorienting and unpleasant, and though the details faded in due time, I was left with a general impression for several hours.

I wasn't hungry, as the din of the imagery had wiped out any wanting for food. I pulled the sheets from the bed and put it back together with a clean set. I am not a superstitious kind of cat, but sometimes I just feel better if I can exorcise the demons from my abode, even if those demons exist only in my head. That said, I would be sleeping in the living room for the foreseeable future. That task finished, I walked into the living room and sat on the sofa for a few minutes, then went and put on my suit and tie in silence, without the usual din of the radio playing in the background. After I eyed the apartment, lit only by the dim light of an onsetting dawn, I made for the door.

I put on my hat, stepped into the hallway and turned the lock. I walked quietly down the hallway, closed doors hiding neighbors I barely knew, then turned and descended the stairs and across the small nondescript lobby. As I walked out onto the sidewalk, a cold north wind blew down the street, making me shiver involuntarily and pull the collar of my trench coat to cover the back of my neck. Thankfully I didn't have far to walk, only a few blocks, and for that and the reasonable rent I could continue to put up with my small and utterly ordinary flat in its utterly ordinary and dull building.

After fifteen minutes, I had walked a few blocks and crossed over to the next parallel street. Even on such an unpleasant and early morning, the walk proved a decent pick-me-up so that as I neared the office, I would be fully awake. Before the office, however, I had a quick stop to make along the way.

As I neared, an unmistakable figure was waiting. Even though day had yet to properly break, she was already there. As always, I heard her before I saw her. Her high and powerful voice proved unmistakable among the droning of New Amsterdam, and despite the foul mood of my awakening I smiled, looking forward to seeing her as I did on most mornings. The eyes attached to the voice saw me and waved, then called out.

"Hiya, Mister Max! Got your daily paper right here, fresh, just the way you like it! Looks like we're in for some cold air out of Canada, so I hope you and Miss Violet stay warm!"

Her name was Lizzie Cahill, street vendor for the local papers, and she was a virtual dynamo of energy seemingly fueled by an endless supply of high-octane gasoline, or perhaps nitroglycerine. She was always energetic, always eager to greet people at her parents' newsstand, and very hard not to like. She could be found on the sidewalk selling papers to the masses before reluctantly heading off to school; sometimes I'd see her at the newsstand in the evenings too, where she would regale me with tales of faraway people and places she had learned about. It could be Norsemen in Scandinavia or New Zealand sheep herders, and if she found a news article that spoke of the places she had learned, her enthusiasm knew no bounds.

Lizzie was unabashedly a tomboy, dressed today in a cream-colored work shirt, felt coat, knickers and suspenders, Argyle socks and leather work shoes, topped off by a floppy newsboy hat. Like her father Sean, Lizzie was solid black with a small white spot at the base of her neck that resembled an oval charm, and she approached the world with eyes of gold, wide and bright, complimented by a

41

lovely smile that only seems to happen in a half-grown kitten such as herself. Her fur had recently changed from fluffy and downy to sleek and shiny, and though she didn't make much of it, I knew that inside she was proud of her looks; though she was a boyish elf in appearance, she was still all girl at heart. She was a bright spot in the often-murky dimness of my life, a little dynamo of joy who always managed to make me smile.

"What's new, kid? Anything juicy I need to know about?" I asked, knowing that Lizzie had gone through the headlines and first few sentences of every article before she ever appeared in front of the newsstand. Her appetite for current events was insatiable. I checked my watch, seeing that it was about twenty til seven; Lizzie would be heading off to school in a little over half an hour, but as soon as she was done, she would hurry back and repeat the process with the afternoon edition. I had no idea where she found the time to skim the newspapers, hawk the latest edition on the corner in the morning and afternoon, pursue her homework, play with friends, and somehow get a good night's sleep. On more than one occasion I found myself wondering if she actually did sleep, or if there were two or three extra Lizzie clones that worked in shifts. It had also occurred to me that if these supposed multiple Lizzies were also telepathic, each Lizzie would always stay abreast of what went on with the others, never missing a beat and keeping their secret lives safe.

"Kind of a slow day, Mister Max," Lizzie replied, looking up at me with two wide eyes. "The usual ruckuses over in Little Dublin, arguments in the taverns, nothing serious, and a restaurant over in Chinatown got shut down. Turned out they were fencing stolen merchandise for the Triads. One of the Councilmen and the Treasurer got caught stealing funds from the city treasury and the mayor is hopping mad about it. He also says the threat of another tuna shortage will bankrupt this city and these crooks are lining their own pockets. Mom says we're lucky because we can still afford to eat tuna right now, but that if the prices get too much higher, we'll be forced to eat sardines!" With that she stuck her tongue out and made an unpleasant face. I silently wondered if she knew what made up the majority of my diet.

I replied, "Let me have my usual, Liz. One Morning Scratching Post and a City Gazette. Nice and hot!" I handed her a half dollar, which left fifteen cents change, enough for a sandwich and a bottle of milk at school. Though I knew her parents fed her well and that she wanted for nothing, I always let her keep the change. As I tucked the newspapers under my arm, Lizzie chided me just a little.

"I hope you find a mystery to solve, Mr. Max! Miss Violet says you need the work to get you off your duff and out the door more! You should listen to her, Mr. Max! She's so pretty and so nice! Gotta get back to the corner, so see you later!"

Newspapers and some light hecklings were our daily tradition, one we both enjoyed. With that she grabbed a paper from the pile on the corner and returned to eagerly hawking it to avid passers-by. I chuckled as I walked to the newsstand, looking to have a quick chat with her mother Victoria before I walked the remaining block to work.

Cahill's News and Magazines operated out of a small corner shop that had suffered a fire several years previous. Though the building's owner feared he would have to shutter the edifice due to damage and the high cost of repair, Sean and Victoria Cahill had made him an offer to renovate the space at cost in exchange for a guarantee to lease the store exclusively to them and at a low but fair fixed price. It was a good deal for everyone involved. The Cahill's landlord received a storefront renovation well beneath the usual cost and at very high quality plus a tenant ready to stay for the long term, while Sean and Victoria landed a great location at a very competitive price with the freedom to remodel and restore as they saw fit for their new business.

They had restored the shop to a high standard with a mixture of bare wood and painted panels, all of which looked very inviting, while the main window displayed both newspapers and magazines which the shop sold. Sean and Victoria had picked the location well, as there was no other newsstand for several blocks in each direction. It took a bit of an investment, but from the outset the newsstand had proven a success, quickly becoming a fixture of the neighborhood and earning the Cahills a tidy profit as well. As I headed inside, I found Lizzie's mother behind the counter, cheerfully selling papers and magazines to a steady stream of customers

"Well Max, I see Lizzie roped you into yet another paper or two! I really should fuss at her for disturbing you so." Victoria said with a laugh. She knew full well that her little troublemaker had me wrapped around her little finger and that I was prepared to do absolutely nothing to change this. She smiled and continued. "Violet stopped by a couple of days ago and wanted to get lunch and go shopping. I hated to tell her another time, but when the new magazines start arriving the place gets hectic in an instant. Sean's inside trying to deal with the last of 'em and take care of customers too; I keep telling him that we should hire on someone else, someone who could take the load off him, but he won't do it. Typical stubborn male, no offense. Says it's our business and that we need to keep it in the family." She paused to hand two newspapers to a customer, then placed the payment in the register with a smile and a thank you by name. "He's worried that if we don't keep building a customer base and a nest egg that Lizzie could be out in the cold one day, and he won't have it. I think he's being a bit obsessive, but he always has planned for the worst."

Victoria's sing-song speech betrayed her Ulster origins, a pleasant Northern Irish brogue that remained in her voice well after she had immigrated and settled in New Amsterdam. In appearance, she was a tortoiseshell calico, a tricolor of black, white and orange in large patches. Though arguably ordinary in looks, nothing about her

44

strong personality could ever be described as such. Victoria was as tough a cat as they came, learning to find her way in a destitute neighborhood when her father died and her mother moved them to Belfast. Her mother taught Victoria to read at a young age and encouraged the young kitten to read everything she could get her hands on. She was a voracious reader; a local headmaster of a private school saw her reading Ernest Shackleton's Antarctic account and began tutoring her after school. Soon an official student, Victoria ranked as one of the top two students and had earned a well-paying secretarial job before graduation. Within three years, she had relocated to New Amsterdam.

Victoria met her future husband a couple of years after settling in America. Also from Eire, Sean Cahill and Victoria O'Hare were soon dating, and after a year and a half, married. Sean's dream was running his own business, preferably a newsstand as he had experience, and Victoria readily agreed. Soon after opening their newsstand, they discovered Victoria was pregnant, and soon gave birth to an only kitten, a daughter, coal black like her father, whom they named Elizabeth Anne Cahill after her two grandmothers. Before long, Lizzy became part of the business.

Without realizing it, I had become lost in my own thoughts. Victoria had said my name twice, maybe three times before I looked up. I shook my head and apologized to her, blamed it on a lack of coffee this morning. She smiled and said, "You know Lizzie always looks forward to seeing you. She won't tell you, but she thinks you're very dashing and brave. Max Persian, the great Private Detective! I think she envisions you solving harrowing mysteries and taking on organized crime. I don't want to tell her otherwise. She's young, so we let her dream." Victoria smiled softly. "She thinks you walk on water, Max. It's just the thoughts and dreams of a young girl, but I thought you should know." I turned to look at Lizzie, out on her corner with a stack of papers, a couple in her paws, eagerly announcing the latest headlines for one and all to hear, and I smiled.

As I turned back toward Victoria, I said, "I'm convinced that her little feet don't touch the ground. It's not just because she moves so quickly that they haven't the time. She is an angel, Mrs. Cahill, a little angel who hides her wings yet floats just above the ground. Most people will never notice, but I do." I winked and smiled, then turned and walked toward work. As Lizzie Cahill's little voice faded into the background, I reminded myself to tell Violet that Victoria and Lizzie said hello. The thought of Lizzie made me smile inside. Funny kid, I thought. Funny kid indeed.

7

I arrived at the office after another block and a half, looking up occasionally at a threatening sky and smelling the scent of rain on the wind. I was just as glad to be heading indoors to the unique charms of my second-floor office. As usual, Violet awaited my arrival at her desk, impeccably dressed and putting a fresh coat of polish on her claws. She looked up and smiled the same radiant smile as every morning, and without a word, for none was needed, she returned to her claws. I headed into my office, hung my coat and hat on the rack, marveled silently at how the non-existent cleaning lady always neglected to wipe the dust from my desk, and sat down to scan the morning papers.

In a half hour or so, Violet would fire up the percolator, come into my office with a hot coffee for herself and its twin for me and sit down, usually in one of the guest chairs in front of my desk but occasionally on the old sofa. When she sat on the couch, I knew she was still unwinding from some social obligation she couldn't figure a way out of. I know she also slept on it occasionally, but I couldn't prove it as she always kept a fresh change of clothes in the big armoire and always folded the sheet and blanket when she was finished. I'd slept on that old thing many times myself, even put up a client or two in the past, and no one ever complained as to how it slept. I had read in the paper that the Winterhavens had played host to an "informal gala" the night before, so I expected today to be a sofa day, perhaps even a 'make up some excuse to boot Max out of the office so I can take a nap' day, but when Violet came in with the usual liquid refreshment, she took command of one of the guest chairs. I'm sure that had she not already committed to her family's soiree, she would have happily lost her lunch over the side of Turk's boat rather than entrap herself with the city's finest, as she made little effort to hide her indifference to most guests. As it was, I didn't want to let on that I knew the couch code, so I said nothing, keeping my amusing secret to myself.

The next bit of happening was our daily meeting, where we talked about our cases and what was happening regarding them, or just as often we talked about our lives as we had no active cases. Violet had taken on this job almost three years ago, after I had burned through a couple of girls already; she had quickly proved herself an astute and capable assistant. By now, we meshed well and knew what was expected of the other. She was particularly useful in providing an alternate point of view, one which I could not see for being too close to the investigation. In addition, her family's associations with rich and high-profile citizens often proved her a mine of useful information I might lack access to otherwise. That she seemed to always know when to operate the great energy fluid machine was an added bonus.

After she sat, I leaned over my desk, my paws crossed, and recounted to her the events of the past 24 hours. She listened to the entire account, soaking it all in, and when I finished, she sat quietly. I had learned through experience that while she seemed to be doing little, her clever mind was sorting through the information I had recounted to her, looking for inconsistencies that didn't add up. After a minute or two she came up for air and looked me in the eyes.

"The key is the trucks. You said that the trucks are rentals. It's a decent bet that the unknown drivers are too. For starters it means that someone is keeping the unions quiet, either with bribes or intimidation. Neither would be easy; the first requires a healthy bit of untraceable cash, while the second requires enough muscle to intimidate a union boss. The trucks alone rule out most of the criminal element in New Amsterdam, and pretty much the eastern seaboard. Just that alone makes me think that Turk Ryder is smart to be nervous. And then the trucks have to be taking the fish somewhere to be dealt with. It wouldn't make sense to just cart it off and throw it away, not if the trucks being rented and loaded, not if the union is being kept at bay, and not if the fishermen are all still getting paid.

Violet stood and began pacing the office. "Max, my guess is that someone is hording the tuna. From what I know of the business, cannery plants and fresh processing centers are housed indoors to escape the weather that would cut into production. The cans last for months on end, maybe a couple of years, but even salted fish can last for a long time because the salt pulls all the water out of the meat and makes it virtually immune to disease. It's entirely possible that someone has set up a salt factory or even a cannery somewhere and has hired these rented trucks to transport the tuna there, paying temporary drivers off to keep them quiet. My guess would be on a salting facility because it doesn't require machines or electricity, which makes it far simpler than setting up an actual factory and keeping it hidden. It still leaves some questions, but it's more than we had yesterday morning."

I had one theory right off the bat. "Violet, what happened to those giant warehouse buildings that your father and uncle built to house the bomber factories during the war? Were they ever sold or torn down?"

Violet quickly replied, "No, they are still there. My dad has always thought that in another few years one of the big auto makers or maybe even another aircraft manufacturer might want to buy a building with a lot of interior space for large-scale industrial production. That's why he's always kept them maintained, repairing anything that would go wrong, so that any new owner could move in immediately."

I stood and began to slowly pace around the office, causing her to pause and turn toward me while I said, "From what I remember, those warehouses and the old airstrip next to them are on the edge of the old industrial district. Not a lot is going on in parts of it right now. There's quite a number of vacant and abandoned factories and warehouses up that way, stuff left over from before the War, some of it going back a hundred years or more. What if

49

someone has set up shop in one or more of those buildings and is using them to process and store tuna until the prices go up, then release some of what they have horded back into the marketplace? A lot of the industrial quarter is still a ghost town, what with the wartime production having dried up, and odds are that whoever might be doing this could set up in a few of them without anyone realizing they are there. Anyone who does know could be paid off in both money and in merchandise. And based on who I saw at the docks, I have a bad feeling I know who is paying the money."

I paused, leaning on my desk with both paws as if to drive home how much I was bothered by this. "We both know that if Constantino Gandini is involved, this case will be a lot more complicated. He's a bad cat and he isn't opposed to pushing people around to get what he wants; you know this from his business dealings with your family. Honestly, it makes me a lot more reluctant to pursue this. There are people I care about that could get hurt and I don't want that to happen." I looked Violet in the eye. "If this came back and you got hurt, I'd never forgive myself. If Joe or the Cahills got hurt, I'd be a wreck. I'm wondering if it's even still worth it."

Violet came and sat on the corner of my desk, her face a show of empathy and concern. "Max, I think you're overreacting a bit, but I'm glad you have concern for us all. But all you saw was Blackie Lawler and Rufus Segovia getting out of a car down at the docks. I have no doubt they were up to something, but there's no way to know what it was. Just because they were at the dock doesn't mean they were overseeing the smuggling of fresh tuna to the industrial quarter in rented trucks. They could have been there for other reasons. We don't even know if the trucks are actually connected to the tuna or not. All we have is the word of two sea captains, albeit ones who know Joe Antonov, and the sighting of two gangsters at the harbor. I just don't think we have enough to even know if Gandini is involved. I'd like to continue a little longer and see if any of the information gathered so far adds up to something before calling it a day. If Constantino is involved, then we reevaluate our position. And I might even have an idea as to how we could go about looking at the warehouses for anything suspicious." She smiled wry, lopsided grin. "We can hide in plain sight."

At the last sentence, I tilted my head, curious at what she meant. "Okay, I'll bite. What are you thinking?"

Violet leaned in further until her smiling face was six inches from my own. "As you said, my family owns those giant buildings. Every so often somebody goes up there to make sure everything is still in working order and to oversee any necessary repairs. So, we go up there and inspect the place ourselves! They usually get inspected toward the end of the month, but it's not that uncommon for someone to show up and take a look around on their own. I've done it myself a time or two when Daddy got called away on business; he knows I like the chance to get away from the hubbub and just be by myself for a while, and anyone we encounter will know who I am and what I'm doing. And since I work for you, I can say that you came along out of curiosity. We can go up there, look around, see what is going on, and we don't even have to sneak around to do it. From there, we can take a cursory look at some of the other buildings, sightseeing, if you will. Do you approve?"

I nodded and said, "That's a good plan. I like that it works as the cover story and doesn't really put anyone in harm's way. I approve. I definitely approve."

Violet smiled and brought up her paw with index finger extended. She said, excitedly "Then let's go!" and tapped my nose twice to the last two words. As Violet moved into the door of my office, I picked up my telephone to call a cab. "We don't need a cab, Max! My car's in the alley!"

As I put the receiver down, I moved to get my coat and hat and asked, "When did you get a car? I know your dad taught you and your sisters to drive when you were young, but I didn't think he'd bought you one yet. When did that change?"

She looked back with a coy smile and said, "*He* didn't buy me anything. *I* bought it myself a month ago with some of the money I've saved up from working here. I figured that since I needed a ride to get here every day, I'd buy something and not have to always borrow one of Daddy's cars to get me here. It's nothing special, just a used Chevrolet, but I made sure to buy one that was taken care of and runs well. It's plain for sure, but it's comfortable and I like it."

Then, her smile turned a bit mischievous. "Daddy said he was proud of me for taking the initiative and he lets me keep it in the garage with his Packards and Lincolns so I don't get wet in the rain. And while I do appreciate his generosity, the look of pure disgust on Iris and Daisy's faces when he let me park it in there is the best part." She rolled her eyes and laughed. "They're such snobs, Max! I know I say that a lot, but it's just hard for anyone else to understand." She lifted her nose skyward and affected a haughty, mocking pseudo-British aristocratic tone. "Oh Iris! We shan't be able to leave the house today lest we rub elbows with unwashed horrible commoners!" Another impression, equally snooty. "Oh dear, Daisy! Don't even speak of such horrors! Just the thought of it and I'll be all day in a bath trying to scrub my fur clean again!"

As Violet laughed, I couldn't help but snicker under my breath; though I always tried to take the high road with such family matters, I had met Iris and Daisy during an earlier employ. My opinion of Violet's older sisters was not particularly high. That Violet took a bit of savage delight in rankling their highbrow sensibilities and sharing the juicy details of her exploits always made me smile inside.

We walked out of the suite and as she locked the front door, I said "You can impress me with your driving in your fancy new car and I'll fill it up with gas. It's not often that a pretty lady drives me!" I tipped my hat with my right paw, dipping my head slightly and smiling with amusement.

She laughed and replied in a mock Southern accent, "Why of

course, good sir! I thank you for your kind and generous offer!" Then she bowed and curtsied in an exaggerated manner, and the laughter I was trying to keep inside burst forth. She took my arm and we walked down the hall and down the stairs to the rear entrance, chuckling to ourselves and enjoying each other's company. We could hardly have been more different, the young and wealthy debutante who wanted to escape the tedious life of high society and me, who lived on the fringes of polite society and occasionally the law, modest in means and rather isolated in character. I secretly enjoyed these times, when notions of class seemed not to matter and the two of us could share in the company of the other, even if only for work. Though I was occasionally urged to ask Violet on a date by both Lizzie and Victoria Cahill, who quietly told me of the high regard Violet held me in, I resisted. Though I toyed with the idea of asking her to dinner to see if something more could happen, I never felt like I could measure up and was afraid of damaging the relationship that we now had. If I mucked up what we had and she left, I would be a far sadder person because of it.

We walked out the rear of the building and into the alley behind. There, its right side hugging the back wall, sat the Chevrolet, a 1941 sedan. The car was clean, chocolate brown in color. The big straight six started quickly and settled into a smooth idle. Violet eased the car up to me and stopped, giving me enough space to open the passenger door and step inside. The tan upholstery, a little worn at the edges, was clean, as were the floors. I shut the door and we started on our way.

As we pulled out of the alley and onto the streets, I stole a glance out the window as the sidewalks passed by, then glanced upward toward the sky. The dull grey clouds had not eased in the slightest; if anything, they had grown darker and more oppressive. The scent of rain wasn't heavy in the air just yet, but the oppressive weight of the low iron sky suggested its possible arrival later in the day. The chilly air, seemingly unwarmed in the past several hours, only reinforced thoughts that bad weather was on the way.

I turned back to glance at Violet, who in turn smiled momentarily at me before turning back to driving, and then I watched out the split windshield as the world passed by. The Winterhaven's big warehouses were located on the outskirts of the city, built during the War on the eastern scrublands on the northeast side of town. It would take us close to an hour to get there as we travelled in the middle of day. My mind mused that by night, with far fewer cars on the roads, the trip from the docks might take as little as half an hour, perhaps less if the trucks hit the lights right and the taxis were cooperative. With appropriated tuna packed on ice, there would be plenty of time to load, transport, and unload before the fish even began to spoil. But all of this hinged on whether or not the trucks were delivering stolen tuna to the warehouses for processing, if that's what they were even doing at all. If we were wrong, Violet and I would have ruled out one theory, albeit a good theory. But tracking clues and evidence often led into dead ends, and it was all part of the business. I glanced at Violet again and wondered if these same thoughts were flowing through her mind, or if her silence concealed something else entirely.

8

After some forty minutes of driving, the dense buildings of the neighborhood boroughs started to give way to larger and more solitary structures. The roads began to curve and the air took on a wetter, heavier feel. We were nearing our destination, a series of gigantic warehouses built to house the machinery and the people who built the large bombers used in the War. The land itself was low, situated about a quarter mile from an ocean inlet, covered in scrub and bramble, and until recently unused for anything.

When an airfield was built here just before the war, the Winterhavens, among others, purchased land nearby and built a number of large structures to house aircraft or even manufacture them. When the Lend'Lease operation got underway, New Amsterdam had readymade facilities for aircraft manufacture. For several years the big buildings were alive with the sound of aircraft assembly, the finished product fueled and flown from the adjacent runway to the Western Front. But soon after the war in Europe concluded, both the airfield and surrounding manufacturing were shuttered, and the area began to deteriorate as some owners either sold what was there or let it sit vacant. And those vacant buildings would be perfect to hide an illicit tuna facility or three. Although Violet and I hoped to see something that told us that we were on the right track, part of me hoped that we would encounter no one at all as untoward things have been known to happen in abandoned areas.

Violet slowed and pulled the car next to the southernmost building, tucked close to a dumpster and some miscellaneous debris that looked to have been there for quite some time. She cut the engine and turned toward me wordlessly. She possessed some very sharp instincts, particularly for someone who had never worked in law enforcement or private investigations and I could trust her to take the lead; she knew these warehouses better than me and would immediately notice if anything was out of place. I nodded to her and we exited the car, holding the latches as we shut the doors quietly. The air was still, the area quiet.

But as we began to walk silently toward a side door, an engine roared to life on the nearby airport runway, then another and another. Several prewar coupes motored slowly onto the wide pavement, lining side by side, their engines rumbling. In front of the line, in between the two middle cars stood a young female cat, clad in jeans, a black leather jacket, and a red bow on her head. As we watched, she raised a red flag over her head and the engines began to rev, then rev again. She swung the flag downward and the cars roared past, accelerating in a steady growing wail of sound. Some eight or ten cars tore down the runway while several figures cheered them on from the sides. At the end of the runway, the cars braked and turned up the taxiway, piling on speed as they blasted up the pavement in the other direction.

I looked at Violet, who smiled back at me. We knew that amateur racers had taken to using the abandoned airfield as a racetrack, and we watched as more cars appeared. This could work to our favor. The sound of the cars would mask us as we looked around the surrounding warehouses, and their presence might keep some of the work crews at bay for a while. We moved to the side door and peered through the small window. Seeing nothing amiss, Violet pulled a ring of keys from her purse and quickly unlocked the door, then the two of us stepped inside.

The interior was cavernous and well-lit by large vertical windows that ran along the sides of the structure. The high ceiling once provided ample space for the tall rudders of bombers, and the entire front of the building could be opened via a set of tracked doors to allow completed aircraft to exit the building. The Winterhavens had spared little expense in creating the best for the war effort. The interior of the building was painted white and large windows planned from the start; both made for a bright and airy interior space in which workers could better see the components on which they worked.

Plus, in the event of a power outage, the interior was bright enough to continue daylight assembly without the overhead lights. This warehouse lacked the upper floor offices in the rear, and instead featured a second set of doors on the far end of the building for partially completed aircraft to be wheeled from other buildings and further worked on in this structure. Four buildings in total were built to house the assembly line, the planes moving from one building to the next. Consolidated Aircraft had used these buildings as a manufacturing plant during the war, but cleared out at war's end. Soon after, the Army Air Force deemed the airfield redundant and shuttered it. Though it had been sold to New Amsterdam, existing airfields closer to downtown meant it was unlikely to reopen anytime soon. The warehouses remained as relics, empty but well maintained in the hopes that someone would yet have use for them.

We casually walked around, the soles of our shoes echoing off the distant walls and ceiling. Without any upper offices, Violet and I could clearly see the massive interior space. Still, we took a few minutes to inspect the doors for any damage, plus the locks on the massive hanger doors. Finally, we checked the fuses in the box and turned on one set of the overhead lights. We spent the next hour or so checking the remaining three buildings in the same manner, and though we expected to find nothing wrong, we couldn't help but feel slightly disappointed that everything was exactly as it should be. Though Violet had casually asked her father about any new tenants, he had told her that there were none and we expected to find just that. We decided to walk back to the car and drive around the larger warehouse and industrial district on the off chance that we might find something that could help our case.

As we made our way to the car, we noted that the sky was still heavy with dark gray clouds and a chilly wind blew off the bay to our south. Despite the threat of the past couple of days, the rain still held off. The racers still sped across the old airfield like dervishes of speed and steel, their cars a constant torrent of engine acceleration and shrieking tires. I felt the squeeze of a paw on my arm and looked over to see Violet looking at me. "We should wait a little while before we start looking again. I doubt anything will happen until it gets darker and my guess is that anyone doing anything illegal isn't going to make it easy to find. We could drive around these buildings for hours and never see a thing. Maybe if we wait here for a while, we can catch someone doing something later in the evening." I agreed.

We reached the Chevrolet and stepped inside and out of the wind. Violet started the car and pulled away from the building. She slowly drove toward the airfield and onto a nearby taxiway. Without a word she pulled the car near some of the spectators' vehicles and turned off the engine. We cracked our windows to get some fresh air, then sat in silence, watching and listening, until Violet spoke.

"There are times I envy you, Max."

I looked over, surprised at her statement and the seriousness of her tone. She looked straight ahead, her blue eyes staring outward through the windshield at nothing in particular, arms crossed lightly in front of her. Though I had known her for a while now, this was the first time that this subject had come to light. Something in her tone suggested that I should treat this with a bit of caution.

"What do you mean? My life is nothing special. I mean, at times it's almost mind-numbingly boring, then it's positively insane," I said. "Compared to your life, to the things you've had access to, my life is so ordinary as to be almost pointless."

Violet's reply genuinely surprised me. "That's the thing Max. I envy an ordinary life. Ordinary people can just go about their lives in their own way and not have to worry about anything else. They can spend time with the cats they enjoy and fall in love with the people they want to spend their lives with, all without any expectations whatsoever. Look at you, Max. You live in a modest flat in a working-class neighborhood and you are free to come and go as you please. You can come home at night and act like a complete slob if you choose, lounging around in your boxers, listening to the radio and eating those awful little fish you enjoy to your heart's content. And you chose your job, something that you are good at and which you reasonably enjoy. I know not every cat chooses their job, but you did, and you chose it without much if any outside influence." She paused for a moment, leaning her head forward and closing her eyes.

"Please don't take me the wrong way, but most people think that being born wealthy is a ticket to the easy life. Maybe for most people it is, but there are things that people don't know about me, things they don't see. I am so very aware of the privileges and advantages that I've had in life, but they have come at some cost. For me, being rich is a form of confinement without bars. I want so much to do something more with my life, to use my influence and my family's fortune to help this city. It's like a hunger inside, a burning desire to do more than what I'm supposed to do, to exceed all expectations. My father, my uncle, they run charities, soup kitchens, places of refuge, many good things. But they never see what is out there on the streets. They work from their offices or are downtown hobnobbing with the social elites, but they never come to the working neighborhoods to see how life really is."

"And for females in our family, that unspoken prison becomes even worse. We are the wives and the daughters, we're to be protected and cared for, and if we try to reach out, to take the initiative, we're told that it's not a "female's place" to make such a big mark. Iris and Daisy are perfect examples of what women are supposed to act like: lazy underachievers in the home and dolled up socialites looking for a husband on the town. I'm one of the lucky ones; so far, my father has supported my efforts to become more independent.

"He has no sons and it may just be that he needs me to take over the family ventures when he retires, but at least I can come to work and get away from all that. He wasn't exactly thrilled when I took this job, but now that he sees what it's done for me, he says that working for you has given me a better sense of what it's like to take on some responsibility. And he's proud of me. Plus, he knows now you won't take advantage of me over my family's money. I wasn't entirely sure he would be happy that I bought this car, but he has been very supportive. But if a time comes when he needs me to start taking over the finances, or God forbid he thinks he's found some cat to marry me off to, I'm afraid what might happen. My father has been progressive with his thoughts and actions toward me, but I don't know how far it goes." She bent her head down and closed her eyes. "I've gotten used to living a more independent life and I don't know if I could ever go back. I can't imagine that I would want to."

When she opened her eyes and turned to me, the tears she was trying to hide began to roll. Her voice was full of heavy sadness as she spoke. "Look at the racers out there, out driving their cars as fast as they dare out on the runway. They live on a ragged edge where they could crash and burn at any moment, but their lives are theirs to control. No one oversees them or tells them what they can and can't do, they just drive and they just race. The first time I came out here by myself, they were at it, flying around their track. I look at them and I see liberation in their speed, a whole field of getaway cars all blasting down the runway, laying down a rubber road right to freedom.

"I see it, Max, and I want it for myself! I want the kind of life where I can wake up and just decide to build a race car out of an old Ford and then drive it as fast as I can. I want to drive it as fast as it will go and then I want to drive it some more, out of this city and away from this place, far and away to where no one knows my name. Maybe someplace out west, where there's still a place without a postcard and a mountain unexplored. I could just drive and drive until I make it to the west coast, all the way out to the Pacific Ocean. I've never seen it, and I want to, so much! I want so much more out of this life than what my sisters and I will inherit, so much more than what is "expected" of me! I want it now, because the wait is becoming intolerable!"

She stopped talking, leaving the engines of the racers and her own heavy breathing the only sounds to fill the silence. She looked down, her eyes closed, and while we sat near one another on the bench seat of her Chevrolet, I felt like the space between could have been a chasm. I had long known that Violet was clever and resourceful, almost from the moment she started working for me, and though she was a young lady of wealthy means, she had proven herself as capable an employee as ten average cats. When I would look at her, I no longer saw a female lady first, but instead I saw the rapier-sharp mind and intelligent wit that I had come to rely on over the past few years. Only at times like this did I see her for the progressive thinker she really was, blazing her own path in a difficult world.

That she wanted more out of this life shouldn't have surprised me, but her ambitions reached farther than I could have known. I wondered how I missed the signs of her discontent, how I could be so clueless about my own employee and partner. Violet was hurting, and I was blind to it. I wanted to comfort her, to let her know that things would be okay, but when I lay my hand gently on her shoulder the words left me. She turned to look at me with those impossibly blue eyes, and though she deserved so much better, the best I could manage was a weak smile, followed by two gentle pats with a paw, then nothing more.

I don't know how long we sat in the car, the silence between us seemingly as impermeable as the Great Wall of China. I didn't know what to say, yet I needed to say something; Violet wasn't just an important employee whom I swapped ideas with and who sometimes accompanied me on many tasks, but she was also my friend, one of the closest I had ever known. Deep inside, down beneath the inner fortress that I had built for protection from a harsh world, down where the essence of soul was stripped bare of its defenses, I knew I cared for her deeply, as something so much more, but I could never tell her, never let her know, for to do so was to risk the very thing I valued so deeply, our close friendship. She was out of my league and would forever remain so, like some beautiful soaring eagle who came, inexplicably, to hold company with a mere common pigeon. Or, I mused, like Mediterranean-prepared Mahi-mahi to my canned sardines. One day she would find a rich man who could sweep her off her feet as she truly deserved, and when that day came, she would leave my mundane world forever.

9

The iron clouds still hid the sun, but the day was beginning to ebb into early evening when the racers pulled to a stop along the front taxiway, and the airfield began to fall quiet. I had been rooting for a black Plymouth, cloaked in bare primer save for a number '3' painted in red on the doors, to win the last race, but out of the final turn it was nipped by a red Ford three window coupe with no front fenders and a flathead under the hood. It was a drag race to the line, where a young calico in a white flowered sun dress, boots and a leather bomber jacket waved a homemade checkered flag. Violet had fallen asleep some while before, at first leaning against the door and window but later laying her head on my shoulder and curling her back legs and tail beneath the steering wheel. Though the air in the car was cool from the outside chill, both my greatcoat and my assistant combined to keep me warm.

With the engines quiet, she began to stir, first yawning, then opening her eyes and looking up at me with only a fleeting moment of confusion. I couldn't resist a bit of fun and said, in a mock chiding voice, "Employee review: It is certainly NOT appropriate for an assistant to fall asleep on the job, but falling asleep while WITH the investigator on the job borders on intolerable! This incident will definitely find its way into your permanent record."

With equally mock indignation, Violet's eyes opened wide, her mouth fell open, and she retorted, "That will be the day! Who do you think does the filing in that office of yours? All I have to do is move any such report to the only permanent file you actually use, that round one that sits on the floor near your desk!" She smirked and shoved my arm lightly. "And why would you let me fall asleep anyway? That awkward silence of ours was going so well!"

I turned my head, looked her straight in her blue eyes and replied in the most truthfully deadpan voice I could muster, "I let you sleep because you always drool a little, just under your nose, and I think that's funny. You snore too, loudly, like a sawmill at full tilt, and I think that's funny too."

With a wounded look on her face betrayed only by the humorous glint in her eyes she replied, "You would pick on things I have absolutely no control over? That's just mean! Low-down, dirty and mean! You are EVIL, Max Persian! Evil and rotten right down to your mean little core!"

By now I couldn't hold it in any longer and burst out laughing, with Violet a split second behind, interjected by the occasional snort. The humor felt good, cleansing somehow, and when we were done, save for the occasional snicker, we took a few minutes and drew up a rough plan as to how we would proceed.

We hadn't expected to find any illicit tuna operations within the gigantic Winterhaven-funded aircraft warehouses, but the inspections had given us reason and opportunity to be in this part of the city. And because Violet had accompanied her father on prior inspections, she knew where many of the larger warehouses and plants within the industrial district lay and had a feel for the areas surrounding them. She took lead on this particular operation, and I was glad for her knowledge. We had laid out a few requirements that someone looking to run a clandestine outfit on this scale would look for. The buildings would have to be sizable, large enough to receive the numerous trucks that hauled tuna from the harbor. They would have to be private, in one of the more abandoned parts of the district and away from prying eyes. Finally, they would probably have to be equipped to operate at night, which meant electric lighting. Our list was short, deliberately so to allow us to stay open to possibilities we both thought of and ones we might find during our search. With that, Violet started the car and we set off.

We began our search in the area around the airfield. Many of the warehouses were relatively recent in construction like the Winterhaven buildings; they incorporated the same types of modern features as those massive structures, plus they benefited from easy access to the highways that crisscrossed New Amsterdam. Some were still in use, but a substantial number stood vacant, mute casualties of the end of war. But our efforts came up empty and we moved on. Buildings further west proved equally bereft of positive results, though the area had good road access and many of the buildings had been refurbished or rebuilt in recent years. The buildings to the north were mostly older, and smaller, constructed primarily of brick with many showing signs of distress. The area was mostly abandoned, and the few wasted and brain-fried souls we encountered did not seem the types to trifle with. Nothing looked promising in the least, and we found exactly nothing of use. Though this was what we expected, we could at least rule out this area as the home of the facility.

Violet and I were growing discouraged as we drove into the oldest section of industrial building. We were by now anything but hopeful. We both knew that some construction dated back into the early 19th century, part of New Amsterdam's Industrial Revolution. These wood and coal-fired factories had been situated here to take advantage of the prevailing winds coming off the water, winds that drove the smoke and soot-filled waste away from New Amsterdam and its wealthy elite. Most of these structures were quite old and long abandoned, and those that hadn't simply fallen in from neglect stood as mute and unwanted reminders of the city's manufacturing past.

By now the sky was darkening, the unseen sun having given up on its futile quest to reach the ground below. The rain, which had threatened to come through the entire day, finally began to fall, first in fitful spitting, then soon in a light but steady stream. The abandoned buildings that still stood hid darkened interiors behind mute windows mostly devoid of glass. Violet turned on the wipers but kept the headlights dark, hoping that anyone doing anything worth seeing would not notice the dark car in the rain and evening gloom.

We drove in silence, slowly past one derelict structure and

then the next, seeming for all the world as if we were the only civilized people in existence. In my mind I knew that we weren't really alone, that these buildings held some of the most desperate and addled of souls, and the thought of their plight and what their desperation could drive them to do made me wish to keep the illusion intact. As the day turned to night, any hope of seeing anything faded and we turned down a cross street with the intent of heading back into New Amsterdam. But as we pulled to a four-way intersection, Violet stopped suddenly. Neither of us said a word, for down the intersecting street about a hundred and fifty feet, a semi was carefully backing its trailer to the brightly lit open doors of an old factory. An old factory that had no business sporting an interior full of lights while its neighbors sat silent and dark.

Violet silently pushed in the clutch and slipped the car into reverse with a slight crunch. She slowly backed up the street and into the alley which separated two ruined buildings to our right. After cutting the ignition, she set the parking brake and turned to me, her voice a rushed whisper, her eyes wide with excitement.

"Max, you saw that, right? You saw a lit warehouse and a truck?" I nodded. "Good. I just wanted to make sure that nothing was playing tricks on me, that the truck was real!"

I chuckled a little, knowing full well what she was feeling. That sudden rush of adrenaline was familiar to my early time as a private eye, that feeling of wonder and uncertainty upon discovering what could be a major part of the case. In truth, I had hoped to find a less active scene rather than the one we just happened upon; I had taken Violet out into the field on numerous occasions, but this would be the first time she had found what was possibly an active crime scene. I had to look around to see what was happening and decide whether this was related to the case, which risked discovery by folks who would rather not be discovered and thus could quickly become dangerous. I secretly hoped Violet would stay in the car and out of sight but knowing her as I did, I held little hope that this would actually happen. For better or worse, we were a team, more so now than ever before.

We quietly walked to the edge of the collapsing building we had parked next to and peered around the corner. The warehouse lay on the other side of the street, its entrance set away from the corner, and by most standards wasn't very large. The truck we had seen was now likely inside, its contents being unloaded behind closed doors. Without the light spilling from the large freight opening, the building was surprisingly dark; it was obvious that the windows had been boarded or painted over to keep the light in and prying eyes out, and it was questionable if we would have even noticed it if we happened upon it now. It looked largely deserted, but careful study revealed at least two guards semi-hidden in the shadows, both wielding Thompson submachine guns. That kind of firepower served notice that this operation was no amateur hour but was a professional undertaking by some facet of organized crime. Violet noticed the guns too and looked over at me with a wide-eyed look that showed her awareness for the very real danger at hand. I nodded, then motioned to the car in one last attempt to keep her safe from danger, though predictably she waved me off with a single cross movement. I knew that the dimming sky and steady rain would go a long way toward hiding us, while the raindrops on old pavement and cobblestones would mask our footfalls, but I also knew that the same conditions would apply to anyone skulking about that might want to do us harm. We would tread lightly and with deliberate care.

With the two goons we could see holding station by the front of the building, we decided to circle around several of the other buildings, taking a circuitous route to our suspect building at a rear corner, hopefully without incident. With luck, we might find a place with a small hole, giving us a glimpse inside to see what was happening. It certainly wasn't a perfect plan, nor one that took into account the sorts of things that could go wrong, but the rain afforded us an excellent opportunity to sneak around that might not come again. Plus, whatever was happening seemed to be unfolding at this moment and my hunch was that it could be transpiring fast. I had been at this job enough to discover that if I put too much thought into any plan, I was just creating useless work. I didn't know how things went for other Private Eyes, but for me, a basic framework of a plan filled in with a healthy filling of "making things up as I go" worked quite well far more often than not. I just hoped that for both my sake and for Violet's that this jaunt would fall into the more often category rather than the not.

As we made our way around the old buildings and across the streets, I was pleasantly surprised to find that the way was dark and deserted. Either the rain kept the guards at bay or, just as likely, none were posted this far from the warehouse. Within ten minutes we had circled around and from a small outbuilding next door we could see the back and part of the side that made our target building. A single door pierced the wall near the corner, though it looked to badly rusted and likely not opened for a very long time. We saw no one else and aside from the rain the area was dark and still. Still, we waited for almost fifteen minutes with our backs to the wall of the small structure, hidden in the shadows of an overhanging roof, but no guard appeared. That single door appeared to be the only rear entrance on this side of the building, as a quick look revealed the back of the building had no doors at all. Though it seemed too good to be true, the only guards seemed to be stationed at the truck entrance. Now our job was to find a place through which to see.

The building featured windows in a horizontal band that ran about twenty feet from the ground. Much of the glass had been spared the wrath of vandals and remained intact, only requiring a coating of black paint to obscure them, though panes and sections had gone missing in places and were covered in plywood. Luckily, this building had been fitted with a metal catwalk that ran just below the windows, and even luckier, upon closer inspection, the windows' paint and plywood had been applied in a hurried and sloppy manner, leaving numerous small holes that were revealed by the interior light. This was good, but I made sure I could get Violet and myself away quickly, for even the best of situations could head south in an instant.

An old self-retracting staircase near the corner of the building served as the way to the catwalk, and as luck would have it the springs that retracted it had weakened over time, leaving the bottom only about four feet above the ground. I reached a paw out and took hold of the rusty metal, then gently eased it to the ground to avoid any undue noise from creaky old hinges. I put one foot on the bottom step, both to help stabilize the staircase and to test the weight the old metal would hold. I eased my full weight on the step and it held fast, then quietly climbed to the catwalk. Once I reached the catwalk safely, Violet quietly joined me, her lighter weight less likely to cause any sound or sudden collapse.

We paused, taking care to ensure that we were not seen, then quietly crept down the old walkway. The bottom of the windows came to my shoulders and to Violet's chin, but on the ground, we had noticed a potential viewing hole about two thirds of the way down that looked to be about two inches tall, an inch wide and at the bottom of the glass. We could take turns peering through it, while I would detail what I saw in a small notebook I kept for such occasions. Through the occluded glass we could hear voices but no telltale signs of machinery; our silence turned critical, for any noise made out here might possibly alert someone to our presence.

We quickly reached the spot in the window. I backed to about 18 inches from the glass, then moved steadily closer, letting the building's interior grow steadily larger and more coherent as I let my eyes approach. I wanted to make sure there was no guard watching on the other side of the window, ready to see a wandering eye appear and seize us for some unpleasant purpose. No one appeared, so I removed my fedora and put my eye to the glass.

Below me, lit by the steady glow of incandescent lighting, I saw workers performing various tasks throughout the warehouse, every one of them involving fish. In the front of the warehouse, a pile of ice and fish sat on a recently poured concrete floor, while on the far side near the pile several workers busied themselves with gutting the fish, cutting them into filets. These were then put into large salt brine vats, in which the coarse grain salt would pull moisture from the flesh. Other workers then removed now-dehydrated filets from other vats and handed them up to workers on large wooden platforms. These laid the filets out close to each other to dry and cure above slowly turning fans and heat lamps. Finally, salt-dried filets were taken down and stacked on tables near the truck, ostensibly to be loaded into the now-empty cargo trailer and taken to another location for storage. The entire interior space was filled, each step claiming its own place in the old warehouse. I couldn't help but marvel at the cleverness of the criminals in charge of this; the salting process required no power and had been perfected centuries before, yet remained a very viable way to prepare the fish for storage and eventual distribution. It was highly organized, efficiently run, and incredibly productive. This salting and curing warehouse was the break Violet and I had been looking for.

I took in as much detail as I could, then pulled away so that Violet could see. The only thing that surprised me was the modest size of this operation; for a city as large as New Amsterdam, the number of fish in this building would not by itself constitute a shortage. A moment later I realized that this was likely just one warehouse among several. Not only would multiple warehouses spread the operation to other points, but should the police disrupt one warehouse, several more were able to keep continue undetected, ensuring that whoever was behind this remained in the business of manipulating the tuna supply for the entire city.

A pair of headlights on the wall below us broke me free of my thought process. I tapped Violet on the shoulder, indicating that I wanted to take a last look before we snuck away. As I put my eye to the glass, I saw the main doors open, but instead of another delivery truck, a long black Cadillac sporting the aircraft-inspired fins of a new '48 models rolled inside. The warehouse doors closed behind it and the left rear door opened. A two-tone wingtip shoe, attached to a leg wearing an expensive dark pinstripe suit, emerged. The chrome tip of a cane followed, while above the door appeared a black fedora with a stark white band. As the rest of the figure emerged from the car, he surveyed the warehouse with an imperious air, looking for anything and anyone who didn't belong there. And though he had not seen us, I knew that we were now in even greater danger.

Two other cats emerged from the passenger side, one a large black longhair in a quiet gray suit and black overcoat ornamented only by a dull watch chain, the other a dark brown tabby in a tan raincoat and suited in dark blue who walked to the back of the car and opened the trunk. From it he pulled a long wooden box, unadorned and unfinished, which he set on an unoccupied table nearby and then carefully opened. From the box, a Thompson gun emerged. He carefully attached the ammunition clip and, in an almost lackadaisical gesture turned the gun upward until the barrel rested against his right shoulder. The smirk on his face spelled trouble.

Though Rufus Segovia often looked overly relaxed and bemused, his reputation as a brawler with a hair-trigger temperament suggested that he could get ugly in an instant. When Blackie Lawler accompanied him, as if to direct Rufus' brand of chaos toward a specific end, his chaotic nature was forged into an instrument of precise destruction. But the presence of the third cat, the one with the cane, changed everything. It took a lot to get Constantino Gandini to venture from his uptown abode to such a plebeian setting, and his presence only reinforced the sense of dread I had felt when that Cadillac drove up. As I pulled back from the glass one last time, I turned to Violet and quietly whispered the words that were screaming through my mind.

"We have to go. Now!"

Violet took one last look through the glass, taking only a second or two before pulling back. Her eyes were wide, her face full of concern. She knew as well as I did what getting caught would mean. But as if to prove that she was no wilting flower, she quickly nodded and moved quickly but quietly ahead of me to the staircase. As we both climbed downward, quickly and quietly as possible, we saw that the outer door below us was still shut, but we couldn't count on it remaining this way. As we reached the bottom we paused in the shadows for a brief moment, long enough to see that no guards had been posted in our absence, then crossed into the shadows the way we came.

The rain that had shielded our approach still fell, muffling our footfalls and helping to hide us from view. We skirted around the darkened buildings and through narrow alleys, moving as quickly as we could while searching for guards, and soon we made it back to Violet's car. In the gloom the car looked inert, dead, like some heavy, metal sarcophagus with something ominous waiting within. But at that moment, the car was like gazing on Valhalla; I had never been so happy to see an inanimate object as I was to see our means of departure.

With key in hand Violet opened the door and waved me across the bench to the passenger side. She then got in behind me, pulling the door to so the dome light would extinguish, then started the car, selected reverse and backed up the street, quietly and without lights. After two blocks, she turned the car right and slowly drove away, only turning on the headlights when she felt she was far enough away. Neither of us spoke. Having seen what was happening and who was behind it, there was little need for speech. It was just as well too, for I didn't want to tell her that a moment before she turned off that side street, I thought I saw a dark figure watching us from where we had parked the car.

Up on the catwalk, Violet and I had briefly whispered about following the loaded truck to its next destination to find where the purloined tuna was stored. That plan disintegrated at Gandini's arrival, at the precise moment when we decided that our lives were perhaps more important than testing the fates' patience. We had already scored a victory by not only discovering a salting facility, but also the identity of the plant's mastermind, the person behind this latest shortage. We had flirted with danger and had come away with a wealth of information. Even in our cold, damp state, waiting for the Chevrolet's heater to warm us, we had come away victorious.

As we drove home, we decided that we would return the following night to ascertain where the dried filets were being stored. We arrived back in the city tired and feeling a bit worse for wear. In her paranoia Violet kept checking the rearview mirror every couple of seconds, and while I really couldn't blame her, I was pretty sure that no one was following us and hadn't been since we left the industrial district a while before. She had met *Signore* Gandini before, often at her family's estate; Constantino Gandini maintained several legitimate businesses and charities in New Amsterdam and often invited prominent families to join with him in these above-board business ventures. She had known that Constantino at least dabbled in some questionable activities, but even since she had started on as my assistant, she had never witnessed this for herself. Now that she had, she was a bit rattled, trying to take stock of what was happening around her. I offered to accompany her home and catch a cab back, but she politely declined. She was a tough one and would probably still beat me to the office tomorrow.

We drove by the office to see if anything untoward was happening, but the windows were unbroken and pitch black. Either someone had been there, someone was up there, or no one was there at all. Either way we didn't stop, but instead I had Violet drop me off in front of Russian Joe's Milk Bar before heading home. As I walked in, I took notice of who was there, but tonight the bar was strictly the domain of regulars. Joe was behind the bar as usual, and I returned his friendly wave as well as those of a couple of the usual barflies.

73

As I crossed the floor, I took off my damp hat, then set it on the bar in front of me. I planted both elbows on the shiny wood surface, closed my eyes, and planted my forehead squarely into my waiting paws.

Taking a deep breath, I took stock of the day's events, from the evidence we had uncovered to my closest associate and friend's tempestuous inner turmoil. Both were proving large bites to digest, and right now I needed some time and a familiar environment to work through the quandaries that had presented themselves; since I wasn't ready to head home to my little apartment and a tin of sardines, I came here. After a day spent in the cold damp gray of a late autumn day, the warm air and the dim light that reflected on the many wooden and glass surfaces that filled the establishment, the bar proved welcoming.

A minute or so later, I raised my head and opened my eyes to find that a tall glass of cold milk had soundlessly appeared before me, as if by magic. I picked it up and poured some of its heavenly contents into my parched mouth, then sighed as it went down easy. I looked to my right at Joe, who, as ever, was drying a glass, and when he turned my way a moment later, I raised my glass in a gesture of thanks and salutations. Without a word, he nodded and flashed a welcoming smile in return. I had surrendered to the realization that I would be here for a while during the short ride from the office in Violet's car and chuckled inwardly that this might be as close to the rest she repeatedly suggested I take.

Sometimes I found that when I couldn't solve a given problem, when I was figuratively (or sometimes literally) banging my head against an immovable wall, I found that if I just put it aside for a few hours that a solution would sometimes come to me, seemingly out of the blue. It was as if my unconscious mind were still pondering the problem and working at a feasible solution, but without the debris that my conscious mind normally fed it. For the record, I have no idea where I got that inane bit of wisdom and insight, but I hope it didn't come from Freud; whatever mild Oedipal complex I may have harbored was my own business. If it was, sooner or later some unpleasantness regarding unresolved feelings might come to the fore, and if I wasn't a basket case already, that would surely push me right over the edge. No, better to just relax for a while with the company of a couple of regulars I knew named Lawrence and Carson, swapping tall tales and bad humor to the tune of cold beverages that kept on coming. Yes, the city may be falling to ruin, but tonight I would drown my worries in a steady stream of cold white goodness and hope that I had the beginnings of something workable by the time I arrived at work tomorrow, because if I didn't, I would have an even rougher morning than the one no doubt facing me after the next few hours. All I could do was shrug and move further down the bar to swap terrible jokes with the other hopeless miscreants who also found themselves in need of a temporary escape.

10

The following morning arrived with the gentle subtlety of a train wreck. Though the day was again cloudy and dim, I had forgotten to pull the shade when I stumbled into my apartment and collapsed on my sofa, and the light in the windows was far too bright. My eyes felt like they contained a healthy portion of sand, while my throat felt dry and scratchy. My night had consisted of several hours spent at Russian Joe's, some of it in conversation with others, some of it by myself, I think. When I got sleepy and could possibly no longer stand, I had Joe call me a taxi to take me home. I had managed to climb out of my suit before I hit the hay, though the stark light of day revealed that it could use a good pressing and possibly a well-deserved spa day at the dry cleaners. This was not going to be one of my better days.

As I pulled another suit from the armoire and dressed, I caught a glimpse of myself in the mirror and cringed. 'You know Max,' I thought, 'you look terrible.' Perhaps today was one of those days where I stopped and bought myself a proper breakfast, the kind that normal people ate, rather than just taking a tin of sardines and stuffing it in my pocket. The clock on the wall said I was still early, so I had plenty of time to don my daily attire with deliberate care. By the time I had affixed my hat and slid into my raincoat, my breakfast plans might well have been set in stone.

Three blocks up from my apartment building lay Hopper's Diner, a corner restaurant I frequented from time to time. Its most appealing features were its 24-hour open time, the consistent if slightly bland fare, and a staff that occasionally treated their customers with something other than thinly veiled contempt, in that order. It was the sort of place that no one actually loved but was cheap and always available. From past experience I knew who would be working, and since my aching brain thought nothing could beat some scrambled eggs with sausage and bacon, I headed there and soon had myself a seat by the window. I always enjoyed window seats, even though today was a bit bright for my lactose-blurred eyes. Because the floor of the diner sat a couple of steps above street level, anyone sitting by the windows could look slightly down and into the faces of the cats passing by, wondering from their expressions and their posture what might be happening in their lives.

In a few short minutes the waitress, a large white and brown tabby named Delia, who seemed perpetually irritated about nothing in particular, came out with a tray that had a plate of scrambled eggs, sausage and bacon and a glass of water to accompany it. As I thanked her, Delia replied curtly as to how awful I looked and recommended that I pull the fedora down a bit further to hide my ugly mug.

As I ate, I thought that Delia may have been one of the less pleasant cats I have known, but at least I always knew exactly where I stood. I finished my plate without interruption, left a modest tip at the table to avoid any cyanide garnishes in the future, and paid at the register. The food may not have been exactly divine, but it was enough to get me feeling a bit better, or at least a bit more like facing another day.

As I left Hopper's, the light of day and the noise of too many cats on their way to work mounted a frontal assault on my bruised senses. I had thought about heading by the Cahills, but today I just wanted to get to the office. What I really wanted was to go home and sleep off my woes, but I had known what I was in for when I started tossing back milks last night. I would live, though I wouldn't like it much for a while. I needed a couple of aspirin and some coffee to resemble anything civilized today and so off I walked to work. If nothing else, work was where the percolator lived. I knew Violet would be waiting, much as she always did, and there were notes to compare and decisions to be made.

After ambling the several blocks in a fog of lactose-induced misery, I walked into my office building and as usual saw nothing amiss in the lobby. No one sat on the old furniture and no one manned the darkened desk. I walked up the stairs and down the hallway until I arrived at my office. As I came to the door, I could see through the frosted glass that Violet had already arrived and had turned on the usual lights. Oddly, she seemed to be chatting with someone, her words mixed with occasional laughter. As I stood outside the door, off to one side so as not to alert her to my eavesdropping presence, I listened for a short moment, convinced she was talking on the telephone. As I shook my head at my own behavior, I reached for the doorknob and pushed in the door. It was then that I quickly learned that Violet was not talking on the phone or conversing with the radio, for in the nearest chair in the waiting area sat Blackie Lawler, notorious mobster and second in command only to Constantino Gandini himself.

As I struggled with the shock, Blackie stood up and faced me. He was a very large cat, larger than I had realized as he stood a full head taller than me. In the medium hue of the lamps, his long black fur seemed so dark as to absorb the light, rendering his green eyes all the more striking, and menacing. But though his size and reputation gave him the air of a potentially violent enforcer, nothing in his behavior betrayed the savagery said to walk beside him; he was calm, at ease with his surroundings, seeming more like a self-assured businessman than a notorious gangster. Violet had been speaking with him with the demeanor of someone who had known him for some time and seemed familiar with and completely at ease with his presence. I was unsure of what would happen in those next few moments, but whatever might unfold, good or bad, I would soon find out.

I entered the suite and quietly closed the door behind me. As I turned toward Blackie, he extended his right paw in greeting. I extended my own and the two of us shook. His massive paw gave me the impression of shaking hands with a bear. "Mister Persian, I am glad to meet you in the flesh. I have heard many things about you."

Blackie spoke with a smooth and melodious voice that seemed wholly unexpected. His deliberate and measured speech seemed so perfect as to be without accent or dialect, but his pitch seemed oddly high for a cat so large. It was as out of character as the grip on my paw, which was strong yet oddly gentle. As we released, I was once again caught off guard and could barely speak.

"I'm sorry for my awkwardness, Mr. Lawler. Most mornings find me a bit more clear-headed. I spent a little too much time at the milk bar last night and really didn't get enough sleep. Lactose intolerance left me with a present when I woke up and I've been trying to shake it ever since. I'm sorry for my rudeness and possible incoherence, but I never expected to see you first thing at work talking to my assistant. Would you mind if I take a few minutes to put a fresh pot on and take a couple of aspirin so that I might be at least semi-coherent for you today?"

Blackie smiled out one side of his mouth and nodded wordlessly. I needed the few minutes to try and put my shambled thoughts in order so that I could communicate effectively with this large black cat now standing in my suite. Something told me that I might need all of the skills I knew when conversing with him and to never underestimate him, not even for one second. As he had turned his back to me for the moment, I flashed a hand signal to Violet that she would join us in my office. Though I didn't tell her why, I needed her to listen and remember what was said; she would probably guess this anyway and would help me as I needed her on a day where I was less than at my best.

I swallowed two aspirin dry and set up the percolator for the full amount. I motioned to Blackie, who walked quietly into my office and sat on the sofa, his large body taking almost half of it. He moved with an air of class and refinement I found wholly unexpected and somewhat unnerving, as if his polish only served to throw his opponents further off guard. Violet entered a moment later and found one of the chairs in front of my desk, though she turned it somewhat to be able to comfortably observe Blackie. When the percolator finished, I came and sat down at my desk, carrying three cups, some sugar and some cream on a tray.

Yesterday's newspapers still sat on my desk, barely read. Blackie glanced at them and made a casual observation or two.

"I generally enjoy the Scratching Post," he said. "Their articles are well written and seem as unbiased as a news publication can be these days. I'm a little less enthused with the Gazette. I sometimes believe their writers will fabricate certain details in their stories just to sensationalize otherwise mundane events in a cheap gambit to generate sales. Their copy editor leaves a bit to be desired as well, with multiple tenses abused and poor, righteous words left hideously disfigured via careless misspellings. One would think that the paper would find someone else who can properly edit, but sadly no, the same person stays on month after month to lay siege to the integrity of the language and perpetrate repeated heinous offenses against innocent consonants and vowels."

He closed his eyes and looked down. "And yet these crimes pale by those committed by so-called radio news broadcasts each day, those blabbering half-wits choking up the airwaves with their ever-repeated stories, delving into the gruesome details of the most horrible events with all the worry of a man having a casual chat with his beloved wife. How times have changed so quickly! A decade ago, a mighty ship of the skies crashed and burned, and the wailings of "Oh the humanity!" filled the airwaves. It was tragedy worthy of Aeschylus and Sophocles, Euripides and Homer. "Sing to me, o Goddess, of the wreck of the great Zeppelin Hubris." And yet now, the most vile and bestial of crimes are delivered with a wink and a smile. "Body found dismembered and stuffed into an oil drum, identity still a mystery for now." No one bats an eye as they turn to the kitchen and ask, "Hon, what's for dinner?""

Blackie smiled, as much to himself as to either of us. Though I got the impression he was allowing me time to recover, he had quickly taken control of the conversation. Though I wasn't entirely sure where he was going with it, I did my best to keep up. The aspirin had begun to quiet the sledgehammers in my head, and the thought of an impending coffee helped to soothe my darkened mood. Still, a certain effort was required to ensure that I heard everything the big cat said, and though it seemed random and unconnected to anything with our case, I kept an ear for any detail that might relate. Though she had stayed quiet, I noticed that Violet did the same.

Blackie picked up the copy of the Morning Scratching Post and held it close to his face, inhaling deeply while closing his eyes. He held his breath for a moment and then slowly exhaled, his bright green eyes almost dilated with pleasure.
He held a smile, then turned to me with an oddly simple question: "Mr. Persian, what did you wish to be when you were still a small kitten?"

Taken off guard, I could only stammer that I had to think about that, that it had been so long that I had all but forgotten. Blackie took the dull pocket watch out of his pocket, flipped the lid open and held it in his hand like a talisman. When he spoke, his voice softened, so much that Violet and I leaned in to hear him.

"I only wanted to be one thing, sir. I wanted to be a printer. I wanted to run the presses, to put something meaningful to paper where only blank space existed before. When I was small my family had little money, and my mother went to work cleaning houses. As for me, I went to school and returned to an empty apartment to spend the afternoons by myself. My father worked the big machines in the print shop, had done so for years, and sometimes he would bring me in and show me how the printing was done. He worked both black and white and four-color process, occasionally setting up special projects for six, eight, even ten colors if the customer was specific about the final product. At first, I found the presses unpleasant. They were loud, full of strange noises that bore into my ears like a drill. And the inks smelled peculiar too, a sort of sickly-sweet nauseating scent that stayed in my nose long after the day was done. But in time the noises became the background hum and the smells became comforting, and after a while I could tell which machine was running with my eyes closed, and which colors were used just by the smell alone.

"My father was a good man, Mr. Persian, an honest man, and when I stood beside him, he seemed a giant. He always encouraged me to read, read the papers, read the encyclopedia, read dime store novels, but most importantly *read*. He reasoned that if people didn't read, didn't stay connected to the printed word, that the written language would slowly die out and society would inexorably devolve into anarchy." Blackie closed the pocket watch and latched the cover with an audible 'click'. "My father was a great man, far better than the one I have become. I wanted to be like him, to follow in his footsteps and to make him proud, but my life took a detour and followed a different road."

He still held the closed watch in his paw, firmly but gently, the grip of someone for whom that single possession meant the entire world. He looked as if he wanted to say more, but the moment had passed. As he sat on the sofa, relaxed and holding onto his watch, his demeanor changed, growing both subtly darker and more menacing.

"Mr. Persian, did you know that you and Miss Winterhaven made a visit to one of the oldest printing factories in New Amsterdam last night?" His choice of words remained polite and civilized, but his tone lost all traces of its nostalgic reverence; now, an icier, more threatening tone crept in. Somehow, he knew we had been there. "It's true!" he continued. "Our fair city had already existed for many decades by the time the Industrial Revolution came knocking. Printing presses had also existed in one form or another for hundreds of years, hand operated devices with moveable type that printed multiple copies of a single sheet, created with individual type. But the growth of New Amsterdam and the need for greater publication changed things. Did you know that the building you peered into was built 120 years ago, and that it was the first building in the city erected exclusively to house large steam driven presses, the likes of which had only been invented recently? There have been some changes to it over the years, functional alterations that have left their marks over time, but the fundamental structure remains intact and usable. I find it fascinating that the building still stands, forgotten by almost all save a few minor enthusiasts such as myself. It should be used to house a museum of press and printing technology! And yet it sits over in the oldest part of the district, completely abandoned and empty, just as it has for years and decades before."

Blackie smiled a cold grin, his saber teeth bared. "I don't know what you two were doing out there on such a wretched evening. Me, I was there to research the building as part of a larger history of printing architecture I have been compiling. I would have never seen you except that I happened to catch you moving through the rain out a window and kept a curious eye on you until you drove away in Miss Winterhaven's Chevrolet." Blackie, still smiling, still baring his large teeth, leaned forward on the sofa, fixing me with his cold green eyes as if in the final stages of a hunt.

"Miss Winterhaven tells me that after your footrace in the rain, you felt cold and tired by the time you both returned to New Amsterdam. She also told me that rather than drop you off at your apartment, you asked to be dropped off at the bar a couple of blocks away, the one run by that ex-Merchant Marine sailor named Joe Antonov. Word is that you stayed there a few hours before calling a taxi to take you home, and that while you were there you had a few cold ones to drink. It would certainly explain why you look like you were treed by a coyote; a nice lactose hangover is never a fun way to start the day. But besides the hangover, there's one additional gift hiding at the bottom of every glass, Mr. Persian, and that is memory impairment. You may think you saw something in that building last night, but I was there too, and I can assure you that that factory is as empty as the Savior's Tomb. It's the *leche*, amigo, and it packs a powerful punch. It makes you remember things that never were."

At this, Blackie slowly stood to his full height and moved closer to my desk. "Through the years, I've found that it's usually better if one keeps one's hallucinations to oneself, lest one get into trouble. People can get the wrong idea if they take your mistaken accounts too seriously, and that sort of inconvenience wastes everyone's valuable time."

The black cat turned toward Violet. "Miss Winterhaven, it was good to see you again. Please give my regards to your father and tell him and your mother that I look forward to seeing them at the party. I certainly hope you will attend, though I know you at best tolerate such occasions. I also believe you should bring Mr. Persian as well, as it's possible he has never before attended a high society gathering. I think he would enjoy himself immensely, stepping out of his old apartment on that worn out avenue, wearing some fancy clothes and rubbing elbows with many of New Amsterdam's most influential citizens."

Blackie turned back toward me, now as relaxed as before. "I know for a fact that my closest associate and my esteemed superior, Messrs. Rufus Segovia and Constantino Gandini, eagerly await the chance to meet you, Mr. Persian. After all, they always prefer to place a face with a name, and your name has come up several times as of late. It seems you are a popular man in New Amsterdam and your admirers would relish the chance to meet you. I hope you do not disappoint. The Winterhaven Winter Gala is the talk of the town! And who knows, the Winterhavens have a top-notch staff for these occasions, and one of them might even sneak a few sardine tins in, just for you!" With that, Blackie offered his paw for a departing shake, then offered Violet a peck on each cheek and an unexpectedly warm goodbye. We followed him as he moved toward the front room, pausing only to grab his coat and hat before seeing himself out into the hall, closing the door quietly behind him.

11

After Blackie Lawler had walked down the hall and down the stairs, Violet turned to me with clenched paws and tears welling in her eyes. "He knew we were there," she said. "He knew we were there almost the entire time. We were so careful, so vigilant, and it made no difference! Did I cause this, Max? Would he have known if it had just been you instead of both of us?" She sighed deeply and sank into the guest chair, her head bowing as her eyes clouded and assumed a downcast gaze. "We were *right there*! We had the proof that would have seen it all opened wide! We saw it all and we saw Constantino Gandini himself there! Now we have *nothing*!" With that, Violet put her face into her paws and began sobbing. As her body was wracked with frustration and guilt with every breath, I tried to think of the words to say to comfort her, to reassure her that none of this was her fault. Though at a loss for words, I put a paw on her shoulder and said her name, my voice as quiet and reassuring as I could make it.

"Violet, look at me. I need you to look at me. It's important." As she looked up, I put my paw under her chin and pushed up with gentle pressure until her eyes looked into mine. "It wasn't your fault. It was never your fault. It could have been any one of a hundred things. You did everything right, everything you needed to do, but sometimes these things happen and the situation goes bad in an instant. There are just too many variables, too many little things to go wrong. There's no way to tell just what tipped Blackie Lawler to us, but it was probably something tiny and simple, like a glint of light off a wet coat at just the wrong time that tempts someone to look in that direction." I held out my paw, beckoning her to stand. "If you do this long enough, you learn that while you win a lot of 'em, you lose some along the way, and sometimes those losses are the ones that keep you awake at night. It's the nature of this business; if you take a tiger by the tail, occasionally it will give you the teeth. It's how you deal with the losses that makes or breaks you."

I looked at her, seeing in her how this particular loss tore at her insides, seeing the unrest and malcontent she felt. I knew that right now her mind swirled with a tempest of thoughts and feelings, and that there was nothing to be gained by either of us today. I gave her the day off with pay, practically ordering her to leave through her reluctance. As she made to go, I gave her strict instructions to do anything she wanted with the day so long as it didn't involve returning to the office or anything to do with the investigation. She slipped her coat over her shoulders and turned to look at me through one of the office's panes of glass. Her blue eyes were drying, though a redness and a hint of a tear remained. I smiled at her and nodded, and a moment later she closed her eyes for a moment as she nodded in return, then quietly walked out the door. I walked back into my office and stood at one of the windows, not moving until I saw her car pull from behind the building and drive down the street, away from the office. She had dealt with enough bad news for the day and a break from the action would likely do her good.

As I watched Violet drive away, I decided that a break would also do me good. Blackie had startled me in more ways than one. In my line of work, I expected the cats that hired me and the cats whom I investigated to know my name and some details about me. I hadn't expected Blackie to rattle off fact after fact about me and about my life, down to seemingly trivial details such as my love of sardines. He had studied me and had me largely figured out by the time he had entered the suite. His control of the entire conversation was deliberate, as he hammered home the extent of the knowledge he knew about me. It was clear that his boss Constantino wanted to silence me cleanly rather than take action against me at this point, but Blackie had made the danger all too clear just in case I hadn't quite gotten the message.

I donned my coat and hat, then turned off the lights, I stopped by the door and took a deep breath, stretching my back for a long moment. Feeling a bit better, I walked out of the office, locking the door as I went. Today was finished, and nothing remained that couldn't wait until tomorrow. I decided on a course of action, one that I hoped would distract me from the troubles at hand for a few hours. A few minutes later, after a short delay at the Cahill's newsstand to say a brief hello to Lizzie, Victoria and Sean, I walked through and softly closed the door to my small apartment. I turned on the radio, which slowly warmed to the sounds of the big bands and returned my suit to its hangers in the armoire. Five minutes later, I lay on the sofa, lazily studying the insides of my eyelids while the sounds of the late George Gershwin faded into the background. Five minutes after that, only the hazy boundaries of sleep lay ahead.

12

The rhythmic percussion sounded on the edge of consciousness. It stopped, then started again in the same tempo. After this continued for several times, I grew aware that someone was knocking on a door. I quickly realized that the door was mine; I opened my eyes to find myself staring at the ceiling. The knocking sounded again; this time accompanied by a muffled yet familiar voice, Violet. She had never visited my apartment, much as no one I knew had been here since I moved in years ago. Still, there was a first time for everything.

I rose from the sofa and glanced at the clock. A quarter to one. I had been home for about three hours and asleep for most of that. I walked to the door, unlocked it and opened it halfway to beckon her in. Only when she looked at me and suppressed a chuckle did I realize that I still sported my usual apartment attire of boxers, an undershirt and black socks. As I shut the door and locked it, I shook my head slightly, mentally chiding myself for my carelessness. Violet had changed out of her office attire into a comely number comprised of khaki pants tucked into a pair of brown heeled boots, an olive sweater and a black beret. She walked and stood near the end of the sofa, and after gesturing for her to sit I quickly walked into the small bedroom and pulled out a pair of linen trousers, suspenders, and a raw silk button-down shirt. I pulled a pair of scuffed and worn brown shoes from the bottom of the armoire and walked back into the main room and sat on the other end of the sofa, loosely tying the laces as we began to speak.

"I have some good news, Max, depending on how you look at it," Violet said. Her use of the word 'depending' made me wonder just how good this news really was, but I was soon to find out. "I went home from the office to talk to Daddy about you attending the gala, but by the time I arrived and spoke with him, your name had already been added to the guest list for our charity fundraiser this

Saturday. We tried to call you, but we couldn't get through, which is why I drove here. Max, is your phone out of service?"

I merely pointed to the table next to her, to the black telephone with the receiver off the hook. "Some days, kid, I just want to sleep," I replied with a shrug.

She frowned a rebuke, but quickly resumed her conversation. "It's a black-tie affair, so you're going to need a tuxedo, and given the rarified company in attendance, it needs to be a nice one. Daddy called his tailor and put him on notice, so we're going to have to head over there and let him measure you so he can get to work. It's a bit pricy, but if we write it as a work expense, Daddy will reimburse you for the costs. You see, he's hired you to keep eyes and ears open while you are there. He doesn't think this tuna shortage is happening by chance either and he also believes that elements of organized crime are involved. He especially thinks that Constantino Gancini is heavily involved if not at the core of it all, and he wants to help end the shortages.

Daddy has long held doubts about Constantino, about how he funds his enterprises. He says Constantino tries just a little too hard to appear as a benevolent industrialist, as if he has something to hide. There are rumors among the high society circles that he is little more than a common thug, and those are the cats who don't see what we see." Violet leaned in slightly, her eyes wide and her whiskers curled just a little forward. "This could be a huge help to the investigation. If we are able to get close to Constantino and his entourage, we might just overhear something useful. We might even hear one of them slip and directly mention the tuna, however unlikely that might be." She then smiled with a mischievous glint in her eyes. "And besides, you'll get to see me dressed to the nines, like you've never seen me before. Even I have to admit I look pretty good in a formal dress!"

I took a minute to digest everything Violet had said to me, and the more I considered what she had said, the more I was convinced that she was right. Though we had lost our best clue when Blackie Lawler had seen us at the salting facility, we had a new opportunity to pursue. Constantino Gandini was surprisingly difficult to talk to in person, for he usually stayed cloistered in his mansion, fortified in his workplace among his gun-toting minions, or ensconced in an armored Cadillac. I could never just walk up and question him on any normal day, but the Winterhaven's charity gala would prove the perfect neutral ground to introduce myself and engage in some polite conversation.

The event would be held in the large ballroom, nestled well within the Winterhaven property and well-guarded against outside intrusion. Guests moved freely amongst each other. Their parties had a well-deserved reputation for being private affairs for those involved; the guards were employed primarily to keep the media and the paparazzi well away from the guests, but lately they were being armed with pistols and extra ammunition, and some guards were rumored to also keep Derringers as backup weapons. Benjamin Winterhaven only hired ex-military as his guards and he paid them well for their services, and as a result even the most agoraphobic of his attendees found that they could rely on the security forces to keep the event safe and orderly. Even though members of the Gandini syndicate arrived armed, they felt comfortable enough to leave their weapons discretely with an anteroom attendant once they stepped inside, though they likely also kept a Derringer or two hidden away just in case.

"I think you're right." I said, looking her in the eye. "The charity gala will make an excellent place to try and gain back what we've lost. Even though Constantino will be expecting us both there and will no doubt be prepared, the chance to talk to him directly is far too good to pass up. And I can bring you in as a sort of secret weapon. He knows you work for me, either from idle chatter or from deliberate information, but I doubt he knows just how much you know and how closely I work with you. And while I can't just throw you on him, you are a pretty young lady and will be all dolled up, and with any luck you might just distract him into making a small mistake. It's possible that a small mistake could lead to bigger rewards, so we need to be on our toes and listen." I stood up, still feeling a twinge of the night before, but the few hours I had put away had done wonders for my head. "The first thing I think we should do is pay your family's tailor a visit. We only have a short couple of days before the gala, and I'm sure he'll want all the time he can get."

A short time later, while she drove, I used the time in the car to question Violet as to her relationship with Don Gandini and his underlings. She told me that of the three that always appeared at the big Winterhaven events, she seemed to be on the best terms with Blackie Lawler. Though he possessed a fearful reputation as a vicious and brutal thug, to Violet he always stayed very polite and cordial. Violet felt comfortable around him in social settings, though she held serious doubts that she could force Blackie to slip in conversation and reveal anything of consequence.

With Rufus Segovia, any conversation was a bit more strained. She noted that while Rufus tried to appear distracted, even bored, in reality he remained ever vigilant and as a result tended toward a brittle and curt nature. He always kept scanning and re-scanning the grounds, always careful of every detail in his surroundings. His nervousness stepped up a notch at night, which meshed with rumors on the streets that Rufus didn't see well in dim conditions and took steps to compensate. Violet found him a multi-layered puzzle, full of mystery below the surface. She regarded Rufus as the hardest to talk to, and because of this she knew very little beyond what she could observe and what she had heard. Violet regarded Rufus as the wild card of the three simply because she knew so little about him, even after years of interaction in social settings such as these.

As for Constantino, any conversation with him usually had at least a dual purpose. The formidable and shrewd boss always kept his own cards close while enticing his partner in conversation to reveal things about themselves, often without realizing they had done so. He liked to appear in exquisite clothes, usually wearing a modest amount of jewelry and carrying a ball-topped cane. Violet noted that while Constantino was ever polite and only spoke in calm and measured tones, underlying his character was an intensity and drive that came out of hiding once she learned to spot it. It seemed to her that he disliked excessive idle talk, preferring instead to converse and plan with other legitimate businessmen in New Amsterdam. She found that the overriding theme with Constantino was his desire to be seen as a legitimate player in New Amsterdam's affairs, a captain of industry for all to see and admire. She knew that even though Constantino Gandini was Al Capone, John Dillinger and Bonnie and Clyde wrapped into one package, he nonetheless kept most people in the dark as it came to his true occupation. There were always low-level thugs who could do his dirty work for him, while Constantino basked in the daylight of legitimate business, keeping the appearance of an honest tycoon while keeping his less honest activities hidden deep in shadow.

We arrived at the tailor and parked the car in the pay lot next door. Once inside, Violet quickly learned how little I knew about tuxedos and hand-fitted clothes in general. My suits were store bought, relatively inexpensive and easy to alter to fit my proportions. I generally wore dark gray, though in a moment of fancy I purchased a dark blue suit with thin pinstripes; I rarely wore it to work, though it served well for semi-formal occasions with a less expensive crowd. I had worn it on a date once, but the date ended with a drink thrown in my face and a taxi ride alone for yours truly. I had not ventured on any such social occasions very often since. Nights were almost always spent in boxers and an undershirt, relaxing on my old sofa and listening to the radio. Sometimes I fell asleep right there, eased into dreamland by a combination of big band and jazz. If I felt energetic, I turned off the radio and climbed into bed. I owned a couple of pairs of linen trousers and a few casual shirts in the event I decided to leave without a suit. This constituted most of the outerwear I owned.

I had never attended a formal gala, and I had certainly never owned a tuxedo. I casually suggested to Violet that a white jacket with black pants and bow tie would look dashing, much like some spy in a European movie. She laughed, though as politely as she could, and informed me that I would look positively debonair if people mistook me for a member of the wait staff. A black jacket it would be. Violet recommended a conservative cut in order to not stand out much, allowing me a certain measure of anonymity to move about the event, a decision I strongly agreed with, though I held firm on my decision to pair up the black tux with a pair of black and white Italian wingtips I had seen in a nearby store; I felt the bolder choice of shoes would add a sense of daring and interest without compromising the quiet nature of the tuxedo. And to be truthful, I had always wanted a pair. The event would be held on a Saturday night, a little over 52 hours from the time we left. I was to report back tomorrow at 2:00 for a fitting and any further alterations. No one expected any to surface, as the cat was simply that good.

The gala would begin at 6:00 in the evening, though Violet intended to commandeer a limousine and driver and pick me up from the tailor's shop, giving us a couple of hours to prepare any rudimentary plans we might think up. Though I would arrive at the Winterhaven mansion hour early, Violet and I would sequester ourselves into one of the upstairs rooms to work until almost half past six, when the Winterhavens would appear to formally welcome those guests who had already arrived and officially announce the charity they would benefit. As with every year, this would be the Warm Blankets Orphanage for Kittens, a charity particularly close to Benjamin Winterhaven; his brother Silas could not father kittens, so he and his wife had adopted four orphans from Warm Blankets.

Both Benjamin and Silas opened their homes each week to

give the kittens a place to come and play, and both contributed to the funding of the orphanage. The gala would also help other smaller orphanages with charity windfalls. It was an event that always drew a crowd, and one that always brought Constantino Gandini to the Winterhaven mansion, for no honest businessman would miss the chance to help orphan kittens in search of forever homes. Though Blackie Lawler had suggested my attendance as a challenge to see if I would come, I hoped to turn the tables and use the occasion as a way to learn about and subtly undermine Constantino's operation.

From the tailor's shop, Violet and I drove a few blocks for some Chinese takeout, then back to my apartment for dinner and planning. After parking the car in the narrow courtyard behind the building, we entered through the rear entrance and climbed the stairs to my floor. As we entered, the pale late afternoon light outside had begun to fade, leaving the apartment darker and colder than usual. I turned on the light in the kitchen, then another in the living room as Violet pulled the small containers from the anonymous paper bag. After turning up the radiators slightly, I walked back into the kitchen and reached into a cupboard to pull out a pair of plates, noting with amusement her realization that I only owned four. I pulled two forks out of a drawer, though she politely refused hers, preferring instead the chopsticks that inhabited the bottom of the bag. My apartment held just enough room for a two-person table, which held notes and diagrams from past cases across most of its surface. I quickly collected the papers into a pile by the wall, then attempted to be a gentleman and pulled Violet's chair for her as she came to sit down.

Just as I came around the table, I remembered something that I hoped would go over well; walking back to the refrigerator, I pulled two bottles I had bought from Russian Joe. Both labels read 'Granjas de Fangio - Leche California" and both were single serve. Both were there because occasionally I liked to end the day with something a little more exotic than our local fare, something that spoke of a little class. I set them on the table as I walked into the living room, bringing back two candles in jars and a box of matches. I passed the table again, this time to turn off the kitchen light, dimming the apartment to a warmer and darker hue. Violet watched me intently as I did this, curious to see what would happen next, and when I lit the candle jars and set them between us, I said jokingly, "Donnie Chang takeout, California milk, cheap candles in jars, what could possibly be more romantic?"

She laughed, then snorted, which only made her laugh more out of embarrassment, which made me laugh, which made her snort and laugh some more. As we finally calmed down enough to start eating our dishes, hers, a rice, meat and veggie concoction I didn't recognize, mine a simple General Tso's chicken over rice, I looked at Violet and reflected on what a strange few days had transpired, strange even in my business. She had always adapted to the quick changes and rolled with the proverbial punches and had once again shown a genuine knack for this sort of work.

In our conversations over the years, Violet had told me that she had attended a boarding school for a few years, relatively isolated from the larger world for much of the time. But in that time, she had obviously learned a great deal, and after she graduated, her parents took her to places far around the world where she had put the knowledge to good use. Her knowledge of obscure facts never ceased to amaze me, but her fine eye for observation and her ability to connect facts together was uncanny; she often saw details I overlooked and could think far enough outside the box to put together strong theories. Like everything else, this was a learning process, but Violet's growth and development in her natural abilities was impressive. Her work complimented my own very well, and not for the first time I realized that I had come to rely on her not as a secretary or an assistant, but as an equal. She was a female in a world that tended to marginalize females to more domestic roles, but she had proven long ago that she could work with me as my counterpart. In this sense, I no longer viewed her as an underling but as a full partner in the business, one whose name certainly belonged on the door.

And now, here she was, sitting in my apartment, eating Chinese food, looking at me with her large blue eyes and smiling out of one corner of her mouth. At this moment, seeing her with that beret pushed to one side, one ear sticking up, hearing her talk and hearing her laugh, all I could think about was how she was truly remarkable and how even though we were associates and friends of a sort, I did care deeply for her. I realized that though the knowledge was far better kept to myself, I would walk to the ends of the earth for her, even die for her so that she may live. And in this if nothing else, I was content.

After dinner was finished and the leftovers packed away in the fridge, we walked to the living room and sat on the couch. "So, what does the great and enigmatic Max Persian do when he's not at the office?" Violet asked. "How does he spend his evenings in his apartment?"

I looked her in the eye and said, "My evenings are quiet. I come back to this apartment and close the door on the outside world and watch the outside light fade into darkness. I have a simple dinner, enough to get me by, and after that I usually sit on the sofa, right where you're sitting, and read a book off the shelf. Most of the time it's nothing profound, just some character-driven pulp novel I find at the corner store. It both helps my mind unwind and makes it easier for me to look at my case in a constructive manner. Please don't laugh, but lately I've been looking for ways to improve my own work, so I've been reading this." I reached around her and handed her a copy of Doyle's 'A Study in Scarlet'. "It's probably a bit silly, but occasionally I feel like some of Holmes' and Watson's greatness might rub off on me, if only in some fleeting manner. Osmosis perhaps, when I fall asleep reading it and the text lands on my face."

Violet smiled, then replied, "Your choice of reading material explains your vocabulary, Max. Sometimes you use a word or phrase that seems out of place but knowing that you read a variety of materials is comforting, because I read a lot of different works in class. You have some of them on your bookshelf. I hope you don't mind, but I glanced at titles when you were busy. Melville, Conrad, Trevelyan's History of England, those are all serious reads. They're the sort of literature that will keep the mind oiled and working."

She handed me Doyle's detective novel, which I put back on the end table, then said to her in a mock sheepish manner, "I haven't exactly read Trevelyan. I saw him in a thrift store a few blocks over and thought it a shame to leave it behind. Looks good on the shelf, doesn't it?" She snickered, then laughed outright. I wasn't sure if I was actually that funny or if the milk had influenced her sense of humor. "But when I start tiring, I almost always do the same thing. First, I either turn on the radio or put a record on the phonograph. Next, I turn off the lights and let the outside illuminate the apartment. Then I stand in front of the window and look down at the world outside. Cats occasionally walk by, cars and trucks drive past, just small slices of life passing. The streetlights are bright enough and the music is soft in the background. I just let my head clear, try not to think about anything at all. Sometimes it's the only thing that can come close to emptying my mind."

Violet nodded as she sat for a moment, then turned off the lamp beside her and got up from the sofa. She walked to the radio and turned it on, filling the dimmed room with the big band station I had most recently set it to. With the only light in the apartment provided by the two candles and the dial on the radio, she walked to the window and gestured me to come stand with her. I crossed the floor to accompany her, and in silence we stood, watching the world pass into nighttime on the street below. After a few minutes, an instrumental version of Glenn Miller's "Moonlight Serenade" began to play. I felt Violet's right paw take my left while her left reached across my shoulder and behind my neck. Somewhat startled, I looked at her to find her looking up at me and smiling.

"Please dance with me," she spoke softly. "When I was a kitten my mother and father would dance, and I always wondered what it was like, especially with someone I care about. No one will see you except me." I smiled to her and nodded, then put my right arm around her side, paw at her back, and took the lead as I slowly swayed in time with the music. I looked at her, looked into her blue eyes and found to my surprise that in the dim light she was even more beautiful than during the day. I thought again how lucky I was that she had come into my life. As the song ended, she smiled up at me and I smiled at her, and she drew me in for a hug. When she rested her cheek against my shoulder, I lightly placed my chin on top of her head. After a few moments we let go, both of us stepping back to find some fresh air.

Violet looked at her watch and exclaimed, "Max, it's getting late! I should be getting home; they'll need my help to get the final arrangements for the gala set." I told her that she should stay the night, noting that those California leches were stronger than she realized. "And where am I supposed to sleep?" she asked. I pointed toward the bedroom, saying "The bed has clean sheets, the armoire has room for your clothes, and the other door leads to the bathroom. The comforter is cozy and the fan makes a nice hum. Even your car will be fine. My landlord's a night owl and keeps the loading dock open while he fixes things under the good lights. Most important of all is me knowing that you are safe and not crashed and bleeding in an intersection." I reached over and took the beret from her head, placing it gently in her hands. "You'll be fine here."

Violet looked at me and asked, "Where will you sleep?"

I pointed to the sofa and said, "There's a blanket and a pillow just for this purpose." I didn't tell her that I slept on that couch most of the time anyway.

"You're right, Max. I'm getting a bit sleepy and you make a good case for crashing here instead of on the road. I hope you don't mind, but I'm going to turn in a bit early." Violet turned and walked into the bedroom and started to close the door, but then opened it halfway and stuck her head out.

"Max," she said quietly. "You're one of the good ones. Thank you for caring."

She then smiled and slowly closed the door. I retrieved the blanket and pillow from the coat closet and set them on the sofa, then while two candles burned and the best of the big bands played on the radio, I quietly walked back to my window, knowing that while the rest of the world moved on outside, my own little world was as close to perfect as it had been in a very long time.

13

The first stirrings of consciousness did not come willingly, but rather by the influence of an outside force. I dreamed of noise and battle, a maelstrom filled with the sound and fury of Valkyries, the Norse figures who choose their warriors from the fields of battle and bring them to Valhalla to be ruled in the afterlife by the great King Odin. They had taken flight on the sounds of French horns and trombones, coupled with the whistling winds of flutes and violins. The images that filled my sleep-addled head depicted the tall, muscular female cats, long blonde braids and tails streaming behind them as they flew on winged steeds. Wielding intricately engraved swords, they pointed into a chaotic scene of battle on some endless, nameless plain, choosing those who would live and who would die, who would come with them to Odin and who would depart to Freja, to dwell in the heavenly field of Fólkvangr. And amid the feline destruction and the final breaths of a warrior tom cut down before his natural time, the souls of the departed formed opposing lines on the battlefield once more, not realizing that they were dead and destined for a far different fate.

Though my eyes remained closed, I regained enough of my conscious self to recognize Richard Wagner issuing forth through the record player. Though the images were beginning to fade, the memories of fantastical dreamt imagery remained strong in my mind, reminding me why I never listened to *Ride of The Valkyries* first thing in the morning. As I opened my eyes, I saw yet another noble female figure, this one a smiling blue-eyed Valkyrie in a knit beret. Violet, standing triumphant like a victorious warrior, smiled for all the world like she had gotten away with something. She leaned in, then said, "I went easy on you, Max. Most mornings I listen to Beethoven's Wellington's March or Tchaikovsky's 1812 Overture. I've found that the sound of cannon fire wakes me up in such an exhilarating way."

I turned and sat up, elbows on knees and head resting in paws. "You, Miss Winterhaven, are a sadist, pure and simple. If I bother to play anything, I pick Vivaldi or Bach. Or better yet, I turn on the radio and let all that jazz give me a reason to get up."

Violet took on a mock wounded look, her face a frown. "*I'm not reason enough for you to get going in the mornings? The thought of my smiling face waiting in the office doesn't make you want to just leap out of bed and race into work? Oh Max, I'm crushed. Devastated even!*" She threw one of her paws over her eyes in an overly dramatic gesture. "Oh Max, I can't go on! What shall I do?" I laughed, which made her laugh too. Then she snorted, which restarted the laughter on both our parts.

"All pulp drama aside," I asked, "I'm surprised you are still here. I would have thought you'd have left to head back and help with the setup by now. Granted, there's a lot of worse ways to wake up, but I'm just surprised. Did you let your folks know you wouldn't be home?"

Violet laughed, managing not to snort this time. "You know I'm not a kitten, Max. My parents know not to worry if I don't come home some nights. But if it makes you feel better, I snuck out and called Daddy after you fell asleep and told him where I was. He says he doesn't worry, but I know he still does. You were just lying on the sofa, pretty far gone and snoring. Daddy asked if you were running a wood chipper." I frowned at her, she winked, and kept on talking. "Besides, neither of us are going to be in the office today but we still have work to do. It makes sense that I spend at least part of the day with you to prepare for the gala tomorrow night. And we can start by finding a quality diner and getting some breakfast!"

I found myself agreeing with her, particularly about breakfast. I also thought that I should let her pick the establishment, as my usual place could be rather off-putting; as if the staff's occasionally hostile antics weren't enough, their supposed grade A sausage tasted a C- at best, and during one of my last visits the cook had broken open an egg and found a beak. I thought we could do better, certainly.

As my clothes from last night were folded neatly over the back of a chair, I felt no shame in wearing them again, only ducking into the bedroom to change into fresh boxers and undershirt before getting dressed. After switching the suspenders for a leather belt, I grabbed a loose-fitting flat cap from the hat rack and placed it between my ears. Violet smiled at me, and together we left the apartment. As we walked down the stairs that led to the back alley, Violet looked me over and commented "That's a different look for you Max. I'm so used to seeing you in a suit and fedora that I keep having to double-take just to realize you're the same cat! I like it, to be honest. I wish you'd wear this more often. It takes ten years off of you!"

I looked over at her with a sideways glance, my eyes drawn tighter than usual and noted that if she hadn't scared ten years off me with her vicious Germanic sense of humor, I wouldn't have to dress younger. She smiled as we stepped off the stairs and out the back door. Though the morning sun had been shining for a couple of hours, the back alley, surrounded as it was by buildings, lay largely in shadow. Though the air was chilly, the lack of wind made it easily bearable. And as usual at this hour, the garage door was open, the lights on, and Louie, my landlord, was huddled over a table in an unbuttoned flannel and rolled up sleeves, a space heater going by his side.

He looked to be rewiring a generator for his truck, but with Louie, a self-taught mechanical prodigy and possible erstwhile mad scientist, one could never quite be sure. He looked up as we passed. "Hey Max. That your Chevy outside?"

"No. Hers," I replied. "Problem?"

Louie smiled, revealing a mouth of somewhat ragged teeth. "Not for you, Max. You're neat, quiet, early with your rent and you only complain when you have a good reason. As far as I'm concerned, you might just be the perfect tenant." Louie stood and walked from behind the table, then looked Violet in the eye. "I heard you pull in last night, Miss. Car's tuned pretty well, but I can tune it better. If you like, next time you're over, leave the keys in my mailbox and I'll get her running smooth as silk. I'll put the keys in Max's mailbox to keep 'em safe when I'm done. '41 Chevy's a good car, Miss. That big, lazy six'll run just about forever if it's taken care of."

Ever the graceful one, Violet replied, "Thank you, sir. I may take you up on your offer sometime." With that, Louie smiled and set back to his work while Violet and I got in the car.

As she started the engine, Violet turned to look at me. "That was interesting. Most men usually offer to open a door or carry my bags, but he offered to work on my car. He seems a bit awkward in conversation though."

As we pulled onto the street, I laughed and replied, "Louie spoke more just then than I've heard him speak in the last year! And he must like you if he offered to work on your car. He's not much of what you might call a 'cat person'. If something in the building breaks down, he fixes it quickly, but he usually works at night to avoid having to speak to anyone. He'd just rather avoid most people, I think."

Violet smirked. "He likes you!"

I replied, honestly, "That's because I don't break anything. Not that Louie knows anyway. I either fix it myself or I call someone to come out while he's sleeping. He gives me a great deal on the rent and I really don't want to lose it."

"What do you know about him?" Violet inquired. "What's his story? Is he hiding or something?"

I shrugged my shoulders and said simply "I don't know. I've never looked into him. He's a very private guy and he doesn't hurt anyone, so I don't see any reason to go prying into his personal business. I think it would be unethical somehow, so I don't do it.

103

Some things should just be left unknown. I do know that he's the most gifted mechanic I've ever seen. It's not just cars, it's anything mechanical. Whatever Louie lacks in personal skills, he more than makes up for with machines. He talks to them, reasons with them, convinces them to work again." I looked over to Violet as she drove and said in my most serious voice, "I think it's voodoo. It must be. There's simply no other explanation." Violet turned to me as we sat at a stoplight, her face a mixture of disbelief and skepticism, then smiled, shook her head and laughed as the light turned green.

I hadn't asked where Violet was headed, but it soon became apparent that she was headed into a nicer part of town. The car ride was silent, though not uncomfortable. It seemed rather more like a comfortable silence between two cats who have known each other long enough to have foregone the need to fill the empty spaces with meaningless conversation. It was possible that Violet had just encountered a hitherto-unknown limitation in my work, though it was a certainty that I was a bit apprehensive about the upcoming gala event and my inevitable meeting with Constantino Gandini.

Unlike my secretive yet mostly harmless landlord, I was thoroughly convinced that Constantino was neck deep in activities that were no good. His actions hurt innocent cats, mostly indirectly, but sometimes directly, and because of this I had no qualms exposing him to the world. In my line of work the distinctions between dirt and grime were often blurry at best, but the distinction could mean the difference between a good cat and a bad cat, one who has some dirt of shame in their past that they'd like to keep hidden and another whose filth and grime may be hidden beneath a veneer of class and refinement, but it is there, just below the surface.

I had heard a story about the Roman Emperor Constantine that seemed oddly appropriate here. Upon the completion of a grand new basilica in the Roman Forum, the Emperor had a colossal statue of himself installed in a large niche at the western end. The head, arms, and legs were carved of fine marble, while the torso was constructed of brick with a wooden framework and finished with bronze. This was fashioned to look like Imperial armor and was fashioned with gold and fine jewels. It was said to be a magnificent statue when seen from a distance, but when one drew close, one could hear the rats inside, scurrying about just under the surface. Thus, the noble visage hid the rotted core that lay within. I wondered as to the significance of Gandini's chosen name, wondering what sort of rats I might hear scurrying beneath when I met Constantino for the first time.

14

Violet brought the car to a halt and backed into a curbside space, bringing me out of my thoughtful introspection. I had no idea how long I had been in my own world, but based on the street we passed, some distance had passed beneath the wheels. Though I couldn't name the part of town, I knew we were in a nicer part of the city based on the relative lack of trash in the alleys and the cleanliness of the sidewalks and buildings. As we exited the car, I put a dime in the meter, good for two hours. Violet looked over at me with a look of mild annoyance, to which I just shrugged. Feeding the meter was the least I could do after she had driven me across town just to get a bite to eat, and if she didn't understand that, too bad. Old fashioned chivalry was something I had learned a long time ago.

I learned from Violet that this diner, the Sunny Side, was long a favorite of her mother and that the two of them had been eating here since Violet was a kitten. In a household overseen by an overachiever of a father, this diner was something that Violet and her mom could share among themselves. We seated ourselves at one of the few open booths and placed our order with the waitress, whose friendly demeanor was a far cry from Delia's usual scowl. I wanted to have a better sense of what to expect and at the Winterhaven's winter charity gala, so as a starting point I implored Violet to tell me more about her family. Though I knew about the Winterhavens, I had seldom met any of them and was curious to know more of their lives from Violet's point of view. She also said that we had some time to kill before venturing to the tailor to try on and, if lucky, to pick up my tux. I could think of nothing I'd rather hear more than a history of Violet's family, and as I expressed this, she smiled and began to tell me a tale of her family, from humble beginnings to masters of industry.

"Mom and Daddy throw several of these galas each year, but this one ranks as the most important, the one closest to their hearts.

They are well aware of how privileged they are in New Amsterdam society and they want to give back to the city, and more specifically, to Warm Blankets. It's not just because Silas and his wife adopted their kittens from there, though it plays a big part. With the proceeds generated, Warm Blankets benefits to the point that they can help other orphanages as well. My parents may be wealthy, but they have had enough experiences of their own that they want to help. That's basically what drives them, their experiences and their hardships along the way."

As two coffee cups arrived, I took a sip. "Violet, would you tell me some about your folks? It might help me get a feel for what to expect if I can know the events that led them here, together. Besides, we've known each other for a while now and I don't know much about them. It will help me to get to know you too."

As she took a sip and smiled, Violet continued. "What you have to know is that my parents are alike in some ways and very different in others. You know some about the Winterhavens, that my great-grandfather Elijah started out in a factory repairing and maintaining the machines. He began modifying and creating his own machines, which he patented, and he grew quite rich on the manufacture of his designs. But at heart he was always a working man and never really felt comfortable with his now wealthy status. He saw how some of his new peers held the working people in low regard, and him with them, and he vowed to keep the Winterhavens aware of the plights of the common man as long as he drew breath."

Violet closed her blue eyes and smiled, saying, "I remember him from when I was a kitten, Max. He was old and thin by then, but his eyes were as bright and mischievous as a boy. He used to make toys, hand carved and hand painted. He kept a woodshop on the ground floor where he would make them to give to the orphanages. My sisters and I would always get a few; I still have a top and a rocking horse he made. And he was always cheerful. I've never met someone so optimistic about the future; I could always bring my

107

problems and worries to him and he always managed to cheer me up. I loved him so dearly, Max. Sometimes I thought he walked on water. There are times I would give anything to talk to him again, or just to feel him hug me. He was one of the good ones."

"Elijah helped raise Daddy and Silas after his son Dominic was killed in a motorcycle crash. He invited Dominic's widow Margaret to live in the mansion with him in order to help raise her kittens, his grandsons. That's how Daddy and Silas grew up, in a giant house with servants and staff, but with no father to guide them. Although their mother Margaret and their grandfather Elijah were there to raise and guide them, they always felt the loss.

They both grew up to be precocious young cats, and when the Great War came to Europe, they rode their motorcycles to the British Embassy and joined the Royal Army. They both saw action and they both survived, but they had aged more than their years and were plagued with nightmares for a long-time afterword, especially Silas. He returned to New Amsterdam, but Daddy stayed in Britain. He thought that aiding in the rebuilding of the country would help him.

"He met my mother just after the war while he was working on the estate grounds where she lived. To hear him say it, Miss Eleanor Jones was the most beautiful cat, the single most beautiful thing he had ever seen. To hear her say it, Daddy looked like a striped brute from East London but spoke with the voice of an angel. They would run into each other while Daddy was working, and as time went on those meetings would become much more deliberate. They started spending more time together and before long they were headlong in love. Unfortunately, someone else had noticed their budding affections and began to make his objections known.

"My mother had few memories of her mother. She died when mom was a kitten, leaving her in the care of her father, one Abraham Tiberius Jones, Eighth Lord of Scarborough. It wasn't an easy upbringing. She learned from an early age to stay unnoticed and out of the way, as Lord Scarborough ruled his estate with a tyrant's hand.

As an adolescent, Eleanor was shipped off to a Swiss boarding school, and there she felt love and acceptance for the first time since her mother's passing. When she returned to her father's estate, she was far more confident and self-assured, which only served to rankle her father further. Soon, the two developed an intense adversarial relationship, and Lord Scarborough seethed in a rage as he watched his only daughter asserting her independence. In his eyes, her relationship with some itinerant worker was an outrage, one he would not tolerate.

"To make a long story short, Mom eloped with Daddy. All she took with her was some jewelry and a couple of small keepsakes; she dared not take more that could weigh her down. They took the train to Southampton and were on an ocean liner bound for New Amsterdam the next morning. She had left everything behind, going from privileged debutante to a refugee in a foreign land, and she knew that she could likely never go back. That's the cat my mother is, a foreigner in an adopted land that she now calls home. Her cousins, her relatives, they have nothing to do with her. She is a pariah, an outcast, and she's had to make her home across the water. She lost both of her parents, Max. My mother may be strong and resilient, but she still misses her mother and still misses what could have been."

Violet looked down at her coffee, her sad eyes just showing the hints of tears. "That man, Lord Scarborough, he undermined Mom and Daddy wherever he could. Those giant warehouses weren't just built on a whim. Before we entered the second world war, Daddy and Silas had secured contracts with Vickers and possibly de Haviland to set up lines to assemble airplanes, far from the threat of Nazi bombs. But soon after the ink was dry the contracts were cancelled.
They were overruled by a Parliament that took issue with "wasting British taxpayer revenue in a boondoggle scheme to build British bombers on American soil, employing inferior American laborers in

building proper British aircraft." Word reached Daddy and Silas soon after that Scarborough was behind the motion. The cat was completely mad, Max, and his madness undermined the war effort of his home country. There were other dealings too, ones that hurt Daddy's businesses for years. How my mother endured him is beyond me.

"So, you have Mom and Daddy, both come from wealthy backgrounds, but they've been hurt too. Daddy saw enough suffering during the Great War to scar him for a hundred lifetimes, though he never talks about it, and Mom grew up lonely and terrorized inside of her own home, then had to abandon that home to be with the one she loved. They empathize with the orphans, the unfortunate kittens that need the help we give. The gala isn't the only way they help, but it is the most visible. To them, it's the most important social event they can throw, and they have turned it into one of the must attend events on the social elite calendar. No one misses this event, Max. All of the city's elites attend and they all mingle with one another, every cat on display for every other cat to see. Constantino will definitely be there, not only to enhance his image as a philanthropist, but also to hobnob with the other elites of the city. This is the perfect meeting place, and we might just be able to get something as he's working the gears of the city."

I took a moment to take in what she had told me. In time, I looked across the table at Violet, whose face held an inquisitive expression. "I've known that they put a lot of preparation and effort into the orphans' gala, but until now I've never known why." A question suddenly occurred to me. "Why did you tell me so much about your family? Their history is not something I've ever read about."

Violet smiled, small and wistful, and replied, "I don't tell many people, Max. When you're the youngest daughter of a wealthy industrialist whose mother is permanently exiled amid a sea of rumors and lies, one learns early on that there are lowlifes out there who will use your past against you. It wasn't so bad when I went to school here, but when I went off to the boarding school in Switzerland, things got rougher. I had a lot of good times and made some good friends there, but there were a lot of ugly cats there just looking to make someone's life miserable. I was one of their targets."

After pausing for a sip, Violet continued. "Daddy insisted I finish out school there, as it was both an excellent institution and the experience would toughen me for the years ahead. But because it was a European school, my family was far away. Even worse was that some of the other students knew British cousins that I had never met; one of them, a cousin named Basil Jones, started attending the school two years after I did. Initially, we ran in different circles and tried to avoid each other, but we ended up in a couple of classes together. After the instructor paired us together for a project, despite both of our pleas, we had to speak to each other and found that we were actually a lot alike. Soon we were inseparable and have remained friends ever since. He's the only cat in the entire Jones-Yarborough family that has anything to do with the Winterhavens. I don't know if you remember, but he came here a couple of years ago, and I think you met him because he wanted to see where I worked."

"I remember," I said. "He was a thin gray tabby, taller than me, dressed in tan houndstooth pants and a cardigan sweater over a white undershirt. Wore a pair of Italian leather boots, low cut and probably expensive. I think he had a flop hat with a pom on top, but he had taken it off before I arrived. As I remember, the two of you got on very well."

Violet looked at me with an incredulous gaze. "How do you remember all that?" She inquired.

I shrugged and said, "I'm a detective. It's part of the job to notice details and remember them for later. I went through police training too, and they're very insistent that coppers learn how to look at what's around them and remember it like it's been locked in a safe. The ability to remember people was also stressed as lawn chairs don't usually rob banks." As Violet frowned, I continued. "Part of why I remember Basil so well is that his visit was unusual. He came specifically to see you."

I immediately closed my eyes and shook my head, realizing how that sounded. "That came out wrong. I'm sorry. It's only that most of our clients tend to quickly forget that you're there, as if you're part of the scenery or a potted fern. I observed the two of you talking and noted how you were both cheerful, even laughing. You had told me he was your cousin, but I figured you were friends as well. Even though I didn't know much of your family history, I knew that there was some event in your mother's past that had clouded relations with the British side, and since his accent stood out, I reasoned that his visit was special. That's why when you asked to step out for a few minutes to walk him out, I gave you the rest of the day off and the next couple too. I thought he was a good cat, that he treated you very well. And even though I tried to run you off for a few days, you still came in the mornings and brought Basil with you a couple of times, even though there wasn't that much to do. I probably didn't tell you as much at the time, but I appreciated both that you came and the brief but engaging conversations the three of us had. I have always enjoyed our talks. It is just another reason I hope you never leave."

While Violet blushed slightly, I took a breath, still a little hesitant as to the task ahead. "We've managed to kill some time and hearing your family history was a nice and welcome distraction, but we've already been through at least two cups of coffee and we haven't even eaten yet. While I'm looking forward to beakless eggs and good service for a change, we should probably get to it."

15

Violet took the initiative. "Max, have you ever attended a black-tie affair before?" I confessed that I had not. Violet nodded and began to bring me up to speed. "The event itself isn't that different from a party over at Russian Joe's. It's just a group of people gathered together to give to a charity cause, kind of like a birthday party except that the recipient is an organization rather than a kitten. The key difference is the formality involved, the attire, the setting, the order and structure of the evening's events. We have the attire, which we'll pick up after we finish here. And just so you know, I had those silly wingtips you insisted on polished and re-polished to within an inch of their obnoxious black and white lives. You'll be able to walk outside on a dark night and see constellations reflected in them." She glared at me for a moment. "And quit smiling, you Philistine, those shoes are simply awful!"

She paused, and I closed my eyes, quietly savoring the amusing moment of Violet's momentary annoyance. When I opened my eyes, she was frowning at me. "May I continue, Lord Persian, or do you wish to continue reveling in your grievous affront to all good taste?" I chuckled, and she smiled as she shook her head side to side. "Anyway, with the attire taken care of, the next thing to consider is the other guests and how the dinner will proceed. Most of the guests come from established backgrounds of wealth, though a few are *nouveau riche*, self-made cats looking to put themselves out there as felines of industry. All of them are well versed in the goings on of these little soirées. The order of events for Daddy's charity balls is simple: in the first hour, the guests arrive. It's really more like two and a half hours, but no one arrives early or even on time as they like to arrive fashionably late." Violet shook her head, then continued. "A jazz band will play on the stage, providing background music throughout the event. You'll be happy to know I've made a few requests that I know you'll like.

"Once everyone has arrived and has had some time to mingle, dinner will be served, and while Daddy's affairs are less formal than most, there are still four courses. First is a fresh salad served with ice water, the usual sort of nibbly, grassy thing. Next comes an appetizer platter, which usually consists of fresh bread loaves and cinnamon butter, a small meat and cracker combination, plus a more exotic fare such as calamari. I know from the kitchen staff that this exact combination will be served, so there's no worry about anything else appearing that might offend your plebian appetite." She paused and winked at me, smiling. "Next comes a single main course, but there will be many different items to choose from. Beef, pork, poultry, seafood, you name it. And yes, tuna is on the list and Daddy had to pay a lot more than usual for tuna. He's hoping that you'll be able to put a halt to what's been happening that's driving up the prices. When I suggested that he add your name to the guest list, he was quite enthusiastic and ready to help. Daddy's looking forward to meeting you in person, Max, and he wanted me to tell you that you are a welcome guest at this and future parties." She smiled, knowing full well that while I tried to hide my discomfort, she could still see that she had managed to skewer me. No pressure there, Violet, no pressure at all.

"The last course is dessert, which will be a selection of cakes, pastries, and other playful dishes. While the guests are enjoying the confections, Daddy will step to a lectern and address the guests. He'll tell his guests about the recipient charity, Warm Blankets Orphanage for Kittens, telling of the wonderful work they do finding forever homes for so many unfortunate orphans of New Amsterdam. He'll also tell them how they helped his brother Silas and his wife Faye bring home four kittens to add to his family and introduce Silas and Faye to make their own short speech. Daddy will return to the podium and finish his speech, imploring those attending to donate to Warm Blankets and other affiliated organizations that help those less fortunate than themselves. He always gets healthy donations too, because his guests are just as interested in maintaining appearances as they are helping the orphanages, sometimes more so."

"Daddy always hosts the gala to help Warm Blankets at the beginning of December, and it always draws a who's who of this city's wealthy and elite. It's a golden opportunity for us to face Constantino Gandini. He always attends this event, away from his rank-and-file thugs, away from his base of operations and on neutral ground for several hours. It's the perfect place to size him up, to see if we can ruffle that fat cat's fur to see if he gives us a clue. If we're lucky, he might inadvertently reveal a key that brings his whole operation crashing down, though I'm not counting on it. If nothing else, we might unsettle him through hints and innuendo that make him think we're a lot closer to him that we really are."

I shouldn't have been surprised by Violet's thorough mastery of the situation, nor at her sheer cunning and powerful intellect. But despite the high expectations I had come to expect from her, she had once again managed to surprise me. Her subtle guile and almost devious planning to manipulate Constantino's understanding of what we knew and were capable of doing to his organization was impressive. Not for the first time I thought it fortunate that Violet was on my side, for had she pursued a life of criminal behavior, she would have become a formidable and dangerous adversary.

The waitress had taken our order a few minutes before, but Violet had been too engrossed in her parents' tale that she only registered my order once it arrived. "I never pictured you for scrambled eggs, Max," she said, amusingly. "You tend to be so basic in your food preferences that I wouldn't have been surprised if they had brought your egg raw and in a glass."

I looked up in mid-chew and swallowed, a slight frown on my face. "I never ate eggs when I was younger. I didn't trust anything that came out of a chicken. But several years ago, those avian monsters bombed my fedora and my greatcoat right as I was talking face to face with a client. From that moment forward, I began eating eggs for breakfast every time I went out, and to my surprise they started tasting good. I almost always get them scrambled too, just to show those flying rats the unspeakable horrors of which I'm capable."

It took a second to register, and then Violet burst out in laughter, then snorted, which started the both of us laughing. When we calmed ourselves to avoid further dirty glances from other patrons, I asked Violet some questions about the events to happen tomorrow night. "You've had some interaction with Constantino Gandini, and you said that he likes to maintain a certain air of flamboyance about him. Is there anything he wears that he values, something like Blackie Lawler's watch? I need a way to strike up a conversation with him, something that would be of genuine interest to him even though we will both know it's a diversion. I don't know enough about his public life and the business interests he maintains to be able to speak to him intelligently."

Violet drew her eyes tighter as she thought, her head drooping as if looking at her empty plate. After several moments, she looked up. "Max, how much do you know about cars?" I confessed that while I knew some, I was no expert, not like my landlord Louie, who could dismantle and reassemble a transmission in his sleep.

Violet continued. "I overheard a conversation that Constantino had a year or so ago. He was telling Tor Svenson that he was looking to buy an old race car. He said it ran at Indianapolis a few times but never won, and that it was front wheel drive. He called it a Miller, said that when he was younger, they were state of the art and he'd always wanted one. I was toying with the idea of buying myself a car and had been studying to familiarize myself with them. It seemed a good idea to know them in case I had a flat tire or was left stranded. Anyway, one of the things I had learned that most cars send power to the rear wheels. That Constantino said the car was front wheel drive caught my attention because it was unusual. When I asked Daddy, he told me that some of the cars that raced at

116

Indianapolis in the 20's and 30's were indeed front drive and that they were built by a man named Harry Miller, whose shop also built the engines that powered them."

Suddenly, Violet took my paw in hers, and I was momentarily startled while she continued. "Max, you're a genius! Constantino Gandini collects prewar cars and has a fascination with ones that are different and unusual. Last year, Constantino started showing up in a prewar convertible sedan, cream colored with dark green stripes. It was sleek looking for an older car, especially a four-door, and I remember him being particularly fond of it because it was front wheel drive, just like the Miller race car. I'm pretty sure it's called a Cord. He uses the car when he wants to make a grand entrance, and my guess is that he's likely to use it tomorrow night. Apparently, he obsesses over that car, and I heard him tell someone that he values that car higher than his Cadillacs or even his Duesenberg. If you can talk with him about that car, ruse or not he will almost certainly engage you in a hearty discussion just because he enjoys talking about it."

With our breakfast finished and our dishes cleared, it was time to depart. I stood from the table and offered my hand to Violet. Before she could say anything, I left enough money on the table to cover both our breakfasts and a generous tip for our waitress. Breakfast had been delightful, both in the company and in the food, which was well prepared with nary a beak in sight. As we walked through the door and outside into the cool overcast of morning, I suggested to Violet that we should stop by the library in order to find some material on Cord and on Miller race cars so that I might bolster my basic knowledge with some books on the subjects. "There's no need for the library," she said. "My father owns several good books on prewar cars in his personal library that I'm sure he would be happy to share with you.

"We won't be able to run by the tailor for a few hours yet, so I thought I'd let you see the house and the preparations going into tomorrow night's gala. But my dad also reads magazines on cars, and I'll bet you already know where he gets them from. So, before we go to the house, we can stop by the Cahill's newsstand and see if any of them have any useful information on Cords or Indy racers plus whatever else we can find. Besides, I know Lizzie would be happy to see you!"

16

As we slowed in front of the Cahill's newsstand, Violet put on her own indicator and deftly parallel parked the Chevy, ending up about five inches from the curb. As I stepped from the car, I spied Lizzie on the corner, a paper in each paw, eagerly shouting headlines into the passing crowds. One cat stopped and leaned slightly, smiling as he took a paper and put a few coins into her paw. She thanked him by name and picked up another paper off her pile and resumed her announcement of the day's events once again. As I walked toward the corner I called to her, ready with my coins to purchase my daily allotment.

Lizzie turned and walked to meet me, a smile on her face. "Hiya Mister Max! Hiya Miss Violet! Would you like your usual today, sir?" I smiled and nodded, then took both papers from her. I passed the appropriate coins into her paw, from which they disappeared into the front pocket of her overalls. "Have you solved any new cases?" Lizzie asked as I walked with her back to the corner. "I'd love to solve cases! Miss Violet told me about how you discovered that one of your clients had kittens with another lady!"

I shot an annoyed look at Violet, who shrugged and said, "*I* didn't tell her! I don't know where she heard it, because she already knew about it when I talked to her!" I just shook my head at Lizzie's impish cleverness.

I stood up straight and said, "Lizzie, I need to ask you a question, and it's very important to an investigation," I said, hoping to change the direction of our discourse. "Where do your parents keep the publications that write about cars? I need to find some quickly and I could really use your help."

I could just see a light coming on in her head as she replied, "Those are inside, with the magazines on motorcycles and farm equipment! We have several magazines and trade publications that deal with all kinds of cars. My dad makes sure to keep them in stock because there are lots of customers who like reading about cars, like Miss Violet! I'm sure she can help you find something because she always stops by whenever the latest editions arrive. As much as she gets, I'll bet she knows everything!" Lizzie turned to look back at her corner, then said, "It's great seeing you both, but these newspapers won't sell themselves!" And with that, the pint-sized dynamo heroically returned to her corner to hawk her wares to a news-deprived public that desperately needed her.

As Violet and I entered the store, Victoria smiled and waved from behind the counter at the front of the store. "I see my Lizzie has found you both and swindled you out of more of your change," she said with a laugh. "Persistent little bugger she is, and she'd off the wool from a sheep without ever lifting shears!" We approached the counter as Victoria asked "What can I do for you both today, my friends? It's good to see the two of you out together, and you, sir, not in that stuffy suit you always wear. You certainly couldn't have picked a better lady to spend your time with, Maxey, because Violet here is a real sharp lady, and easy on the eyes too! "She leaned to me and said in a loud whisper, "You know something else? I've heard she's rich!" At that moment I was glad to be a common brown tabby, as the stripes on my face make it harder to see me blush.

I turned and looked at Violet, only to discover that she too was flustered and hot in the cheeks. I turned back to Victoria, whose expression shone with bemusement and content; this was not the first time her vivacious personality had inspired a mild embarrassment in those she regarded as friends. Indeed, she left no doubt as to the origins of her daughter's own outgoing nature. I couldn't help but smile, as did Violet in her own quiet self-conscious awkwardness.

"We're looking for anything dealing with prewar automobiles," I told Victoria, hoping to change the subject for the second time in less than five minutes. "I'm hoping to find something that deals with a prewar luxury car called a Cord or Miller racing cars, both if possible. I'm looking to find some information that might be related to a case I'm working on, and as Violet usually buys her father's magazines here, she thought we should come in and see what you might have."

Victoria put her paw to her chin as she remembered her inventory. "I haven't seen anything to do with Miller race cars, but I'd wager dollars to horses that one of the current magazines has something with Cords. I'm going by what's on the covers as I ring them up, but I'm pretty sure I saw a magazine that might tickle your fancy. The husband's back there and he knows the way. Crazy cat could find his way to San Francisco blindfolded!" We thanked Victoria as a customer came to purchase one of the more exotic papers resting on her counter, then entered through the door to the counter's left.

Though I had entered the store many times, I never ceased to be amazed at the lovely interior and high degree of craftsmanship contained within. Sean and Victoria Cahill must be descended from master craftsmen, such was the mastery of woodworking evident in the entire store. The outer siding and the heat shattered window that once held midlevel purses and shoes had all been replaced and upgraded, but it was the interior of the store that truly revealed the skill of the work involved. The newlywed Cahills had completely gutted the damage, throwing out not only the warped and burned shelving and fixtures, but also the entire wall facings, replacing them with and handmade wood paneling finished to a degree that would shame that in a palace. Along the back wall, they had designed and created a large mosaic, made entirely of colored glass which depicted a pastoral scene of their beloved Ireland. Lit from behind, it drew the viewer into a world of peaceful existence with a green and fertile land.

The racks, on which numerous publications sat ready for purchase, were also handmade, sturdily constructed from wood and finished to an equally high degree. These took up the front three-quarter of the store, while the rear quarter housed small, round tables, each flanked by small chairs, which beckoned to customers to sit and enjoy a relaxing read. The store was unique and had quickly attracted a loyal clientele, who also marveled at Lizzie's boundless enthusiasm, at Victoria's witticisms and lovely demeanor, and at Sean's quiet intelligence, his degree of perfection, and his ability to not only find everything in the store, but to know everything that was in every publication, every single time.

Sean Cahill stood next to the cart he was unloading, placing new issues on the shelves and tidying up the store as he went. He turned as Violet and I drew close, smiling as he walked over toward us with a paw outstretched in greeting. He was a kind cat with an affable face, short but with a hard and muscular frame that spoke of years of manual labor in his life. His fur was short and black, with a small lucky patch that peeked over the edge of his unbuttoned collar. His emerald green eyes shone brightly and reflected the lifetime of knowledge contained within. His daughter looked exactly like him, only smaller, though she possessed a spirit more like her mother. Often quiet, Sean possessed a gentle nature and a happy-go-lucky air that masked a keen mind with a memory like a steel trap. But his calm demeanor did not mean he lacked courage; a few years prior I learned that two cats had tried to rob the newsstand and threatened his family in the process. One was taken to the hospital with a concussion plus several broken bones from being picked up, thrown into the wall headfirst, then picked up off the floor and thrown into the other wall. The other would-be thug was admitted with a pair of scissors buried in his leg, nearly unconscious from blood loss and the severe beating he had endured. I remember wondering what he would have done if Lizzie had been sitting at a table instead of listening to the radio in the apartment upstairs.

After warm handshakes, Sean crossed his arms loosely and said, "Well, what brings two of my favorite customers in today? Something for work or something for play?" I could see the twinkle in his eye that he hoped we would admit to the latter. None of the

Cahill clan shied from a public opinion where relationships were concerned.

As I shook my head slightly, I replied. "Sean, I'm looking for something that has to do with automobiles, specifically one called a Cord. It's a prewar luxury car and has to do with a case Violet and I are working. We asked Victoria if she had seen anything as she sold the magazines, and when she said she remembered something, we came in here to ask you about it."

Sean nodded and motioned us to follow him a couple of aisles over where he picked up a magazine and handed it to me. "I like to keep up with the automotive world. Cords were unusual cars, nicely appointed, from the same company that owned Auburn and Duesenberg. They were the first to market a front wheel drive passenger car. I've heard that a businessman here in New Amsterdam owns a couple of Cords, an L-29 sedan and an 810 convertible. Constantino Gandi-" Sean stopped abruptly, turning to look me in the eye. In a low voice, he said, "You want to learn about the car because you're investigating Gandini, aren't you?" Violet and I turned to look at each other, but said nothing one way or the other. Sean fixed me with a piercing stare, and I buckled and slowly nodded. Sean drew his brows and narrowed his eyes as he continued. "I've never met the cat, but from what I read and what I see, I've always thought there was something off about him, something beneath the surface. I don't know what it is exactly, but he just seems like he's trying too hard to look like the nice guy boss." He picked up an automotive magazine from the shelf and said, "This is the only thing I have that talks about the cars you're looking into, but it's a fair article that covers them in a basic but decent manner. If you're really looking into Constantino Gandini, you can have it for free."

I was surprised that Sean would give me the magazine, knowing that while the store kept up a good business, the Cahills did not give anything away lightly. For him to give me the magazine, especially without so much as a moment's hesitation, said something about the regard with which Sean Cahill held Constantino Gandini. As I took the magazine from his paw, I remembered something I had heard at Russian Joe's a while back, something that involved Constantino Gandini sending a couple of his goons to persuade a local merchant that informing the police about some illegal activities recently discovered could be detrimental to the merchant's health. I never heard any further info about it, and it soon passed into the back of my memory. Hearing the contempt in Sean's voice made me wonder if he too had heard about Gandini's intimidation tactics; I had known Sean for a while now and I knew he despised anyone who immediately resorted to violence to settle a dispute. I don't know if Violet remembered this bit of history, but the look of ice in her blue eyes said that she, like me, had her reasons to put the screws to Constantino Gandini.

I thanked Sean, and as Violet spoke her farewells, I walked to the front of the store to say my goodbyes to Victoria. After a peck on the cheek, I walked outside and over to Lizzie, for once getting within five feet before she realized I was there. I said nothing, then knelt and put my arms wide, enfolding her in a warm embrace. I could hear her purring in my ear even over the din of both auto and foot traffic, felt her arms wrap around my neck. I wasn't usually so free with my emotions, but the thought of some goon hurting this half-grown kitten just to get to Sean and Victoria over a petty dispute made my blood boil. No one would hurt my friends as long as I could do something about it. No one.

I released Lizzie and looked her in the eye. "You're a good kid Liz. Keep up the good work, because I might need someone to scour the newspapers while Violet busies herself with painting her claws again." She giggled and I pulled her newsboy hat down over her eyes. As she readjusted the hat, I stood, listening to the combined sound of her purring laugh. Since she had started plying papers for her parents' newsstand, I had grown fond of the coal-colored imp, but the realization that my actions could cause her life to be threatened for no fault of her own had brought into fine focus just what Lizzie Cahill and her family meant to me. I still felt a great deal of trepidation regarding Constantino and his minions, but any fear began to fade into the background, pushed aside by my loyalty to people I considered among my few friends.

Having said my goodbyes, I turned to walk toward the car, only to find Violet, arms folded and watching me with a mischievous stare. "I saw what you did there, Max. I saw it clear as day with my own two eyes! You gave Lizzie Cahill a hug and you did it for no other reason than that you could." She slipped her left paw just above my elbow, gently pulling me toward the car. "You should be careful. Any further outbursts like that and people might talk. They might whisper that Max Persian really does have a heart in there somewhere!"

We stopped by the car and I opened the driver's side door for her. She reached to close it, but I held it open. "You're wrong, Violet. Not about me growing a heart, as that's just a matter of anatomy and neither here nor there. You're wrong that I lacked a reason. I just tend to keep my reasons to myself. Besides, all anatomical foibles aside, people have likely spoken about me for a long time. All I had to do was to hire on Benjamin Winterhaven's plucky youngest daughter and the tongues must have started wagging. Now I'm out on the town with the same beautiful lady. I'm surprised our ears have not started to burn away!" I smiled as I closed the door and walked around the front to the passenger side of the Chevrolet.

As I opened the door and sat down, I looked over at my employee and friend and said in a calm voice, "And there isn't a cat around with whom I'd rather spend my time." She turned to me with an expression of surprise, and I could see that under her short white and grey striped fur, she was blushing. I hoped I hadn't said too much, so to break the tension I extended one finger and claw and pointed out the windshield. "Onward, driver! Onward and... that way!" The short laugh reached her blue eyes, which twinkled with delight, and while she drove, I thought that, like Lizzie Cahill, I heard her purr.

17

After several blocks 'that way' I suggested to Violet that we might head over to Russian Joe's later and see if he knew anyone who might know about Cord automobiles. The magazine article I skimmed as she drove proved very useful, but it only covered basic information. I hoped that Joe, who usually knew a lot about most things and knew someone who knew everything about things if he himself didn't, might be able to help me learn some of the quirks about these unusual cars. Considering Constantino Gandini seemed to be a fan of odd cars in general and Cords in particular, I wanted to know enough to be able to ask him something that got him talking. While I would never fool him into believing me an enthusiast, showing an interest in something of his with knowledge that went beyond the basic might make him inclined to talk to me about other things. Besides, I had some interest in automobiles, and the unusual front wheel drive Cords and Miller race cars did pique my curiosity. The interest I had long held for mechanical transportation had paid dividends in past cases, and with a bit of a crash course, I might learn something and gain a way to talk to someone I increasingly wanted to bring to the ground. I just hoped that the crash course didn't involve my knees courtesy of a ball peen hammer.

After our long breakfast and a stop at the Cahill's newsstand, I asked Violet when my tuxedo and shoes would be ready. She looked over and smiled, then said that we were already en route. "Jacques is an amazing tailor, and a lot of New Amsterdam's wealthy employ his services. I expect that he's a millionaire himself, what with the prices he can charge. I know a little bit about his craft, and because he was commissioned on such short notice, the design he chose is simple yet quietly elegant. He was very thorough with his measurements and his preparation, and I'm sure he had it completed within a few hours of our previous visit. He offered to come in early today to check the fit and make any last-minute alterations, but he probably won't need to. Jacques has practiced his craft for years and is extremely good at what he does. The man doesn't make mistakes.

"My father says that Jacques' tuxedos are so finely tailored that he wishes he had more opportunities to wear them, and that his suits fit so well that it's like putting on a set of well-worn leather gloves. I know that you have some reservations about a black-tie affair and wearing a fine tuxedo, but you'll love how it feels and you'll love how it looks. Because it's comfortable, you'll be more relaxed and able to do the wonderful things you do. And if that isn't enough, you'll get to wear those silly shoes with it, and the tux might actually make them look presentable!" The smile on her face positively radiated sarcasm, but also smacked of elegant cuteness, which I didn't mind at all.

After a few more minutes, we arrived at Jacques' shop. Though it was only a quarter after ten and the sign on the door read Closed, Violet knocked on the glass. After a moment, Jacques opened the door and let us inside, then secured the lock after closing it behind us. The large front window was obscured by heavy burgundy curtains that ran behind the shop's window mannequins, and as a result the shop was quite dark. Jacques' sewing machines and tables for measuring occupied part of the rear of the main showroom behind a short wall; Violet had told me at some point that he liked the natural light and watching the cats and the cars pass by outside as he worked. Several lamps burned brightly on the tables, and a single recessed floodlight illuminated a small platform that fronted a three-way mirror, obviously for customers to check the fit of their purchases.

After a few short pleasantries, he walked through an open doorway and into a storeroom, returning a moment later with my tuxedo, pressed and creased with the precision of a fine watch. From a table behind the short wall, he produced a pair of black and white wingtips, polished to a mirror shine. He directed me to an ample sized dressing room just on the other side of the doorway and after a couple of minutes and some assistance with my cummerbund, I stepped into the main room. I heard Violet gasp from the gloom and turned to see her standing by one of Jacques' freestanding displays, her paw raised and partially covering her mouth.

She must have read my dismay, because she walked to me and placed her paws on my shoulders as she looked me up and down. "You have never looked better, Max! You look as dashing and debonair as any handsome young playboy that has attended all of our balls. The only reason I gasped like I did is that you nearly swept me off my feet just by walking into the room!" She took hold of my arm, as if being escorted to the dance floor. "I also owe you an apology. Those shoes work well with the entire ensemble. Black ones would have been too plain and ordinary, but these bring just enough flair to the party to make you look flashy enough to appear interesting, but not so much as to appear gaudy or narcissistic. And the shine on them is flawless! People are going to notice, Max. When you step into the room, you are going to make all the right impressions. And that will make it hard for Constantino to avoid you."

She looked up at me with that mischievous smirk of hers. "That is, if they notice you after the sheer beauty of my dress doesn't blind them first. Some of them might even blind themselves with brooches so as to never to see anything less than sheer perfection again!"

I shook my head, laughing softly. "Come on Oedipus," I said, "Let's get everything ready to go so we can get you back to Thebes in a timely manner. Iris and Daisy won't stand a chance in solving the Riddle of The Sphynx without your radiant help."

Despite herself, Violet laughed, then snorted, which started her laughing again. "Stop making me laugh, Max! You know I snort when I laugh, and when I snort, I laugh even harder!"

I smiled a mischievous smile of my own. "I know. You laugh, you snort, you laugh again, which makes you snort again, which makes you laugh again, et cetera, et cetera. If I could somehow harness you and your laughter, I could create electricity. I could retire a very rich cat for having patented the first working perpetual motion generator. Your laughter alone could power a city block almost indefinitely!" At this, Violet hit my arm, and though her mouth wore a frown, her eyes shone brightly with laughter.

I had to admit, if only silently for the moment, that she was also right about the tuxedo. It fit like nothing else I had ever worn, snug but not tight where necessary, loose enough to allow a surprising freedom of motion everywhere else. As Violet had said, it felt as comfortable as a favorite pair of leather gloves. Though it was wholly a tuxedo, Jacques had picked a black fabric that contained faint grey pinstripes, just light enough to catch the eye in certain lighting. It was a surprising choice, but one that paid dividends in its appearance and in its uniqueness, for though Jacques had designed tuxedos for many of the guests attending the Winterhaven's charity gala, he proudly assured me that he had never used this particular fabric before. Though I didn't ask either Jacques or Violet how much this masterpiece had cost, I could guess that it likely ran at least a month's pay and probably more. I lamented aloud that I would likely never wear such a perfect garment as this again, knowing in my heart that unless I struck oil, truer words may never have been spoken.

After switching back into my casual attire, Jacques inspected the tuxedo and quickly repressed the pants to a chiseled perfection with edges that could have cleaved apart iron bars. After quickly ironing the pleated white shirt, he packaged the entire affair under a loose paper smock, then returned each shoe to the cloth sacks and wooden box they had arrived in to keep their exquisite shine perfect. As a final touch, he handed Violet two skinny boxes containing unfolded handmade bowties, one with a pattern that matched the subtle striping of the suit and one without. Jacques unlocked the front door, speaking a friendly final farewell as he saw us outside, then closed the door quietly behind us and locked it. While he closed his shop and exited out the back to enjoy the rest of his day in front of a soccer broadcast, Violet and I returned to her car, where I discovered that a discreet hook had been added to the roof behind the driver's seat.

When I asked, she said that the dresses worn by the family women were always delivered in a Metro Van owned by the high-end tailor hired to create them; they were too tall to hang in the car and too finely made to ride folded in the trunk or on the back bench. But when she realized that I lacked suitable transport for my tux, she asked her father's handyman to fashion a hook from the roof of her car. The addition was a relatively simple fix, one that afforded a place so my tux would stay as pristine as possible. Though she could have rented a van, Violet had avoided the pointless excess taken so easily for granted that plagued her older sisters like an incurable affliction. In a family of remarkable people, I found Violet Winterhaven the most remarkable of all.

We drove back toward the office, but instead of turning we continued back to my apartment building. As she pulled into an empty spot in front of the building, I asked why we were stopping there, Violet replied, "I thought we could spend a while relaxing in your apartment before heading over to Russian Joe's. He won't be open for a few hours yet and I thought we could listen to the radio and relax a while." She shrugged. "Or we can go have a picnic lunch in the park and enjoy a chilly day to ourselves. Either would be fine, but you'll still need a change of clothes for the next couple of days, so we stopped here."

Caught off guard, I could only ask why I needed a change of clothes. "Because I think it would be a good idea if you stayed at the mansion. You'll be able to see many of the preparations for the gala as they are set, and there will be time to learn the layout of the property and figure out some good places from which to observe events. Daddy can help you with some of it, and I can help with the rest. Plus, you won't have to worry about anything happening to your tux or about getting there. I think it would make things easier for you; if you stay home, you'll sit in that apartment by yourself and worry and stress yourself silly. At least this way you'll have me to talk to and you will already be there."

I had to admit that she gave a good argument, but there was one detail she hadn't mentioned. "And where will I sleep?" I asked. It was a stupid question, and I knew it was a stupid question by the way Violet looked at me. The Winterhaven mansion had several guest bedrooms, all of which were reputed to be finer than the best hotels in the city. I shook my head, amazed that in all of the time I had known her that I would forget that she was the daughter of one of the richest industrialists in the entire Northeast.

I stayed quiet for the last bit of the drive, making sure that I didn't embarrass myself further. After we arrived at my little apartment, we spent a few hours listening to jazz on the radio and eating a basic yet nice lunch. Violet was right; even with her company I was growing increasingly nervous about the upcoming event. When it came time to leave, I gathered some clothes and a few basic things into an older suitcase and turned off the radio. After checking the lights and powered appliances, we exited my humble abode as I locked the door behind me. I realized as we were walking out to the street that this would be the first time I would spend the night elsewhere since moving in years ago. It seemed like only a couple of years, but in truth I had moved in at least eight or nine years earlier, though I couldn't remember exactly when.

I had hired Violet since then, and she had only first seen the inside of my apartment a couple of days prior, while I had never set foot in the Winterhaven mansion. As Violet opened the trunk of her Chevrolet and I placed my suitcase inside, I said to myself that not only have the years started to pass by, but my social life had been on life support the past several years, even by my reclusive standards. As she drove the short distance to Russian Joe's tavern, neither of us spoke. I didn't know what was turning around inside her head, but I was content, even happy, with Violet's company over the past few days. I stole a glance at her face as she drove, but when she turned toward me, I quickly looked away. I hoped that she hadn't seen me admiring her, but from the corner of my eye I saw her smile and couldn't be sure either way.

18

When we walked through the door at Russian Joe's, both Violet and I were taken aback. The first Friday in December was a chilly one and had brought out cats who didn't want to stay in the cold alone. The tables were largely full, with groups of cats engaged in conversation and laughter, while the bar itself was three-quarters full. As we took a pair of stools at the far end, Joe waved to us as he juggled several refills at once. After a moment, he brought us two fresh glasses and leaned over to speak to us.

"I spoke to a cat who spoke to a cat, and the cat you want to talk to about a Cord will be here in an hour, maybe a little less. He'll know Constantino Gandini's car inside and out because he's the one who owned it first! The car was in his family since it was new and he kept it until a year ago. Sit tight, enjoy some White Russians on the house, and when he arrives, I'll introduce you. In the meantime, a mutual associate is waiting for you. She tried your office, but you were out and since I didn't know where you were, I suggested she stay here and wait for you to arrive on other business." His eyes twinkled in amusement. "You remember Miss Aurora Kowalski, yes? She is in my office sampling the napping prowess of my sofa, so if you'll pardon me, I'll step in and wake her. Then it's back to work; the evening is shaping up to be a madhouse."

Joe stepped out from behind the bar and went to the back rooms for a moment, then came back to his post and picked up a glass and towel. A moment later, Aurora Kowalski emerged, covered a large yawn with her paw and walked over to us, setting her sleep-mussed fur right as she did. I shook her paw and introduced her to Violet, then got down to the matter at hand. For a bit more privacy, Aurora led us to an open booth and sat across from us at the table. Once seated and after a quick look around, she got to the matter at hand.

"The trucks I told you about, the ones that have been coming each afternoon to transport the tuna catch, they're gone. Not only that, but the tuna boats aren't coming to port until late in the evening. When they do arrive, the crews are tying them to the docks and heading home instead of offloading their catch." Aurora took a deep breath. "I think they're going somewhere else and offloading their catch there. Just for kicks I called a couple of friends that berth their boats in other harbors and gave them some names to find out if they'd seen the boats. None of them have seen anything unusual. I spoke to Turk after you left to see what he knew, and the two of us have kept our eyes open. Those trucks, those boats, they were at the harbor every single day and now they're all gone. With your visit, I don't think it's a coincidence. I thought you should know."

Aurora paused, and as her smile faded from her face, I noticed that she seemed a bit on edge. When I asked her why, she revealed her worry that she and Turk might have somehow let slip their involvement in my case. Both feared that should their part be exposed to whoever was behind the tuna shortage, they could meet with some unfortunate circumstance. Without delving into the details of our excursion to the warehouses, Violet and I reassured her that while someone had slipped and revealed the investigation, the mistake was ours. We told her that we had been paid a visit, though not by whom, and that the visitor had informed us that our activities had been discovered. We concluded by saying that while she should be alert and keep an eye out for anyone suspicious, she and Turk were probably not the focus of anyone's attention.

I thanked Aurora for the information she had passed to us. She made as if to leave, but then turned to us and regaled us with one last surprise. "Joe told me that you have often commented favorably on the nautical paintings, saying that they look out of place because of their skill and beauty. They should. After all, I painted them!" Violet and I looked at each other in surprise. "Your words are high praise indeed, as most people don't seem to notice them at all. Joe thought the place needed a bit of livening up, so he commissioned me to paint them and paid me very well for my efforts." At this juncture I asked the obvious question, how a fishing captain was also a world-class painter, all the while hoping for an interesting story in the meantime, to which she didn't disappoint.

"I was an artist long before I began working on the boats," Aurora said. "I'm something of a prodigy, if that term can be applied to painting as well as music. A childhood spent growing up on the Hudson River meant I crossed paths with a lot of painters. I was lucky in that when the Depression hit, I was still in grade school, and by the time I had stated my desire to attend an Academy of Art, I was able to qualify for a New Deal program called the Federal Art Project and got accepted into Bard College. After two semesters, I needed money to live on, so I started looking in the classifieds and asking around for summer work. The only people who would give me the time of day were the fishermen on the wharf, so I went and applied to several in person. I told them I wanted to do the work and get out on a boat so I could look back and study the land from the water. Joe Antonov decided to hire me on the spot.

"He ran a tight ship, and the work wasn't easy, but Joe was supportive and fair to some landie cat who had never even been on water. At first, I was afraid. Petrified, even. But I needed the money, so I made myself go out there and did the best job I possibly could. And Joe, he took me on like a project. He showed me how to work a boat, how to handle the fish, but more than that he would talk to me, tell me of his love for the sea and everything in it. He called me into the wheelhouse to show me the dolphins as they rode the wake, encouraged me to get right out on the bow, over the water, and just watch them as they moved through the deep. I learned to *see* the ocean from Joe, learned to see the water as a living thing with all its emotions, learned to see how the creatures within lived and fought for survival. I learned from his example, and because I listened, I'm a better seascape painter than I could have ever been otherwise. I saw the beauty of the ocean and in return, it saw into me."

136

Aurora stretched her back, then continued. "By the end of the summer, I had fallen for the blue ocean, making a promise to myself that while I would finish my program at Bard, I would make sure to always hold the water close to my soul. I came back and worked on Joe's boat each summer, and when I graduated, I moved here permanently and worked it to support my art. Joe was always there for me, always ready to support me in my endeavors. I saved up enough money to finance the Inferno, a beat-up old nag of a boat that I could both fish and use as a floating studio. Joe helped me renovate her with both cash and labor. When I inquired as to how I would pay him back, he asked for the paintings in this bar." Aurora smiled. "I still think I got the better end of the deal, but you'd never know it from him."

As she brought her story to a close, Aurora stood up and begged her leave of us, noting that she had spent a long day on the water and wished only to go to her apartment and collapse for a few days. She gave Violet and I each a polite goodbye, then turned to get her coat and scarf. As she left, I remarked to Violet how the cat called Russian Joe seemed to have the most peculiar and exquisite tastes when it came to friends and acquaintances. Violet smiled and replied, "Well, of course he has exquisite taste in those he knows. With *me* counted among his friends, how could his tastes be otherwise?" She covered her mouth with a dainty white paw, and I couldn't help but laugh.

We returned to the bar to await the cat who had sold Constantino his beloved Cord. As we waited, I turned to Violet. "Two questions," I said. "How did he know we were looking for someone who knows Cords? And what exactly is a White Russian?"

Violet smiled and replied, "I called Joe while you were trying on your tux and asked him for his help. He said he thought he could get a hold of someone and have him meet us here, but even if he hadn't, I thought getting you over here for a little while wouldn't hurt. As for the second question, I have no idea. My guess is that milk is white and he's Russian. Ergo, White Russian. He has a very subtle wit, that one." I shrugged, satisfied with both answers.

"What made you call Joe?" I asked.

"Max, if it's one thing I've learned from working for and with you, it's that Iosef Dmitrievich Antonov knows every person who knows every other person in this city. And if he doesn't, he knows someone who knows someone else who knows the other person. You're not the only one who comes in here, you know, and when I do, I'm continually amazed at the sheer number of people and things that he knows. Besides, you told me early on that if you didn't know someone and I didn't know someone, talk to Russian Joe. And to your credit, Max, you were absolutely right on more occasions than you would know." She smiled an innocent smile, one that seemed to say 'See? I know what I'm doing!' and then reinforced this by sticking the tip of her tongue at me playfully.

Violet and I waited at the bar, sipping our drinks and listening to the broadcast game as we talked softly among ourselves. I learned that during her time in boarding school she had played cricket and had been quite good at the sport; upon returning home she began following baseball to pass the time. Soon thereafter she joined a local women's softball league and within a few months made herself into one of the star players. Only an injury to her knee had convinced her to stop playing, but her love of the game persisted. I had worked with Violet for several years and had never even guessed that she was a baseball fan. Learning about her was fun, but it also highlighted how little it seemed I knew about her. I hoped this would change. As I pondered this, Joe signaled me to bring Violet and meet him at the other end of the bar. Our source of information regarding Cord automobiles had arrived.

19

Sterling Elias walked over and put out his paw to shake, and I realized how physically large he was. It wasn't just that his black and white fur was quite long, but the body it concealed was quite imposing. He greeted Violet and I warmly and motioned her to sit between him and myself; next to him she looked like a dolled-up kitten. When he sat on the barstool, he positively hulked over the bar, and for a second, I wondered how he actually fit into any car. I soon learned that while his body was massive and towering, his personality was quiet and unpretentious, as he was something of a pacifist. Still, I felt an underlying sense that Sterling hadn't always been the most peaceful of cats. Thinking to myself that he could likely pull my arm off at the shoulder, I was rather glad he was.

"Joe told me that you two are looking to get some information about Cords," Sterling said. "I've got to know why, as there can't be more than five people in this city who have any interest in them, you two included." As Joe had vouched for Sterling's character, I felt comfortable giving him some of the reasoning, telling him that I had a meeting with Constantino Gandini the next day, that I knew he owned an L-29 sedan and I wanted to have a conversation with him about this car.

As I spoke, Sterling's eyes narrowed and he exhaled a long, controlled breath. "That car belonged to me. My father bought that car new instead of a Cadillac or a Stutz. I thought it was the prettiest thing I'd ever laid eyes on, and when the war came and I enlisted, he told me that it would be waiting for me when I returned. I got shipped off to England and dodged German lead at Omaha, then drove those Schutzstaffel punks all the way back to Berlin. And through it all my dad never doubted I would come back. I lived through that mess without catching a bullet, and five months after I returned the old man passes away." He paused and shook his head. "While I'm over there putting Nazis in the dirt, he gets cancer."

Though Sterling's yellow-green eyes simmered as he spoke, his body remained relaxed, almost slack. He took a slow drink of his milk, a milk that had quietly appeared when he started his story, then continued. "Constantino bought the car almost fourteen months ago. He saw it on the street and decided he wanted it, simple as that; he can be very, ah, persuasive. Sent a couple of toughs over to talk to me. There wasn't much I could do. One of 'em had me covered with a .45 auto like I used in the War. If I could have disarmed him, I could have broken both of their arms, but Gandini would have just sent more goons and they probably would have shot me up with Thompsons. So, I let it go. Now Gandini owns it. End of story"

Sterling closed his eyes and took another long drink. "My father loved that car even more than I did. After I enlisted, he bought a secondhand Lincoln-Zephyr and almost never drove the Cord; he said he wanted to keep it clean for me when I returned, said it was my car. He handed me the keys the day I came home, went with me to sign the title. He was already getting sicker then, but he said he wasn't going to miss signing the car over to me. The cancer got bad soon after and I drove him to the hospital in that Cord. I drove him in it for the last time when I brought him home. There was nothing more they could do. I'd have driven him to the cemetery in it too, but the funeral people frown on taking cats out of their boxes." The glint in his eye was unmistakable. "I never wanted to let it go. Meant too much to me. Machines can become part of the family too."

Sterling took another drink. "I'm sorry folks. You didn't come down here to see me cry in my milk. You came to get some questions answered." He turned toward us and put one large paw gingerly, nonthreateningly on Violet's shoulder. In a low voice he said, "Joe has a pretty good sense of people, and he tells me that you two are all right. He might have even told me, without saying the words, that you might just be looking to take Gandini down a few rungs. I would like that very much, folks, very much indeed."

He withdrew his paw to his lap, there to pull a set of keys

from his pocket. "I had this set made well before Constantino took the car. They'll open both the doors and the trunk if the locks haven't been changed. I hope you might get the opportunity to be alone with the Cord, and if you do, you might use this smaller key to find some useful paperwork. My father built a few hidden compartments into the car and I would be happy to let you know where they are all hidden. I told those stooges to tell their master where they were, showed him with a key. My guess is that Gandini uses them to keep certain things hidden. Who knows what secrets lie hidden within?" With a gleam in his eye, Sterling handed Violet the keys, which she quietly slipped into a pocket.

For the next hour and a half, we learned as much as possible about Cords in general and about Sterling's L-29 in particular. Joe had provided us with a gold mine in Sterling, as the cat was a walking encyclopedia about Cords and all manner of prewar cars. Because he had owned the same car favored by Constantino Gandini, indeed the same exact car, Sterling knew all of the idiosyncrasies of that vehicle, things such as the fiddly nature of the inboard brakes and how he always had to set the right side to brake slightly harder than the left. But his revelation that the car contained secret storage nooks in the passengers' compartment made the keys given us even more valuable to us than gold. I noted to myself the importance of paying a visit to the Cord during the event.

When we felt we had tapped Sterling for all the information we could possibly need, the three of us sat and shared in each other's company for a while. Though Violet touched not a drop, I put back a couple of mugs and Sterling, half-lost in a past of war, loss and glory, sent at least nine noble milk soldiers, possibly more, on to *leche* Valhalla. When he began to feel tired, Violet called two of her family's chauffeurs to come and take both him and his car home, implying a nice bonus would come to their next paycheck. Afterword, she spoke to Joe and asked to pay for our drinks, Joe shook his head and smiled.

"No charge tonight, pretty lady. Even though Mr. Sterling Elias drinks like a fish in the desert, he's here on business tonight with two important clients. I have an idea of what you're working on, and I don't mind doing my part to help. You are both good people, Mr. Persian and Miss Winterhaven, and because of that, your drinks, as well as those of your esteemed guest, are on the house." He smiled as we stood and said in a low voice, "Good luck tomorrow. Maybe you'll let ol' Joe know how it went!" With a half-smile I nodded to the clever barkeep, then turned and let Violet lead me out to the car.

Violet started the engine, and the weight of the past several days lay upon my shoulders. I felt tired, and not just because the *leche* was going to my head. Most of our cases unfolded in a slower and more controlled manner; we get hired for a specific job, we research and observe, we put what we found together in a coherent way and we present our findings to the client. If we're lucky, we've found out what we were hired to find to the clients' satisfaction, but sometimes the outcome wasn't what was expected.

As Violet drove, I remembered a case in which a young lady had hired us to keep an eye on her husband as she feared he was in some sort of trouble with some of our city's less savory types. The two of us had followed him at a distance, just making sense of his movements to see where he went. After a few times, it became apparent why he would come and go from their apartment at unusual times and why he took unusual routes to his destination, sometimes by taxi, sometimes by subway, but always to the same destination. Then we had to give his wife pictures of his multiple rendezvous with another young kitty. To say that she was devastated would be a gross understatement; I later learned that she packed a truck and left New Amsterdam for her family's farm in Iowa, never to return.

I learned this because her soon-to-be ex-husband exploded into the office like a raging bull and screamed everything to us. It's easy to remember such things, especially as it was one of the few occasions I'd felt forced to draw a weapon. When he charged into my office with murder in his eye, I pulled a Colt 1911 pistol from the holster I had mounted under the desk and clocked him in the side of the head with the base of the grip. I only noticed when he was down that Violet had pulled a Derringer and was training it on him as he moaned.

Having persuaded him to calm himself and sit in one of my chairs, Violet and I listened as he poured his life story out to us while I kept him at gunpoint. When he was finished, he just hung his head and cried. We let him leave and never called the police; it was an awful case all around and any legal action would have just prolonged the misery for everyone. Sometimes there are no happy endings, and the best thing to do is to wash one's hands of a bad situation and move on.

I looked over at Violet, her eyes on the road and her hands on the wheel. There was one silver lining to that horrible case, I thought. That was the first time I began to think of Violet as a partner, not just a secretary. Perhaps, I thought musingly, when this was over and we went back to something approaching normalcy, I would call the painter and put her name on the door as a detective in her own right. Smaller letters perhaps, as she would be the junior detective and because Winterhaven is longer than Persian, but her name should appear on the door nonetheless. In my sentimentality it occurred to me that I was glad that she had taken the wheel. I suspected those *leches* were a bit more potent than I was used to. At least I would probably get a good night's sleep. Though I didn't want to make an imposition of myself, the thought of a soft bed in the Winterhaven mansion sounded more appealing by the moment.

By the time we arrived, I had fallen asleep. As we pulled into the drive, Violet gently shook me awake, and though groggy, I came to enough to be able to walk into the house rather than be carried. I forgot about my duffel until I saw a butler retrieve it from the trunk along with my tuxedo from behind the driver's seat. Violet gave the butler some quiet directions, to which he nodded and came to my side. "Shall I escort you to your room, sir? Per Miss Winterhaven's orders, it is ready and waiting for you." I accepted his assistance with as much grace as I could muster and let him lead me through the mansion and up the stairs until he stopped outside an open door and politely ushered me inside.

As I surveyed the room, my ward hung my tuxedo in the walk-in closet and set my shoes in a cubby on the right side, then quickly unpacked my clothes and set the duffel on a shelf in the closet. After placing my leather toiletries case in the bathroom, he turned and said, "Our night staff can press your clothes and hang them on the outside of the door for tomorrow," indicating two small pegs. I told him that I would appreciate this. He also informed me that if I chose to leave my shoes outside the door that they would be polished and set outside the door beneath my clothes. "Is there any specific time you wish to awaken? The morning staff would be happy to knock at the appropriate hour." I shook my head gently and spoke a soft no, thank you.

As he moved to the door, the butler paused, smiling. "Miss Violet has told us many good things about you, Mr. Persian. It is a pleasure to finally meet you. If you need anything, the night staff will be there to assist. My name is Claude, and I will be here in the morning to help with preparations. Goodnight and sleep well, sir." As he left, he pulled the door quietly shut behind him.

After looking about the room again, I took my shoes off and set them in the hall as they looked a bit rough, then re-entered the room and closed the door. I unbuttoned my shirt and let it fall to the floor, soon to be joined by my trousers and socks. Now clad in just my boxers and undershirt, I stretched and lay down on the bed, its blankets and sheets pulled down invitingly. The last thing I remembered was my head hitting the pillow, then blackness. Violet told me the following day that she had stopped by a few minutes later, hoping to say a few last words about the charity gala, but she had found me snoring on top of the sheets with the light still on and

144

oblivious to the world. In her mercy she put my legs under and folded the bedding over my unconscious body, then picked my clothing off the floor, turned off the light, and closed the door behind her. If I dreamed at all, no memory remained.

20

I opened my eyes, briefly disoriented and wondering where I was. I remembered the evening spent at Russian Joe's, then sat up to take a bearing of my surroundings. I quickly remembered that I had spent the night in one of the Winterhaven's guest rooms, and immediately after remembered that my clothes had ended up lying on the floor. Now, they no longer lay there in their wrinkled glory, so I walked over to the door and opened it slightly. My clothes hung pressed from the hangers on the door's outer face. I could smell that they had been washed during the night too, an unexpected kindness. I turned and looked at the clock on the nightstand, which read about 7:45 AM. Later than I normally slept, but not so late as to be rudely decadent, I hoped.

The remaining events of the previous evening had come back easily, and no milk headache had reared its ugly head, so I walked into the bathroom to get myself ready for the day. I didn't know if the maids would make the bed or not, but both out of habit and a desire to act polite, I made it up as I best imagined it, then drew back the curtains to another cloudy day. My window, tall and somewhat narrow, looked out onto an expansive yard, closely cut and generally immaculate.

My room, like all of the guest rooms in the mansion proper, lay on the third floor; based on European precedents, Benjamin Winterhaven and his family lived on the second floor, the *Piano Nobile*. Violet had mentioned once that while the third floor was most usually called 'the third floor' the architect had called it the *Secondo Piano Nobile* as it was furnished equally lavishly to the main floor below. Like many English manors built during and after the Renaissance, the ground floor held the 'servants' rooms such as the kitchen, plus more modern additions such as a laundry room and other utilities.

The outer façade of the mansion had been designed in a

restrained classical style; as with its English antecedents, a large staircase fronted the building, set in the center and modelled after a Roman temple front. Inside the triangular pediment sat a sculpture ensemble featuring Venus and Mars, accompanied by Bacchus and Minerva. Along the rear, the theme was mirrored save for the staircase and portico. Instead, a semicircular room bulged outward from the ground floor, its roof forming a large balcony from the main floor sitting room that Elijah Winterhaven had constructed for himself, while two staircases curved around the sides to the ground. I couldn't help but hold a slight jealousy against Violet that she spent endless hours of her childhood discovering the mansion's mysteries.

I looked around to make sure the hall was empty, then took my clothes and shoes inside. I put on my clothes and took a look at my shoes; as promised, my shoes were polished to a rich medium brown that had removed the nicks and scrapes on their leather hide. Someone had even thought to replace the worn and mismatched laces with new ones, a nice detail. As I put them on, I marveled once again what sort of lifestyle a bit of wealth could afford. Now fully dressed, I walked down the hall in search of both breakfast and someone who could bring me up to speed on what to expect for the evening's affair.

I walked out of the room and turned toward the main stairs. They terminated at the balcony on which I now stood, looking down into the main entryway of the house. Behind me, a large guest lounge beckoned through open doors, and I couldn't resist a look around. As I went in the room, I saw several cases lined with books, while comfortable chairs beckoned. An ornate chess board and a globe rested on a Rococo table, while a large phonograph stood in the corner. I walked to it and looked at the recording set to play. Tchaikovsky's '1812 Overture'. I shook my head; Violet had probably left that just for me.

I descended to the ground floor of the mansion and walked the short distance to the Gala Hall. I found myself in a utilitarian storage room, then a short hallway that I guessed led to the main hall. At the end, I stepped through a set of doors into a corner of the great room. I gazed about and I saw a stage on the opposite wall, with a large staircase on the wall to my right. The large room buzzed with activity. The Winterhaven's staff and caterers engaged themselves throughout the room and onto a piazza beyond the rear glass and doors. Outside, large and temporary frost-resistant greenery sat in massive pots no doubt selected for this evening. Beyond the piazza, linked by cobbled walkways, lay the centerpiece of the garden, a curious building set apart from the mansion. Built in a classicizing style yet featuring a glazed roof and dome, the building resembled a cross between a Palladian chapel and the Crystal Palace. Though my morning hunger was growing, my curiosity overcame me and I stepped between the workmen and out into the piazza.

Activity outside mirrored that in the great hall behind me. One worker a large urn filled with a small conifer tree on a dolly, while another exited my view through a service door with his own empty hand truck. Several other conifers of various sizes had already been wheeled in and sat as yet unsorted near the doors. Further outward, landscapers placed low, broad pots along the edges of the main path at regular intervals, while maintenance crews busied themselves laying electrical cords and small lights on either side of the same path. Still more workers installed spotlights throughout the grass to illuminate the surrounding architecture. Across the piazza I saw that preparations continued into the glass-roofed structure, and letting my curiosity get the better of me, I walked down the wide main path and inside the building.

To my surprise I discovered that this unusual construction was a substantial interior garden, not only much wider and deeper than I first suspected, but entirely comprised of glass on the upper half. Had the day proven sunnier, the whole of the interior would have basked in the glory of a summer's day, even now at the end of November. Even with the doors opened wide behind me to allow free access for the workers who came and went, the interior was comfortably warm. About twenty feet inside the door on a wide pedestal stood a marble statue of Venus Victrix, her name and that of her sculptor, Antonio Canova, inscribed on a plaque facing the doors. The Roman goddess reclined, her head propped with her right paw, an apple held lazily by her left, while a loose garment gently circled her waistline, leaving the cat bare above the waist. She looked in a comfortable repose, as if enjoying the many scents of her garden surround. I had noticed the sound of trickling water when I entered, and as I walked slowly around the sculpture, I saw the source, a sizeable fountain at the end of a short path.

As I meandered along, I glanced up at the trees that reached toward the glass ceiling above. After a moment spent wondering why they looked different from area foliage, I realized with a start that the trees had not nor had they ever grown naturally here. Tall, thin cedars made it apparent that the greenery towering above me was of a Mediterranean origin, and though I failed to recognize the other varieties, it was clear that the Winterhavens had created an Italic oasis of their very own here in New Amsterdam. The size of the trees above me gave an excellent indicator of the height of the roof, which I realized was considerably higher than I had first surmised.

As I ambled further into the greenhouse, closer to what I assumed was the building's center, I came upon a magnificent fountain, its figures carved of stone and topped by an obelisk, its surface adorned with Egyptian hieroglyphs. Set in the center of a small clearing, the stone spire reached high above me, higher even than the surrounding vegetation, while above it the glass ceiling took the form of a large dome, the entirety of its form rendered in patterns of stained glass, its center left open in an oculus. All I could do was to stare, at the fountain, the obelisk, the multicolored hues of red, blue, yellow and green, the audacious magnificence of the thing. That feline minds could conceive of this, that feline paws could have built this, was almost more than I could take in.

149

What was I doing here, in this house of riches, and what could I possibly hope to gain, so hopelessly out of place among people who could throw away a lifetime of my wages and never notice? I felt the nagging itch of self-doubt many times before and had always worked through to the case's conclusion, but this time the itch was fast becoming a rash. I believed myself in over my head, struggling to make sense of a world beyond my modest life, and for the first time I felt the urge to run far away.

In my dark self-reflection, I didn't hear the footsteps on the paving stones that should have told me I was no longer alone. I found myself standing next to an older cat, of average size and build, dressed in casual attire. I looked at him only to see his head tilted back, eyes fixed into the dome. After a minute or so he closed them, slowly brought his head to level, then let a long sigh escape from his body. Only then did he turn to look at me, his green eyes betraying a high intellect as he sized me up. His face, covered as it was in brown and white medium length fur, reflected curiosity and kindness, and though I only knew him as a man of means, I reasoned him someone with whom I could get along. Working in the profession I had chosen, deciphering a cat from what little I could observe had become something of an art which I had acquired an amount of skill. But I could be wrong.

"It's all a bit silly, isn't it?" said my new acquaintance with a wry grin. "Bernini's 'Four Rivers' in Rome. I couldn't very well buy a landmark, but I could have a replica made of Carrera marble by Italian stone masons, then shipped here and reassembled. It's a three-quarter scale reproduction and still the dome had to be added to clear the top of the obelisk, so of course I went a bit overboard on that too. This whole scene is really a bit over the top, but my wife and I wanted something to remember our Italian honeymoon by. Honestly, I think we should have stuck to postcards."

He smiled, then turned to me in full and extended his paw. "Benjamin Winterhaven, sir. It's a pleasure to meet you."

Extending my own paw, we shook as I replied, "Max Persian. I guess I don't need to tell you that your daughter Violet works for me."

To my surprise, Mr. Winterhaven laughed and said, "Oh no, believe me sir, my youngest daughter has spent many hours keeping her mother and I updated on the happenings of one Max Persian, Private Detective! I think that when she tells of your shared exploits she is as giddy as a schoolgirl, except that she was never giddy when she was a schoolgirl. To be honest, I wondered what she was thinking when she applied to work with you, but she is happier than I've seen her in a long time. I couldn't be happier for her, plus it's given that independent streak she has a reasonable outlet. I was surprised when she came home with that Chevrolet, and even more surprised that she bought it with the wages she earned working for you. I'm happy she did though. Shows initiative. Heck, she's even conned the mechanic who services our cars to show her how to work on hers!" He smiled and put a paw on my shoulder. "Mr. Persian, you have my gratitude. The changes in Violet since she signed on with you have made me proud, and that means a great deal as a father. I owe you, sir, I owe you."

Though I'm seldom left speechless, that moment was an exception. Not only had I laid my plebian eyes on an object of incredible beauty (and no doubt equally, incredibly expensive) but I had just met Mr. Benjamin Winterhaven, at once one of the wealthiest cats in the country, but also the hitherto unseen father of my capable employee and closest friend. Occasionally in life, events occur that are outside of the norm or so bizarrely random that one is left fumbling to make sense of it all. This moment in time left me struggling to process the events of the past few minutes. After a moment that seemed like a minor eternity, I said, haltingly, "Please call me Max. I'm very uncomfortable with being called Mr. Persian right now. The past couple of minutes have really been a bit much to take in."

After laughing softly, he said in a warm voice, "I understand. At least I think I understand, which probably means I'm clueless. My close associates call me Benjamin. I just never was comfortable being 'Mr. Winterhaven.' Mr. Winterhaven was my grandfather. But my friends… my friends call me Ben, and seeing that this might just be the beginning of a beautiful friendship, I'll count you among my friends… Max." He smiled, then cocked his head slightly to one side. "I'm curious. What is Max short for, if anything? Names are such funny things, so full of meanings and the like, and yet they usually get shortened to a friendly nickname." I was finally beginning to relax in the realization that Benjamin Winterhaven was surprisingly personable, even normal.

"Maximillian," I replied. "Long and chocked full of excess letters and syllables. The guy who painted the letters on my office door would have gone on strike if I'd told him I wanted 'Maximillian B. Persian, Private Detective' above the suite number. So, Max it is."

As I shrugged, Ben laughed and shook his head. "I can see why Violet likes you." Still smiling, he turned back toward the piazza. "As much as I'd like to stay and meditate in front of my favorite fountain, there's work to be done. Violet let me in to your plans, and you'll have my support, 100 percent. Our unspoken friend needs to be taught a good lesson, maybe more." With that, we walked back toward the main hall while Ben started detailing the particulars of the buildings.

"My grandfather built this estate because that was what was expected if one was of wealth, even new wealth. But he was always a bit embarrassed by how ostentatious it all was, and that was before the gala hall and greenhouse were built. He figured that he could put it to use, though, and so put some of his expertise into the design." After a couple of minutes, we had arrived in the banquet hall. Ben stopped and gestured the room with a sweep of his arm. "This great room is all his doing. When it was built, critics either loved or, more often, hated it because of the Rococo décor and the ceiling art that was modelled after Tiepolo, all pastel colors and soft forms. At the time an 18th Century ballroom was well out of fashion, as mid-century Romanticism was still the rage. Even a Neoclassical room steeped in stories of antiquity wouldn't have been out of place. But my grandfather didn't care about what was popular; he had been to Venice and northern Italy as part of a tour of Europe and he copied what he liked. Those vases along the wall were all made and painted when the estate was built. He enjoyed reading works of antiquity and had scenes of the Greek tragedies painted in both red and black figure styles."

I paused Ben to ask a question. "What was his favorite piece of antique literature? I've read a good number of them myself."

Ben smiled and replied, "Violet has told me that you enjoy reading and have an impressive knowledge of the classics. My grandfather enjoyed The Odyssey a great deal, and the plays of Plautus. But his favorite was The Anabasis."

I smiled, then pointed to one of the black figure vases. "I recognized Xenophon from the scene on that vase. I've never seen anyone paint a battle between Greeks and Persians where the word 'Trebizond' and ships feature in the background. Whoever painted it did a remarkable job with the subject matter. I don't have the background in fine art that you and Violet have, but I recognize the themes and stories in a lot of the paintings I've seen. I'm glad I'm here to see these works and hear your stories behind them. I'll be able to use them in conversation if the opportunity arises."

"The current garden was one of my father's late additions," Ben continued. "Originally the garden stretched outside and behind this part of the building and off to either side until it ran against the trees. The inner courtyard is formed by the central part of the original garden, with some of the paths and statuary still intact. But he never felt comfortable with it all, and when his son, my father, saw a picture of the Crystal Palace in London, my grandfather jumped on the opportunity to build his own in the middle of the grounds. Gave

153

him the opportunity to let the rest of the gardens go to fields and trees. Cheaper to maintain, he said. The garden structure has been enlarged a couple of times, but it still keeps to the spirit of the original." Ben closed his eyes and smiled. "As a child I spent a lot of time in there. I still do when I can. I spent far more than I should have on that Four Rivers fountain, but it's one of the few things I've spent a substantial sum on and I do enjoy it so very much. Do you have anything like that, Max? Anything that was a major splurge but brings you a great deal of pleasure?"

"Yes," I said. "I bought a French armoire several years ago from a former client who noticed me eyeing it when I paid a visit to his house. It's a later Rococo piece, very finely made, and I spent several month's salary to purchase it at a discount. It sits in my apartment and is as out of place in my bedroom as a cactus in a rainforest. But it makes me happy for some strange reason. I can't even explain why."

Ben smiled. "Violet has told me that you hold the leather chair and the old sofa in your office in similar regard. Such are the simple things in life, Max. There is no rhyme, there is no reason. Some things just make us smile."

Ben sighed and said, "I wish I could spend more time talking with you, but these charity events take up all of my time and energy. I expect Violet will find you in about half an hour or so, but until then and while you are here, the grounds are yours to explore. You met Claude last night; he's been here a long time and has become both an outstanding butler and a close trusted friend. I told him in general terms why you are here, and he's ready to help. He said that assisting you in your endeavors sounded, quote, 'like the kind of fun we had back in the War.' His kind of fun was gathering intelligence for the British before the US joined the Great War. In other words, he was a spy. I don't know what he did during the Great War, but I imagine it was... exciting. Two wars he and I have lived through. You'd think after all of that violence and bloodshed the feline world would have had enough. You'd think so, but you'd be wrong."

He hung his head slightly and shook his head. "That's why we need these charitable events more than ever, Max. People like me need to aid others who are in dire straits and need the help. And if Constantino Gandini is half of what you and Violet claim him to be, then he needs to rot in a cell." With that, Benjamin Winterhaven checked his watch, said his goodbyes and left me to my ways. As I didn't see Claude that moment and didn't wish to bother the staff, all of whom appeared very busy, I set about scrounging up some breakfast myself. As I thought about the events of the past half hour, I continued to mull over what I had learned. Ben had given me a great deal of information in a short amount of time, and I needed someplace peaceful in which to process it.

21

Half an hour later, my stomach full of leftover chicken, I walked back to the garden. The footfall of my shoes on the stone sounded a cadence with each step. Past the Canova statue and its graceful reclining figure, I walked back to the Four Rivers fountain and around it once, looking for the paths that radiated from it. The volume of the water was such that eavesdropping would be nearly impossible from a concealed position, a fact I tucked away for some possible future use. I stopped, looking across the small open space to the foliage and paths on the opposite side, then walked slowly, repeating my examinations. My goal was to ascertain what areas might conceal a snoop from view, imagining how a body could best conceal itself among the Mediterranean greenery along the various paths. As I discovered these potential hiding spots, I worked out in my mind where I should stand so that such conversations would remain safe from interception.

After taking stock of my actions and concluding that I had done as much as I could, I set out to quickly explore the paths. Because they meandered through the vast garden, I thought a rapid study of the layout and monuments along the way could prove useful. Unlike the great room, whose open layout afforded a view of those within, the garden's twists and turns presented a myriad of places to hide in leafy shadow. I wanted to know where the smaller fountains were located in case I needed an alternate meeting site or even a place in which to hide something. After a short walk, I came upon one. Though much more modest in scale than the grandiose Four Rivers, this tile-clad cascade (from Spain, a plaque read) still towered some fifteen feet high, water pouring from each of its eight sides into a similarly octagon-shaped pool. The sound, while quieter than its larger relative, still provided enough volume to mask a conversation held at a normal volume.

I decided to take a different path toward the back of the

garden to see where it went. It was narrower than the main thoroughfares, being only wide enough for two cats to walk side by side. The flowers and shrubbery were also closer and the path wound between the numerous trees, bringing the observer closer to the permanent occupants of this structure. Had the sun shone, this path would have remained shrouded in a dimmer semi-darkness that in another setting provided the setting for a romantic interlude. Today, however, it only served to more effectively conceal any potential baddies from detection. Though I would make a concerted attempt to not stray from the wide and open main trails, knowing the basic layout of the garden could prove useful if I had to run and hide myself.

After another short walk, I found myself at the rear of the interior. A second fountain flowed; its design identical to the first. I took brief stock of the shadows in the trees and plants, noticing with some surprise that the entire area was noticeably brighter than that which I had so far seen. Behind the fountain, only a few trees grew, and about fifty feet behind the bubbling water lay a door, its surface painted to mimic the greenery nearby. I gently pulled on the handle, but the door was locked tight. As I looked to the left, I noticed a railing that led to a smaller door. It was largely hidden by some tall bushes unless one came almost on it as I had. Stepping quickly to the door, I gently pushed on the painted surface.

To my surprise, the door opened to a service hallway, its plain walls a striking contrast to the garden's lushness. I stepped through, making sure to hold the door open while examining the other side. The door had a handle to open it from the hallway, but it also could be locked from the same side. I would have to politely request a key to this door, as it might just provide a means of escape should any of Constantino's goons get a bit trigger happy. Though I knew they would not bring any obvious weapons, they would still be carrying something, perhaps a Derringer in an ankle holster. No gangster took the chance of showing up to a firefight unarmed.

I turned back into the garden and walked along the rear wall, passing by the door as I walked. The entire back wall was clear of trees and plants by about twenty feet, presumably to aid employees and delivery personnel in bringing in large items. What surprised me was the presence of an even larger hanger door, its panels made almost entirely of glass. Out of curiosity I walked to the door, whose lowest level of windows started at chest level and stretched up to the ceiling. Looking out, I noticed a sizable paved area large enough for articulated trucks that stretched off to the left. On the far side of this, I saw a garage inside which sat two Cadillac limousines and a blue Ford panel truck, presumably for errands of some sort, while an open space betrayed the presence of a fourth vehicle between the two limousines and the truck. A young gray and white cat in breeches and argyle socks walked around one of the Cadillacs, washing it from a bucket and drying it with a towel. I doubled back to the hallway door, went through and soon found another door which led outside. As it was unlocked, I exited and walked toward the cat in the garage.

"I'm hoping you have a moment for a quick question," I said. He looked up and set down his bucket, then walked out and shook my outstretched paw. "This is my first time at Mr. Winterhaven's charity gala," I continued "and I was curious as to where all of the cars go during the event." He looked at me with a suspicious gaze, to which I quickly raised my paws and said, "My name is Max Persian. I'm a guest of Violet Winterhaven. I'm also her boss, for what that's worth. If you need to check with Mr. Winterhaven, I'll wait. I'm on the guest list."

The young cat smiled and nodded, then said, "So you're the Max Persian she told me about! Miss Violet told me you might come 'round snoopin' about the cars." His brogue was pronounced, but somewhat different than I had heard from either an Irishman or a Scotsman. "She's a great one, always polite to us hired hands and askin' about our families and such. Trust me, you got the best of the kitties with that one!" He looked around quickly. "Miss Iris and Miss Daisy, sometimes they can be a bit stuffy." I couldn't help but chuckle.

"By the way, my name's Malcolm, and before you ask, I'm Manx, direct from the Isle of Man itself!" He turned around to reveal that, true to legend, he lacked any bit of a tail. "A lot of us there are like this, just born this way or with a very short tail. I actually have a very small stub of a tail, but it's much easier to just close off me trousers." He paused and cocked his head slightly. "Oh, I hope I didn't just run me mouth off tellin' you rubbish you didn't want to know. I guess I'm used to most people being a bit curious."

I smiled and replied, "You don't need to worry, Malcolm. I was curious and I would have asked."

Malcolm smiled, then turned and pointed at a hanger-like structure that abutted the pavement next to garage. It's sliding doors were closed, the outside sheathed in aluminum paneling. The building looked inconspicuous save for its size, and its placement and construction indicated that it was meant for a utilitarian purpose. "That buildin' there is where the cars are stored during the events. With the weather bein' what it is during the winter, Mr. Winterhaven figured that he should have a place to store his guests' cars that was secure and dry. When he helped finance the hangers at the bomber airfield, he had his architect design that bugger for use here. There's a service garage in the back that lets me service the fleet and keep 'em runnin' like thoroughbreds too. He keeps a few old cars back there, ones that he doesn't usually drive that often but wants to keep in tip top shape for when he feels like it. Some of us employees keep our wheels stashed in there too when there isn't a big shindig comin' up. But tonight, it'll be full of expensive things that don't belong to us. And ol' Malcolm will be in there with 'em, keepin' 'em safe and making sure they don't get into any fights." He smiled a wry grin.

"Now, the Lincolns are generally pacifists, but they really don't like anyone else trying to break away and go do something else. The Rolls Royces and Cadillacs like to think they're better than the other, but they generally play well together. The Mercedes keeps trying to invade the Delahaye's parkin' spot. He already took that Tatra over there's space too! There are usually two Hispano-Suiza's and they just both try to stay neutral. The real troublemaker's the Chryslers, because they keep tellin' that poor Pierce-Arrow that he's dead." Malcolm looked over at me and winked. "But in all seriousness, that's where the guests' cars stay, usually with room to spare. I'm curious why you're wondering though, Mr. Persian."

Before I could reply, I heard a familiar female voice behind me. "A little clandestine activity may be afoot, Malcolm. One that may involve a particular car belonging to a particular guest of ours." I turned and saw Violet leaning against the doorway, head slightly down and a smirk on her face. "Max, I see that you've been up to no good and consorting with known hooligans," she said with a witty smirk. "And you're no better, Mr. Corlett, weaving yarns and spinning fables about those innocent automobiles! Max, that horrible cat once told me a tale, a rags to riches story and then proclaimed it to be about my lovely Chevrolet!"

She walked over to Malcolm, arms outstretched, and enfolded him in a firm embrace. "He's about to tell us that 'hooligan' is either English or Irish and that I should not lower myself further by not insulting him in proper Manx Gaelic. Watch."

He nodded, then said, "It's true, Max. She should be using the word 'riftan' instead. Means 'troublemaker' all the same, but it's a proper insult for this Manx gentleman!" After grabbing her shoulders lightly and giving her a smile, Malcolm chuckled and started toward the auto hanger with Violet and I in tow.

As he neared the building, Malcolm drew a keyring from his pocket and flipped through until he found the correct one. He inserted the key into a lock on a nondescript door just around the corner of the building, then went inside. A few seconds later, the sound of an interior lock disengaged and the two main doors began to slide apart. Violet smiled and waved a paw toward the doors in the universal gesture of 'after you', then followed me into the building. Though windows lined the top of the walls like the warehouses we had investigated, the interior was dim and quiet with only the sounds of our soles hitting the concrete. Malcolm stood by the side door, and after a moment or two flipped the switches that turned on the overhead lights that brought the interior into focus.

The building was almost empty save for some tools and equipment at the rear of the structure and a small number of automobiles. I walked toward the back of the building, noting by the pattern of oil the relative placement of cars when parked. Many were parked nose first toward the walls, others parked nose to nose in the center, leaving two distinct aisles by which to maneuver them. The cars kept in the back also piqued my interest. Two of them were Ford Model A's, a two door and a four door; a third, a Stutz that was missing its engine, but two of them, an old Duesenberg sedan and some sort of monstrous Bentley that looked like it might have conquered Brooklands, gave me a spark. After asking Malcolm, I was assured that both cars not only could be moved but also started and ran under their own power. As I noted how the rear of the building was less well-lit, especially in the right rear corner near a large hydraulic lift, an idea began to solidify inside my head. After quickly consulting Violet, the two of us called over Malcolm and the three of us discussed our thoughts on bringing our particular idea into being.

After a few minutes spent examining the building's interior and formulating rudimentary beginnings of our plan, Violet and I left Malcolm to his work and started to walk back through the garden. I told her of my idea to use the fountains as private meeting areas so that we could converse without being overheard. She nodded in agreement and showed me several places to hide sprinkled throughout the greenery that could be used to eavesdrop on our adversaries in turn. As she and her sisters had wiled away many hours here playing hide and seek, I had no doubt that no guest could possibly know the nooks and crannies as she did. As we came upon the massive Four Rivers, I held up a moment to see how loud we would have to speak to be heard. Though a minor detail, it could work against us if we got careless; we would have to remember to always face the fountain or each other to talk.

As we neared the front of the greenhouse, we came upon the reclining kitty by Canova. This time Violet paused, taking a few moments to admire the graceful sculpture in the light of the late fall cloud cover. "My mother saw the original on their honeymoon and fell in love with it then. There is a small replica in her bedroom that she bought while they were there. My father contacted the same sculpting team who replicated that colossal fountain and commissioned them to replicate several classical statues. He didn't tell my mom that the Canova was one of them. When it arrived in port, he had it placed in storage until the night before their wedding day when he paid a skilled crew to install it before morning. He orchestrated the whole thing and he pulled it off, and the look on her face was priceless."

I just shook my head in awe and said, "I would have just taken her out for steak and tuna, but in truth I'm not very romantic."

Violet looked at me and after a couple of seconds began to laugh, then snorted. "Max, I'm sure you're plenty romantic, but you have more common sense and a better sense of humor," she said in between bouts of laughter.

When she had regained her calm, she said, "I love this garden, but I think Daddy spent far too much on it. The money he spent on this statue alone could have been put to much better use. I just think about how Warm Blankets could have benefitted from what he spent on vanity projects. Daddy isn't a bad man, far from it, but I don't think he realizes just how much some people are struggling out there. I didn't have much of a clue when I started working for you, and because I grew up here, I probably never will."

Violet turned to face me and look me in the eye. "Knowing that Constantino Gandini is out there basically stealing tuna from the mouths of the cats and kittens who really need it makes me so angry, Max. My father inherited his family's fortune and increased it with shrewd business dealings, most of which I hope were legal and above board. But Constantino is a thief. He's a rich and powerful thief, but he's basically still a thief. On top of that he is a bully and a thug. That's why we must find something, anything, to help bring him down."

I reached out and rested both paws on her shoulders and gripped them lightly but firmly. "You know I hate to make promises in this business," I said, looking her straight in her deep blue eyes, "but this is as close as I may ever come. This case started as a simple means to an end, to earn the reward money and put it toward the business. When we began, I had no idea how it would come to affect you, and to be frank, this case has affected me too. This shortage is a city-wide crisis, and if it continues this way a lot of innocent people will face hardships they shouldn't have to face. Every morning, I buy a paper from a family of hard-working folks who have built their business from the ground up. What will happen to them if tuna prices continue to climb? The Cahills are lucky; they are pretty well equipped to ride out an economic storm, but there are a lot of others out there who aren't as well off, who put most of their paycheck toward food and rent. Constantino Gandini has already profited millions and millions from shady deals, and to see him profit on the suffering of others makes me see red. I promise you that I will do everything I can to bring him down, and that I will stand by your side to do it. You're the best friend I have, Violet Winterhaven, and that's just what friends do."

A moment later she pulled me into a tight embrace, her paws wrapped around my back and her head resting on my shoulders. She sighed, then whispered, "You're the best friend I've ever known, Max. You're so much more of a cat than you know, and I love you for it. I have for a long time." She kissed my cheek, brushing against my whiskers as she pulled away, smiling, her eyes glistening with tears like morning dew. She reached and took both of my paws in hers and said simply, "Now you know." She held my paws for a few moments longer, then released them and motioned me toward the doors and the cold overcast day beyond. I silently wished for all the world that we could stay longer in the garden, just the two of us, but we had work to do, and time was of the essence. Reluctantly, I walked with Violet out into the chilly afternoon air.

We spent the rest of the afternoon between the ballroom and a private lounge on the second floor of the mansion, a room seldom seen by guests but useful because it contained detailed plans of every building on the estate. This room formed the part of the mansion where the Winterhavens actually lived, and as such the secrets of the rich and powerful family resided here rather than in the parts accessible to guests. While hard at work, I had lost track of the time and was slightly startled when Daisy burst into the room with all the subtlety of a tornado to inform Violet that guests would be set to arrive in an hour. When I said hello to her, she rolled her eyes and walked out; though the necessary reminder might have been announced to us against her will, Daisy's cordiality and affinity would not be offered forth so carelessly.

"Are you sure she's not adopted?" I asked Violet, not for the first time.

She laughed and replied, "Unfortunately I don't think so. She looks almost exactly like our mother when she was that age, but she has all the manners of a warthog. I don't know why you bother with that one."

As I gathered my notes to read over before I readied myself, I said, "It's simple. Every time I greet her, she gives me the stink eye and lets me know what she thinks. If I ever greet her and she's friendly, I'll know something is wrong, like she's been switched with some doppelganger and will know how to respond. Daisy's honesty

164

is the one thing I can count on every single time, because in its rude consistency, I always know exactly where I stand."

A moment later, Violet's eyes grew and she laughed uncontrollably, and each time she began to stop, a large snort would set her off again. After what seemed like half an hour of this, she finally regained control of her speech and said, "Maximillian Bruce Persian, while you are one of the more intelligent men I have ever known, you are most certainly the most subversive. It's cats like you that cause unrest." She smiled and shook her head; she told me to go prepare for our evening together while I have the time. As Violet's escort for the evening, I also needed to be ready in the next two hours, but my preparations were far less extensive. As I headed to my room, I thought on our plans, flexible enough to account for changes yet firm enough to give us a set of objectives. Everything was set, and it would soon be our time to shine, even if in secret.

22

I returned to my room and closed the door behind me with a soft click. In such expensive surroundings, it felt wrong somehow to leave my clothes lying on the floor, despite the actions of the previous night. I took a minute to hang them in the closet while my shoes went to rest under them. Since I had a bit over an hour before I needed to meet Violet before our introduction, I decided to take a shower to be as clean and comfortable as possible.

With the daylight beginning to fade from the sky, I pulled the curtains to, plunging the room into dimness. I turned on a lamp on a small table near the window, slipped out of my undergarments and placed them on the shelf next to my wingtips. Turning to the bathroom, I turned on the light, then decided against it and flipped the switch off again. Even with only the table lamp in the bedroom for illumination, my eyes seamlessly adjusted to the dim of the bathroom. I reached for the knobs to bring a warm stream of water; shortly, the warm vapor began to collect on the mirror, and I fumbled for the switch to turn on the exhaust fan.

As the warm water hit my fur and soaked through to the skin beneath, I leaned my head back and closed my eyes. I felt relaxed, perhaps surprisingly so, but a hint of tension remained in my muscles and in my bones. The weight of what could happen this evening bore on me and with it the possible outcomes, both good and bad, that might occur. This case was like no other I had worked on, even when I was younger and a bit more brash. I had never taken on organized crime and approached these particular adversaries with a healthy dose of respect. To do any less would be courting disaster, not just for myself, but also for everyone around me.

As I turned up the hot water, my thoughts shifted to my long-suffering assistant. One misstep, one wrong judgement, and I could put Violet in serious danger. Constantino Gandini had a reputation as an unforgiving and callous opponent, while Blackie Lawler and

Rufus Segovia were known far and wide as ruthless enforcers ready to empty a Thompson gun first and worry about the consequences, never. And that was just the two gangsters whose presence was expected; if anything had reached Constantino about any activities from a certain private detective agency recently, he might just opt to bring more goons to the party. And even with his security force at work, Benjamin Winterhaven knew that he could not possibly find every weapon that Constantino's cats brought, and he wasn't the only crime head set to arrive. Though this fact could be used to our advantage, counting on their willingness to oppose Constantino and his crew could prove a gross error in judgement as they might just join him instead. The only people whose support could be counted on was Benjamin Winterhaven, Violet, and Claude, though all I had to go on was Violet's and Benjamin's word, which I trusted. For their own safety, everyone else in attendance had been kept in the dark.

I leaned into the tiled wall underneath the faucet as the heat ran down my back and off the end of my tail. I reached up and adjusted the shower head so that it aimed at the back of my head and neck. As I took several slow breaths, I pushed back at the worry and doubt that had been slowly building inside. I had to stay calm and not let my panic get the better of me, for there were many people counting on me to perform at my best. I closed my eyes again and envisioned something so beautiful, so serene, that to gaze upon it was to gaze upon Olympus, Nirvana and Valhalla all in one.

This day, a picnic in the shade of a Japanese cherry tree in full bloom, a clear blue sky above and the perfect visage of Fuji-san in the background. Resting on a low table, two plates of bone contain filets of halibut garnished with lemon butter and a hint of basil, each with a small helping of baked shrimp and tartar sauce on the side. Two glasses of a fine cabernet sauvignon await, their chill causing droplets on the sides to run down the stems and onto the white tablecloth. A single pink rose, a shade between *amicitia et amor,* sits in a cobalt blue vase between them, moving only slightly in a

167

delicate breeze. I am happy, without a worry in the world, for I am here with her. For this one moment, we are together and all is well, perfect, even divine. I smile, and with a slight giggle my smile is mirrored in her face. I reach cautiously, tentatively for her paw, feel its warmth under my fingers and against my palm. I gaze deep into blue oceans, her eyes so bottomless, depths so far away. I have admired you from the moment we met, and to know you has been to love you. I would live for you, and I would die for you. If only to be near you, to say your name my-

Knock! Knock! knock!

"Mister Persian! The gala shall begin in thirty minutes! Miss Violet has requested your presence!" said Claude from behind the bedroom door.

I hung my head, still longing for my hopeless fantasy, then held it upright and thanked him for his courtesy call. As I turned the knobs off, I shook my head at such bad timing. I crossed the bathroom and turned on the lights, blinking momentarily at the glare. Two cream-colored towels hung on a bar, and as I took one and thoroughly dried myself, my tabby fur stood out in all directions. When I reached for the second towel, my fur was now only slightly damp, after the second, clean and dry. I reached for the small leather case left on the counter the night before and retrieved my well-worn brush to quickly put every inch of fur back into place. I brushed my teeth, rapidly yet thoroughly, as the smell of this morning's breakfast would hardly make a suitable impression when smiling those pointed canines. After returning everything to place and turning off the lights, I made my way to the closet to retrieve my attire.

After donning my tuxedo and wingtips, I took a quick look in the mirror and marveled at my appearance. One item, however, was missing. I reached in the pockets and found a bow tie, made of the same faintly pinstriped material as the jacket and trousers. Violet must have slipped it there knowing that I might forget it. Unfortunately, it was now wrinkled from being folded, and as I looked around for an iron, a knock sounded at the door a second time.

I quickly opened the door to find just the cat I had hoped to find. "Am I ever glad to see you Claude!" I exclaimed. I showed him my bowtie and explained my dilemma.

He smiled, took the tie and said, "I can fix this, sir. Please follow me and we'll get this little number all sorted out." Though in a tuxedo himself, with tails no less, Claude pulled down an ironing board, its broad end hinged like a Murphy bed to the wall. Behind it in a small cubby sat a black and chrome iron, which Claude deftly removed. He unwound its cord, plugged it in and turned it on in one easy motion, and as the iron came up to temperature, he laid the wrinkled tie on the board. After a moment, he put his paw near the iron's surface, then dipped his fingers in a glass of water that seemed to appear from nowhere and spritzed the tie with his fingertips. He then picked up the iron with his other hand and quickly ran it across the wrinkled fabric. After another moment, he held up the tie to reveal, to his satisfaction, that the adornment was smooth and presentable.

He clicked the iron off and unplugged it, then moved directly in front of me. In a matter of seconds Claude's nimble fingers had the bow immaculately tied around my neck, neither too loose nor too tight. He quickly ushered me toward a full-length mirror in the room to admire his handiwork, then humbly apologized. "Though I'm sure that you could have tied an equally impressive knot sir, I took the liberty as time is of the essence. I hope you'll understand."

I chortled and replied, "I would have taken half an hour and it wouldn't have looked half this good, Claude. Watching you is like watching an artist at work. Please don't tell Violet that I can't tie one of these things though. I'll never hear the end of it."

Claude smiled a wry grin with one side of his mouth, then raised his right paw to his chest and bowed. "On my honor, I swear that the secret of this clandestine affair will accompany me to my grave." As I smiled at his wit, Claude winked, then brushed my shoulders with white gloves he had somehow adorned without my noticing. He ushered me through the door. "Miss Violet has read me in as to your activities tonight, sir, and she will read me the riot act if I fail to assist. Not that I would dream of shirking any noble request, of course, but if you find yourself in need of a second, I would be honored. I'd like to kick *ut irrumator praetor* Gandini down a long flight of stairs for what he's doing." He quickly looked over at me to find a look of amusement across my face. "My apologies, sir. I didn't realize you also knew Latin."

"Only some colorful phrases that resulted in rapped knuckles from the rulers of angry nuns," I dutifully replied. "It's surprising how little tolerance they have for that sort of thing."

We walked through the house and crossed into the ballroom, then stopped. Claude turned to me and said, "A few of the guests have already arrived, and more will arrive in the next fifteen minutes or so. Miss Violet is waiting in the upstairs lounge at the top of the grand staircase and has requested that you join her there. The two of you will be announced and make a grand entrance down that staircase." He turned to me, smiling. "Let her set the pace, as she will guide you along. You'll be entering to a roomful of guests, though not all will have arrived. Your entrance will follow that of Miss Daisy and her companion. Miss Violet will help you along, and you'll manage just fine." He drew in close with a serious expression, staring me directly in the eyes. "There is one more piece of advice, Mister Persian, one of vital importance."

I moved closer, knowing that his years of experience were about to tell me something crucial to the evening. Claude then placed his gloved paws on my shoulders as if to underscore the seriousness of the next statement.

"Don't trip."

After a moment, he winked again and I burst into laughter.

"Miss Violet is waiting sir," Claude said cheerfully. "I've

seen the dress she is wearing just before I came to summon you. She told me to tell you that she hopes you approve."

As Claude continued into the ballroom, I mounted a side flight of stairs that led to the private upstairs area. These several rooms provided the family a place to wait before being introduced to the guests and descending the grand staircase. The guests themselves came through the ballroom's main entrance after disembarking from their cars. After entering, guests passed through an ornate entryway and into an anteroom where their coats would be taken and stored in the large closets to either side. At the far end from the doors, a lectern stood guard, it's attendant ready to announce each guest as they proceeded into the main banquet hall. At the same time, their names were entered into a large book for posterity. Such formality was rarely used, I was told, but for certain events it had become customary. For tonight's gala, the annual December charity drive in benefit of the Warm Blankets Orphanage for Kittens, all the stops came out.

As I made my way into the upper halls and rooms behind the long wall of the ballroom, I noted both the opening that led to the grand staircase and the richness of the paneling and inlay that lined the walls. A few last-minute preparations were being made, with white-coated staff ensuring that every last detail was in place. One of them, a young cat barely clear of kittenhood, rushed up to me, verified who I was, then led me to one of the rooms where I was to wait momentarily until my introduction. As he opened the door for me, I could scarcely believe the sight which lay before me.

23

Violet stood toward the rear of the modestly sized lounge, her paws clasped in front of her, a shy smile on her face. She wore a floor-length dress in rich purple, its sleeves a matching thin mesh with a wide neckline that provided ample room for the sapphire cameo around her neck. Pleats allowed for a close fit at the waist, while matching low-heeled shoes poked out from below the bottom. On her head she wore a slender tiara, not immediately noticeable but for the sparkle from the array of small diamonds, amethysts and sapphires along its width. She looked at me with her deep blue eyes and the full effect was like meeting her again for the first time. The cat who before was always pretty had transformed into someone of radiance and pure beauty. To look at her was truly to gaze upon royalty.

I took a few moments to find my words. "Violet, you look absolutely lovely. Beyond lovely. I've known you for years and I never knew you looked like this. I mean, you've always looked like this, but you look different now. Different in a good way. Umm, like a flower that's opened, not that closed flowers look bad, I just mean—"

She put a paw over my mouth, giggling all the while. She smiled as she said, "You talk too much Max. You're going to get yourself into trouble someday."

Mumbling around her paw, I could only say, "Em forry." She giggled again and withdrew her paw. "I'm sorry Violet," I said, softly. "I was just caught off guard by how amazing you look. You told me a couple of days ago that I would get to see you in your formal dress, but you never warned me how taken aback I would be due to your gorgeousness!" At that, she became slightly embarrassed and self-conscious, so I drove the issue home. "I wondered how we would move about and carry out plans, but now I know how we'll pull it off. You'll distract them while I, now completely invisible and unnoticed, will have free reign to do whatever needs doing!"

I saw the tips of her ears turning red, even through her fur. "Do you really think I'm that pretty?" she asked shyly.

I smiled at her while saying, "Violet, you've always been a lovely cat from the moment I met you. You could be in this dress or walking round with a barrel strapped over your shoulders for all I care. You're beautiful because of who you are, the person inside who cares about people and has her own dreams and ambitions. If I was ten times the tom I could be, I could never be half of what I see every single day. It just so happens that all of that beauty has now been given form and flight, and I was momentarily caught off guard." Violet crossed her paws in front of her while looking a little down and sideways out of shy embarrassment. A moment later, she put her paws on my shoulders, reached up on her tiptoes and planted a kiss on my cheek. "Max Persian, there are times when you say the sweetest and most awkwardly wonderful things to me!"

I looked her in the eye and shrugged, then said, "It doesn't hurt that you're a real looker anyway, sweetheart!" Though she rolled her eyes and shook her head, inside Violet was bursting with happiness. The smile on her face, despite the eye rolling, betrayed her.

A knock on the door announced Benjamin Winterhaven's entrance. He came alone, and though without a jacket, he looked every bit the captain of industry that he was. He gave his youngest daughter a quick hug, then turned to me and shook my paw. "The introductions will come shortly," he said. "Violet may have told you this already, but when they are about to start, my wife and I will take to the hallway you just came through, then Iris, Daisy with their companions, then you and Violet will line up in that order as the girls will be announced in order of their birth. It's pretty simple really. You'll walk to the head of the grand staircase and stay for a moment as your names are announced, then descend at a modest pace. It's all a bit of formal silliness really, but the guests love being announced as they enter. Violet will guide you through it, so there's no need to worry.

Once you're through with your introduction, you two will meet and greet for ten or fifteen minutes, then you'll have time to see what you can dig up. If you need anything, anything at all, you ask me or Claude, but don't tell anyone else, guests or staff, what you're up to here. My staff is pretty good, but there's no telling who Gandini has bribed or coerced in this house in order to acquire information. You have my best. Now, the game has been set and the players are starting to arrive. All that's left is to put the pieces into motion and see who wins!"

After shaking my paw again, this time with both of his, Benjamin left the room and us to a few moments of privacy. I went to sit on the leather sofa, but Violet stopped me, saying that it would put wrinkles in the material of my tux. A moment later, I began to pace the room, my arms crossed and my eyes drawn. Violet chided me again, reminding me that crossing my arms would wrinkle the elbows. Such waiting around before any occasion always proved excruciating for me. After a couple of minutes spent pacing in silence, I turned to Violet, who stood almost motionless in the middle of the room. She appeared lost in her own thoughts, perhaps planning how to carry out some of our planning. I was less productive, just hoping that we would line up soon and get these introductions over with so we could start.

As I thought, I chuckled quietly. This was so typical of Violet and I, she the calm and rational planner, I, the more impulsive and spontaneous doer. Though different, we suited each other well. Without my impetuousness, Violet could over plan, while her intelligent restraint had certainly spared me unpleasant situations by keeping me from running headlong into trouble. And yet here I was, alone in a room with her and free to say whatever I desired, and I had gone silent. I looked over at her, and as I did, I wondered if some rash action at this moment might be in order. But I never got to act, for a white-coated staff member knocked on the door and announced

174

that we were to line up in the hallway as introductions were imminent.

Violet and I left the room for the staging area that was the hallway. As we found our place, I saw for the first time the rest of the Winterhaven family as they filed out of the various rooms nearby. Violet's older sisters wore equally stunning dresses, Iris in a deep blue and Daisy in maroon. I realized after a moment that the three sisters had dresses which matched their flowery names; all three were quite stunning, though Iris and Daisy seemed far more intent on talking amongst themselves, leaving their hapless companions looking somewhat confused and lost. I turned to Violet, who had noticed me looking at them, and shook my head slightly as I shrugged; the two older sisters had darkened our office on several occasions, usually together and seldom pleasant. I used to wonder how they could possibly be related to Violet and thought sometimes that they must have been lost during a family vacation and been cared for by a family of monkeys, as wolves would be too noble for the end result. As I began to ponder ever more improbable scenarios, Violet and I were ushered to the end of the hallway to take our place at the top of the grand staircase.

Although I had seen the extensive preparations as they came into place, nothing could have prepared me for the grandeur of the scene before me. The room had been transformed through clever use of light and sound; the natural light was fading quickly, while the electric lamps shone at a medium brightness that gave the expansive space a more cozy and intimate feeling, while on the stage a band played a mixture of big band and jazz in the background. Round tables, their white tablecloths centered with floral arrangements and lit candles, had been placed near the stage while allowing a space in front suitable for dancing. The decorations I saw along the walls, almost garish in the daylight, took on an entirely different look and mixed a festive air with just the right amount of formality.

A reasonable number of the guests had already arrived and

mingled in small groups as the formal introductions unfolded. They themselves had been announced as they entered the grand hall through the vestibule by a richly voiced black cat hired specifically for this purpose. On cue, we stepped onto the head of the staircase. I felt the eyes upon me and stiffened with discomfort. As if on cue, Violet took my paw in hers and gave a reassuring squeeze as if to let me know that I would be fine and that the evening would work out.

We took our place at the head of the stairs, gazing out upon the scene below, and I noticed that the band was playing 'Moonlight Serenade' and that we were lit by a pair of spotlights placed into the ceiling. I glanced her way to find her looking at me with a sideways glance. "I knew you would be nervous, so I had the band play some Glenn Miller just for us," she said in a hushed tone. As I smiled, our names were announced: "Miss Violet Winterhaven and Mr. Maximilian Persian." We then descended the steps to a midway landing, paused for a moment, then turned to the right to arrive at the main floor. As we reached the last step, the next name was called.

A decent number of attendees had gathered near the bottom of the stairs and greeted us. Though some were unknown to me, I recognized several by name if not by the photographs I had seen in the paper. Most knew the members of the Winterhaven family on familiar terms, and though I did not know them personally, they were cordial, even friendly. Violet greeted guests with handshakes, hugs, kisses and combinations of them all. As she did, she introduced me, though in a superficial manner that left me easily forgotten. She was in her element here, and I felt desperately out of place, though at least I looked the part. I noticed that as the Winterhaven families were introduced, arriving guests paused behind the announcer until the family members had descended the staircase; only then were guests introduced, then the announcer returned to the next family member. It seemed a bit complicated and rather stuffy, the sort of traditional formality that I neither understood nor fully appreciated. I was relieved when Violet took my arm and led us toward the back wall opposite the stage.

We settled near one of the large lamps that stretched from floor upwards to a height of about 25 feet, their light illuminating the ceiling above. As she took my paws in hers, she leaned in as if to kiss or tell a secret. "I've spoken with Malcolm and he has the garage set. The Duesenberg and the Bentley are sitting near the right rear of the garage with a single space between them. Constantino's car will be parked in between them, partially hidden in the dark area near the lift. I'm going to wager that it will be you playing Sam Spade in those hidden compartments. Let's hope that our particular falcon may be hiding in the crevices." She leaned back and turned us so that her back faced the band. "Constantino Gandini is always fashionably late and always seems to draw a crowd when he appears. My guess is that he'll arrive in the next few minutes. What are you planning?"

I took a deep breath and hoped my fur concealed my furrowed brow. "I plan on ambushing him as he walks in the door. If I wait in the entryway, I can see when he and his goons show. I will try to get outside without looking too conspicuous and start a conversation about the Cord. We both know he's very proud of that car, proud to the point of arrogance, and having someone with whom to share his knowledge should appeal to him. He'll know that I'm no expert, but if I come off as someone interested in a curiosity, I should be able to hold my own. I doubt it will be anything more than car talk, but it's possible that Gandini will let slip some detail about that car which might help us somehow. If he's due soon, I need to get up there and wait for him. Any suggestions as to how I can wait without seeming too suspicious?"

Violet nodded. "There are some benches that circle inside the walls. Sit on one of those facing out the doors and tell anyone who asks that you feel a bit queasy and are just waiting until it passes to go back inside. Constantino will pull that car around so that the right side is facing the doors. He'll be able to get out and walk straight in, so I'd recommend sitting in the back to look straight out. The staff

177

knows not to bother you, so distractions shouldn't be an issue." At that, she squeezed my paws and said, "Good luck, Max. You can do this." I smiled, then I turned and walked toward the entrance.

I found a place on one of the benches and sat down. Feigning an upset stomach worked like a charm, keeping curious and overly helpful guests at bay while allowing me an unobstructed view out the main doors. Though I leaned forward with my elbows on my knees and my head facing down, I could see as the guests arrived. The range of cars surprised me. Some guests arrived in the newest and most state-of-the-art Cadillacs and Lincolns on the market, while others arrived in Chryslers or Mercurys, Buicks or the occasional Packard or Hudson. Most were newer models, but occasionally an older car appeared, resplendent in running boards and sweeping fenders. After a small while, the cars started to run together in my mind, appearing and disappearing like some segmented snake, only parts of its metal body visible. I wondered if I might not be getting sick, as my mind began to wander from the task at hand. I sat up, trying to snap myself out of whatever funk I had entered, trying to stay focused.

And then the car appeared.

24

Though it was two decades old, the Cord's bygone styling and immaculate condition only served to glorify the stately machine. In the lights which illuminated the front circle of the Winterhaven estate, the car almost seemed to float across the brick way, its wide whitewall tires and cream paintwork giving it an almost ethereal effect. Sterling had mentioned that his father had modified the engine and drivetrain, and as it motored slowly toward the door, I could feel as much as hear the low rumble of the engine. It stopped in front of the door, and both the right front and left rear doors opened. From the front, Rufus Segovia emerged and took station outside the car, while from the rear Blackie Lawler's large and shadowy frame took a moment to gaze back toward the front gate, then walked around to the right side of the car and opened the rear-hinged door.

Flanked by his two most trusted henchmen, Constantino Gandini stepped out of the car. Though smaller than his bodyguards, Constantino nevertheless took center stage. He palmed a cane finished in black and gold, and in addition to a finely cut tuxedo and expensive looking wingtips, he sported several jewel-encrusted rings on his paws. Even at my distance inside the foyer, I could see that one of the gems was an emerald of such value as ten years of my salary. Though Blackie Lawler and Rufus Segovia each appeared formidable and impressive, one look revealed who really ran the show.

I knew what I needed to do. Standing up, I strode out onto the columned portico beyond the front doors. My heart was pounding, especially when I saw that Blackie Lawler had recognized me, but I knew I had to throw caution to the wind if I were to bring our plan to fruition. I led with an innocent question. "Excuse me, *Signore* Gandini, but may I have a moment to admire your car?"

Constantino looked at me, curious. After a moment, he flashed an alligator smile and replied, "Certainly! I'm quite proud of her and enjoy showing her off." He ordered his driver to remain while we gazed upon the Cord. I was surprised at his pronounced Italian accent, an indicator of the Old World he had left behind. He walked to me and stood by my side as we both admired the sedan. I introduced myself, though we did not shake as he did not offer his paw. He either did not regard me as worth a shake or he knew who I was and what I was up to. I hoped it was the former, for as I looked to Blackie, his narrow eyes looked suspicious, even contemptuous of my inquiries. The malicious half-smile on Rufus' face gave the impression that he would enjoy hurting me if so ordered. All I could do was forge ahead.

"I've only ever seen one other Cord, an 812. It was a spectacular car. Hidden headlamps, supercharged straight eight and front wheel drive. That's what intrigued me, the front drive setup. Like the old Indy racers from before the War. I knew there was an L-29 somewhere around here, and now I've finally seen it." Inside I was shaking, but I hoped it didn't show. Constantino and I slowly circled the car, its idling engine sounding a bass note both quiet and low. It sounded both menacing and powerful.

Constantino stopped and turned to look at me. "What do you know about the Ruxton?" he asked. I paused for a brief moment, then replied, "It was also a front drive passenger car. They didn't sell many of them before production was discontinued. There were lawsuits over the name and other issues, and if I remember correctly the L-29 came on the market about six months earlier and sold in greater numbers." Constantino seemed impressed, nodding his head slowly.

A few seconds later, he looked me in the eye. "I have heard your name in certain circles, Mr. Persian. You're a private detective of sorts, no? I know that you employ Miss Violet Winterhaven as your assistant, and I'm assuming that is why you are here. But I can't help but wonder if you are here to learn, to investigate one specific person and their interests. For now, I will assume that you are here as a companion to a friend and nothing more, and that your interest in my car is out of knowledgeable curiosity, as you seem to know what you are talking about. I respect that you came to me in the open, not slinking around like a snake in the grass. We are now new and friendly acquaintances, ones who I'm sure will see each other in the future." He offered his paw to me, which I took in my own with a firm but friendly shake. "I'm sure we will meet again soon, Mr. Persian. Until then, enjoy the party! The Winterhavens pull out all the stops."

Constantino turned from me and signaled to his underlings to escort him inside while the car slowly drove toward the parking facility. Though Rufus never glanced at me, Blackie looked squarely at me as he passed. Surprisingly, his expression no longer reflected hostility or intimidation, but rather bemusement and curiosity. After they passed, I remained outside for a few moments, my only company the silent attendants manning the steps and the insects that flew harmlessly around the exterior lights. I took several deep breaths of the chilly air, calming my racing heart and somewhat frazzled nerves, then after a minute or two returned inside to the Winterhaven Charity Gala and the myriad of cats in attendance.

By then, most of the guests had arrived, rendering the ballroom rather crowded for all its size. I recognized a Benny Goodman tune emanating from the band, though exactly which one was difficult to tell. I moved toward the rear wall, under the staircase where a single round table had been set on which raged a casual poker game. Next to it sat a roulette table, its wheel glistening in an electrum finish. Finally, a semicircular blackjack table sat, the dealer's back to the staircase underside, which was ironically painted with a perspective landscape of the Monte Carlo harbor. It was here that I found Violet, eagerly calling for cards and then moaning as she lost. As I neared, a gentleman sitting to her left with a red bowtie stood up and left, putting a hand on her shoulder and saying a friendly goodbye as he left. He nodded and smiled as I moved to take the now vacant stool on which he sat, while Violet remained oblivious to my presence as she lost another hand.

"Have you ever considered holding on eighteen?" I asked.

She looked over and smiled. "I thought gambling was supposed to be about risk-taking, Max, not always playing it safe. Playing it safe is good a lot of the time, but all safe and no risk hardly seems like any fun at all!"

I looked at her and asked a rather obvious question, but one to which I lacked any answer at all. "How is any of this legal? Isn't anything larger than a basement get together subject to regulation?"

Violet's response came in the form of a laugh, a cheerful sound as rich as the cornets on the stage. She looked at me and smiled, then said, "It's not really gambling when all winnings go to Warm Blankets. The players may win, but they leave with nothing more than they brought to the table. That way, they only gamble if they leave with winnings, which they don't. Anything over their initial amount goes toward the charity collection, as does all House winnings. City Hall may frown on this for all I know, but they'll never do anything to solicit the bad press that would ensue if they shut down a source of charity to an orphanage. Newspapers tend to go overboard on that sort of thing." As I nodded and smirked my comprehension, Violet smiled and winked, then laughed softly. Her laugh sounded like the ethereal song of the divine, at least until she snorted, put her hand over her mouth and laughed softly in embarrassment. I shook my head sideways and chuckled as I gently took her arm and ushered her outside into the courtyard.

We walked about halfway to the garden and turned to look back upon the ballroom. The lights that I had seen being installed were shined on the house, spotlighting certain details in the architecture and casting them in high relief. Two statues on either side of the porch leading inside were lit from the side, their feline features cast into strong relief. One depicted a beautiful cat in a form-fitting dress, caught in mid-stride with her left paw extended

182

outward. Her face smiled with an otherworldly calm and grace, while her long fur seemed frozen in place as it blew in an unfelt breeze.

The other sculpture depicted a shorthaired tom, robed in a loose-fitting tunic that left part of his chest bare. His right paw extended partway toward the viewer and held a large wineglass, so carefully carved that the viewer could see its volume within. His left paw was held at the center of his chest, while at his bare feet rested a box overflowing with grapes and three bottles of varying sizes. His head was cocked slightly to one side, while his face wore a bemusing half-smile that seemed somehow inviting, even beaconing. Behind them, the Neoclassical architecture of the mansion seemed to glow with the dimmer light, enough for the house to seem radiant from within but dim so as not to overpower the statuary. The entire effect was quite stunning, even beautiful, and I had taken two steps toward it before Violet's voice broke me out of my reverie.

"Aphrodite and Dionysus. Love and Beauty, Wine and Earthly Delight. Daddy commissioned them shortly after he began hosting these charity events in the hopes that they might inspire further enjoyment and generous donations from whomever was in attendance. They're completely original, unlike a lot of the statuary he has bought, carved by an Italian immigrant who was apprenticed to a Florentine Master. His name was Ernesto Battista Milano, and his work was absolutely brilliant and crossed several styles; Daddy served as his patron until he died. He died young too, only about my age, and very few people realized just how talented he really was, and now so few ever will. He had a defect in his heart, one there since he was born, and the coroner Daddy hired said his heart was a ticking time bomb. He could have died just after birth or he could have lived to a ripe old age, but it happened to fail on him when it did. Daddy and I both look at them with a twinge of sadness, for we knew how far Ernesto could have gone and what beautiful things he could have created. At least these two are of lasting permanence that will outlive us all. He deserved that much, I think." As I looked over at her, I saw that her eyes were moist. When I asked if there was anything I could do, she smiled sadly and turned away with a soft "No."

A moment later she looked back at me as she dried her eyes with a discreet handkerchief and said, "I can't help but feel sad when I think about Ernesto. He was a wonderful person, the kind of cat who was happy, seemingly all the time, and that happiness brought out happiness in others. At that time, I was in a rough place in life, and all I wanted was to dig a hole and bury myself inside. When I met Ernesto, I was returning from Europe from my first year at the new boarding school. I was relieved to be home because I wanted to get away from that place, but once I got here my two sisters ganged up on me. You have no idea how horrible they were back then Max, but the things they did and said to me sounded just like things The Royals might come up with.

"But a week after I arrived, I met Ernesto when he came to take measurements for the statues. I started talking to him and he was like a being from another planet, so I asked if I could come to his shop to learn what he did. I couldn't believe he said yes, and for the rest of my time at home I spent as much time as I could at his studio. He even taught me some very basic techniques and let me try them on those statues. My work was later smoothed out when they were finished, but I can say truthfully that I helped make them both. When it was time for me to return to Europe, I didn't want to go. Even though my sisters taunted me mercilessly when I was home, my mother was busy with our social lives and with running a house and all its staff and my father was out a lot of the time with work, I enjoyed the time I had spent. It was all because of Ernesto. He was such a revelation; someone whose outlook really had an impact on me. Even though I'm not a lot like him, he gives me something to strive for, a better self to realize."

She looked at me and I could see her blushing slightly underneath her fur. "He was also the first cat I ever had a crush on. I wanted so much to be Mrs. Ernesto Milano, to sculpt beside him and to face the world together. I remember when Daddy called me with the news. He passed away five months after completing these statues, and they were one of the few large-scale projects he was able to complete. I couldn't believe he was gone, someone so young who left such a lasting impact on my life. Remembering him is like seeing only footprints in the sand after their maker had long disappeared. The struggle comes in remembering the footprints after the tide has come and washed them away."

We looked at the two statues in silence for a few more moments, then Violet turned to me, shaking her head as if to rid herself of old cobwebs. "I'm sorry Max. Every time I walk around this place, I see ghosts. This party has me feeling a bit nostalgic, but dwelling in the past won't serve our present. Daddy saw you out talking to Constantino Gandini. Tell me how it went."

I took in a breath, then released it as my shoulders sagged. I replied that I had gotten to speak to him directly, closely watched by both Blackie Lawler and Rufus Segovia. Though I had spoken to him, I didn't think it had gone well, and if anything, the meeting may have done more harm than good. He had known who I was from the start, and was suspicious as to my presence, even though our professional status was also known. As I spoke, I noted how Constantino seemed to know that I would be in attendance, and even tested me as to my knowledge of his Cord. Though I thought I passed some sort of test, I couldn't help but feel that Constantino was on to the plan and would have one or both of his lieutenants watching me like a hawk. I hoped it was Blackie, for the predatory look that Rufus had flashed toward me had chilled me to the bone.

I took a deep breath under dark clouds at the boundary between twilight and night, then looked at Violet. "The best chance of finding something on Constantino Gandini is parked in the garage. Somehow, I need to get in and unlock the compartments that Sterling told us about. The advantage right now lies in that Constantino

185

doesn't know that we know about them, though he won't assume it as a certainty. The problem is those two goons and their ability to keep me in sight, as well as Constantino himself too. I'm not sure I can evade all three of them to get out there without some assistance, but outside of you and your father, there is no one whom I trust enough to ask for help. I'm not sure what to do next, but whatever it is, it needs to happen quickly."

Violet's eyes narrowed as she thought quickly. "You may not have to do anything Max." I looked at her with a sideways glance of puzzlement. "Think about this for a second," she said, holding her gloved paws in front of her, index fingers raised. "Constantino knows that you've taken an interest in the Cord. He's already nervous because he thinks there is a possibility you either know about the compartments or will stumble across them as you search the interior. No doubt Blackie and Rufus, at least one, if not both of them, have been tasked with keeping you in sight at all times and to stop you if you make a move. Constantino can't keep a steady eye on you, but he will be attentive as to where you are. No doubt one of them is watching us right now, even though they can't hear us. I'm going to wave my arms from time to time, so look increasingly distressed as if we are starting to have an argument." She shook her right arm firmly as if to make a point. To play along, I merely shook my head.

"The beauty of this situation is that all the attention is on you. Those two won't let you out of sight, but it also means that they won't be looking for someone else. They'll keep a steady eye on you, but that allows another cat burglar an opportunity at the car without as much chance of detection. You become the distraction, keeping the attention to yourself while someone sneaks into the car and looks for incriminating documents. It's simple, it doesn't actually alter the plan much, and it can work."

I thought quickly, remembering to wave my paw in mock indignation for my watchers, then asked her how she thought it might proceed.

"That's the genius part," Violet continued. "You will do exactly what you planned to do all along, which is to break into the car. You'll head through the greenhouse, stopping along the way to admire the sights, which will give Blackie and Rufus plenty of time to follow. When you get near the back wall and make a careful move toward the door, they will stop you. They may use some persuasion, but they won't dare hurt you, not here and not at this event. If they did, it would reflect poorly on Constantino and they won't chance that. And while they think they've stopped you; I will break into the car myself and see what I can find."

My gesture of surprise and irritation was genuine. "What do you mean, you're going to break into the car? Violet, do you know how dangerous that would be? Catching me in the garden eyeing the back door is one thing, but if either of those two catch you in their boss' car, they will kill you there, wrap you in a tarp and throw you in the trunk. No one would ever find you!" I appealed to her in desperation. "Violet, you can't do this! It's not just about the missing tuna or the criminal racket in this city. It's about a beautiful lady who means too much to too many people, and they can't afford to lose you! *I* can't afford to lose you! There has to be another way!"

Violet's blue eyes, usually as calm as a bright summer sky, turned dark as the tempest of a raging sea. "There is no other way, Max. Claude is clever at a lot of things, but he's getting older and I can't rely on him for this. Malcolm is young and loyal enough, but he is impatient and impulsive; I fear that he would do something that would lead to him getting in over his head. I can't risk him for this either, even if he did know the entire plan. And my father?" Her paws shot outward in a gesture of futility. "He is the only other person here who knows most of what we are up to, and he's the host of the party! There's no way he can do this, and I would never ask him to. I know just as much as to where those compartments are hidden as you do because I was there with Sterling same as you. I am the only other person here who knows what you know, and I'm the only other person who knows what to look for." She gripped her paws into fists, claws poking through the gloves and into her pads. No doubt the gesture and the argument that spawned it was real.

"I'm going to walk out in a fury and retire to my room. Wait ten minutes, then start moving toward the car." I opened my mouth to protest, but was immediately shut down. "Don't argue with me, because this is how it's going to happen." Then she slapped me, hard, and as she turned to storm away, she snarled one final command. "It's started. Do your part." With that, Violet stormed off and inside the ballroom. A guest I did not know came up beside me and said something, but I barely heard him. I said nothing in reply, then went to sit on a bench off to the side of the main path, contemplating the masterpieces of Ernesto Milano and wondering how such a carefully crafted plan could sour into chaos so rapidly.

25

After a few minutes, I stood and walked toward the sculpture of Aphrodite. The figure, clothed in sheer cloth, looked down and to the left slightly in an expression of caring affection for her love. Her two arms lay across her chest, paws slightly apart above crossed wrists, while she took a small step forward. Hers was a look of serenity and calm, so out of place in the ever-chaotic world and I couldn't help but look up and upon that lovely face to try and make sense of this day. Violet and I had disagreed with each other before; two people who had worked together for several years were bound to. But I had never seen the look of unbridled anger in her eyes before and I wondered what would happen from here. It seemed that she felt I didn't take her abilities seriously, and nothing could be further from the truth. Violet Winterhaven was the most capable person I had ever worked with, in fact, the most capable person I may have ever known. But the stakes in this case were higher than any other we had worked on and it seemed to be spiraling out of control. I wasn't worried about Violet's capabilities as an investigator. I was worried about her safety as my friend.

A part of me wanted nothing more than to take Violet with me and leave this place, to pack what we needed and head far out west, someplace big enough for dreamers, but also for those looking to vanish into a new life. I had long thought of moving someplace with mountains, tall peaks with sweeping vistas, with clear skies and open spaces. When I was a kitten, I had heard romantic stories about the west, of the people who went in search of the things they couldn't find in the east. Of fame, of fortune, of land and the seemingly limitless bounty it had to offer.

I heard stories of the darker side too, of cats who were already there when settlers arrived, cats who fought like lions to hold on to their lifestyle and livelihood. In the end they failed, and in that failure were reduced to abject poverty on the absolute fringes of society, living in squalor on some of the least profitable land in the country. The west was, for me, a place of triumph and tragedy, of fanfare and failure, of the heights of ecstasies and the depths of woe, wrapped together by an arid land that challenged the best and did not suffer fools lightly.

It was a recurring dream I had, pulling up stakes and heading off. Several years before I had nearly put down payment on land just outside Flagstaff, Arizona. It was just after the War ended and the country was beginning to shift from wartime production to civilian manufacture. The war had proven lean times for me, and to make ends meet I had taken a second job at a five and dime. I called it a second job as a matter of pride, but in truth that job was the only thing between me and impending homelessness.

Toward the end of the day, work was slow, and I prepared the store for the next day with time to spare before we closed. I read the papers as the day wound down, keeping up with the latest developments in Europe, when one day a particular article caught my attention. It spoke of the day when the war would end and the boys would come home, of the events that would happen and the opportunities that would come to be. It spoke of opportunities out west for the intrepid few who could venture there, of new mineral development and advances in farming, both animals and crops. It painted a glowing picture of pristine wildernesses and snow-capped peaks, of pure rivers and the cleanest air.

I longed to leave New Amsterdam behind and start anew, and through some careful research narrowed my ambitions to cities in Arizona, Colorado, Idaho, and Montana. I settled on one of two cities, either Bozeman, Montana or Flagstaff. What turned me toward Flagstaff was the presence of a cousin in Phoenix who helped me narrow in on a site to build and could tell me some about the town. I was set to put money down, but I was let go from my second job to make way for the owner's son. I had hoped to work another six months to recoup some of my outlay, but as this was no longer possible, I stayed in New Amsterdam. Luckily, the private detective business soon picked up enough to afford me the means to stay where I was. My cases were small time, but they paid the bills and even allowed me to bring on my receptionist and secretary full-time, albeit at virtual slave wages. Though I had never told anyone, I had hoped to move west once I felt comfortable with my finances, but even though I reached that point eighteen months later, something kept me from going.

I had realized that this something had a name, and that name was Violet Grace Winterhaven. When I hired her during the early going of the War, I had placed an advertisement in a few of the local papers for a part time receptionist. At the time, business was still modest but steady and I needed someone who could answer phones and help with my chaotic organization system. I received a few calls and booked a handful of interviews, but all of them balked at the wage I could, or rather couldn't, pay them. What small pool of applicants I had found soon dried to nothing when I received a call.

When I interviewed Violet, she was enthusiastic and wasn't put off by the pay, so I hired her on the spot. She asked when she could start and when I told her that she could have at the filing cabinet, she took straight to it, interview clothes and all. I had to smile because she was so ready to go. In the next few weeks, she proved herself the perfect office counterpart, so much so that I did everything to ensure that she would stay. Over the ensuing years, I came to rely on Violet for her skills and work ethic while also surprising myself by growing increasingly fond of her. At some point I realized that I cared deeply for her, much to my own surprise and fear, and though I never said as much, I wanted to spend my time with her and make her as happy as I possibly could.

And now she was willingly putting her life in danger, all for a cause. She was angry with me to be sure, but she misunderstood my reasons: I didn't want to hold her back, rather, I genuinely feared losing her. The backstreet rumors surrounding Constantino Gandini and his henchmen told of a ruthless lot of gangsters and thugs whose willingness to commit wonton acts of violence and terror were fast becoming the stuff of legend. Blackie Lawler had garnered for himself a well-earned reputation as a cold-hearted enforcer, and Rufus Segovia's mixture of a volatile personality with a near-psychotic enjoyment of physical violence had made him a physical embodiment of pure terror. And though Constantino sought to ape the appearance of a respectable gentleman, at his core lay a savage and vicious animal whose desires for wealth and power could never be satiated. They might see me moving my way toward the garage, but if Violet were caught breaking into the car by any one of them, she would surely meet her demise. Constantino might mask his nature with the fine trappings of respectability, but underneath the velvet glove lay an iron fist ready to destroy anyone who stood against him. Even the daughter of a wealthy businessman.

But, as Violet had said, the plan was already in motion and nothing I could do could stop it. The only thing I could do was to stick to Violet's plan and lure the eyes away from her and onto me. The enforcers knew I was interested in the car and they knew I was interested in Constantino's affairs, plans for which might be kept in that car. A cat like Constantino didn't get to the top and stay there without a healthy serving of paranoia, and that was what Violet was counting on. I was the bait that would draw the fish away from the wiggly worm. I checked my watch in a casual but obvious manner, took one last look at Aphrodite for good luck, then turned and walked toward the garden. I silently hoped that Violet remained safe throughout this ordeal and that we both lived long enough for me to tell her once and for all how I truly felt.

After bidding Aphrodite a silent farewell, I began walking toward the greenhouse. I felt that not only Blackie and Rufus were watching me, but Violet as well. I was sure that she was now making her way to arrive at Constantino's Cord and the secrets it contained. Hopefully that slap she gave me and her blatant displeasure when she stormed off into the house served to draw attention to her in such a way that it looked like she had retreated to her private quarters. It meant that distracting Blackie and Rufus fell to me, so I had to make it look good. The plan, such as it was, had begun, and though I didn't like it, I had a part to play.

26

As I walked across the garden and toward the greenhouse, I turned to look at some of the decorations in the lawn and by the paths. I caught sight of Rufus on one glance, walking behind an older couple, but I made no indication that I had spotted him. I didn't see Blackie at all, which led me to believe that while Rufus kept an eye on me from a closer point, Blackie was holding back to see me from afar. I couldn't help but chuckle under my breath because even though I knew they were there, and they knew that I possibly knew they were there, the three of us played a game in which we pretended to remain unaware of the others. It might have been fun except for the high stakes involved in the game's conclusion, and the fact that my adversaries likely had firearms to draw on whereas I had only my wits.

As I came to the greenhouse, I opened the door and walked inside. I walked straight ahead to the statue of Venus Victrix and stopped. I took a few minutes to both admire the statue and try to get a bearing on my opponents. Though I was on the main path through the garden, the surrounding secondary paths radiated out and wove through the interior. Thankfully, I had taken some time to inspect these paths and to observe the way the light fell through them. The only difference now was that the lights inside the greenhouse had been switched on, which altered the appearance of the garden substantially. Even so, I had made sure to remember where gaps in the plants appeared, gaps that both allowed Blackie and Rufus to spy on me and also to allow me to see them as silhouettes.

I turned from the statue toward one of these places, ostensibly to look at a variety of rosebush, but in reality, I was checking gaps to see if my pursuers were watching. Sure enough, I spotted both of them within twenty seconds. I saw who I thought was Blackie on the path and watching through a gap in the undergrowth, while Rufus surprised me by appearing about twelve feet up a tree. He was surprisingly well concealed and had an excellent view of the statue and anyone near it. This told me that I must not underestimate them for one second, for to do so would be the end of our well-laid plans.

I turned back to the statue and walked around it to the other side, thinking that the longer I took getting to the back of the garden, the more time Violet would have to search Constantino's car. After a minute or two, I started back down the path, not wanting to give my two followers any reason to abandon me. Still, I walked down a side path, feigning an attempt to lose them. As I rounded the path out of sight of the Venus Victrix, I increased my pace and looked over my shoulder every so often. Sure enough, I glanced a shadow on the ground behind me though I never heard the footfalls that accompanied it, while in the foliage behind me and to my right I caught a glimpse of form and movement that betrayed an imperfect attempt by one of my pursuers to conceal themselves. I was glad that I had reconnoitered the layout as well as I had; most of my adversaries were not nearly so skilled in avoiding detection, and only a bit of attention to lines of sight and places to hide allowed me to see them at all.

My plan was to draw Blackie and Rufus with me along the west side of the garden, first to the fountain along the west wall, then to the northwest corner of the structure where the smaller of the service doors was located. I didn't plan beyond this because I expected my two shadows to emerge from hiding and confront me, stopping me from leaving the greenhouse and reaching the garage. I was gambling that they would merely stop me and force me to turn back instead of kill me outright, but I had no way of knowing for sure. Between the vegetation and the fountains, the sound of a gunshot might not carry to the front of the building, and it was entirely possible that no one else was inside at that moment. Though I didn't relish the thought of being shot, I was glad that Violet was in far less danger than I.

When I reached the fountain, I sat and removed a shoe.

Something had gotten inside and was pressing against the bottom of my foot in an uncomfortable manner, and it gave me a few moments to look again for my fan club. This time I never saw Blackie, though I did spot Rufus in another tree, barely. I returned the wingtip to my foot, stood, and tied the laces. I didn't stop to dawdle any further, but once again took a side path toward the rear. Now I walked with purpose, looking back for effects' sake, not really to find anyone. I knew they were there now and felt no need to find them among the plants, plus I wanted to give them the idea that I had realized that I was not being followed and was thus moving uninhibited toward my objective. I didn't know if they would actually fall for this, but at this point such thinking didn't hurt.

As I neared the end of the final path, I slowed, giving myself a moment to look out and see what I was in for. As I emerged opposite the door, I was surprised to find that I was alone. I looked about, suddenly fearful that my ruse had been discovered and that they had passed me to get to the garage. Just before I had decided to head toward the utility hallway and the door that led to the service buildings, I heard footsteps behind me and the metallic click of a gun.

"I wouldn't go any further, sir."

An unfamiliar voice spoke. I slowly raised my paws and turned around, making no sudden movements, looking to come face to face with my adversaries. But only Rufus Segovia stood before me, as Blackie Lawler was nowhere to be seen. Though I had seen Rufus from afar, I was surprised when I saw him up close and personal. He was, like me, a common brown tabby, albeit taller, but what struck me was his build. Even under formalwear, I could see the unusual stockiness of his frame. His torso was like a barrel, thick and weighty, while his arms and legs seemed to bulge in spite of the custom fit of his tux. His chest bulged with muscle, while his neck was large and solid, as if his head sprouted from a tree trunk. He looked more feral than anything else, stocky and powerful but

196

seemingly lacking in grace. Even more unsettling was the expression on his face. Rufus had a reputation as unhinged, even maniacal, but the cat before me wore calm, even serene expression. His gold eyes bored into me, sizing me up in an instant. The thought that he might possess a sociopathic personality flashed through my mind, and I knew that I should err on the side of caution if I wanted to walk away from this.

"My employer told my associate and me that you might take a walk, a walk to take another look at his car. He's flattered that you appreciate it so much, that you see it for the unique piece of machinery that it truly is, but he does have doubts about your reasons for wanting to learn about it. He was worried you might try to spirit it away so you could keep it for yourself, maybe learn its secrets along the way." He flashed an Arctic smile, one that never reached deeper than the surface of his face. "You see, Mr. Persian, my employer really likes this car and doesn't want anything to hurt it in any way. He doesn't like people milling around it alone unless he explicitly trusts them. Unfortunately, he told me that as he just met you, he really doesn't trust you enough yet. Therefore, he sent me to 'persuade' you to come back to the party, to talk more shop with him if you like. He even promised to take you for a ride in it if you so desire, as he doesn't meet many people who understand why it's so special."

The cocked pistol in his paw was a two shot Derringer, small but with plenty of firepower in the hands of someone who knew how to wield it against an unarmed opponent. Rufus looked down at it, then back to me and cocked his head slightly. "We should be getting back now, sir. Even with the heaters the temperature usually drops to about 50 degrees in here after sunset." I hoped that Violet fared well, for there was nothing more I could do. I had been thoroughly checkmated.

My hope was that I had distracted them long, but I wouldn't know for sure until later. I nodded my surrender and told Rufus that I would go with him. I decided not to insult his intelligence with some bit about how I just wanted to see the car, for we both would have seen through the lie. I walked over to him and lowered my paws as he lowered the pistol and released the hammer.

Rufus leaned in and in a low whisper said, "We'll walk together, sir, we can even chat, but if you try anything, I'll tear your head off." I replied that I believed him. I didn't ask Rufus about Blackie, not wanting to reveal that I had known they were there, but his absence troubled me. I hoped that Violet was all right.

27

As we walked back into the ballroom, Rufus put his left paw on my shoulder and leaned in, as if we were old friends. He told me in a friendly yet menacing way that I should stay in the ballroom and not wander off and get lost, claiming that it was for my own good. The irony of his statement was not lost, and I assured him that I would enjoy the gala. I meant it too; our gamble on finding information in Constantino's car was a one-shot affair and couldn't be repeated even if I wanted to do so. Although I was currently alone, I resigned myself to try to enjoy the party. After a few minutes spent at the margins, I felt a tap on my shoulder and turned. I had hoped it would be Violet, safe and sound from her clandestine excursion, but instead I found Claude, who smiled and slipped two sardine tins into my paw.

"Dinner will be soon, and though I'm sure there will be delights aplenty for you to sample, Miss Violet wanted me to make sure you had these. Just in case." I thanked him, then asked him if he had seen Violet in the past half hour or so. I told him how I had angered her and how I needed to apologize to her and smooth troubled waters, but he merely shook his head. "I saw her when she came in from the lawn," he said, "but she went upstairs into her quarters and I've not seen her since. My guess is that she's still up there and hopes not to be disturbed."

Claude then leaned closer, taking me into his confidence. "I've known Violet for a long time, sir. She is passionate about the things she loves, even if she doesn't always realize it. Her anger is like gasoline: volatile and explosive, but it burns itself out quickly. You will be able to apologize soon enough."

I thanked him, and as he walked away to focus on other matters, I looked at the tins in my paw. Her thoughtfulness never ceased to amaze me, and I realized anew that while I was surrounded by a roomful of people from her class in life, none of them could tell me if she were even safe or not. All I could do was wait, and at times such as this, I really despised waiting.

The evening continued in this sullen manner. Though part of me wanted to leave and return to the sanctuary of my apartment, my concern for Violet meant that I would stay. Time seemed to slow to a crawl and still she had not come back. I tried not to show it, but my worry only increased with each passing second.

After an eternity of fifteen minutes or so, dinner was announced. The guests and I made way to our seats, each labelled with our names, and as I neared the table, marked for the three Winterhaven daughters and their companions, I saw that Violet's place at the table remained empty. The courses were read aloud, and while delicacies such as shrimp scampi and baked halibut would have sounded appealing under different circumstances, I felt no desire to enjoy them. My stomach was tied in knots with worry. Not even the thought of delightful little fish tins in my pockets could tempt me, so I sat quietly and kept my worries to myself. I saw Claude, running from here to there, fixing what may be wrong on an entrée, but every time he looked over at me, he shook his head. I dared not ask Benjamin Winterhaven as to the whereabouts of his daughter, both because as host he was extremely busy with the details of the gala, but also because I didn't wish to alarm him, as it was entirely possible that he either did not know what had transpired or that Violet was waiting for an opportune time to rejoin the party.

I had thought that she would have appeared by the time dinner and dessert were winding down, for this was when her family set in motion the events that opened the stage for donations. The Warm Blankets Orphanage for Kittens was understandably an important institution for her family, particularly as her cousins had been adopted from there. The orphanage held a special place in Violet's heart, and I had thought she would not want to miss it. What truly concerned me was when Iris leaned toward me, asking if I had seen Violet as her father was looking for her. All I could say was that

I had not seen her recently and that I didn't know where she was. When Iris rolled her eyes, groaned and muttered to herself that Violet always made everything difficult, I began to fear that she was truly missing. I began to fear the worst.

During the fundraiser, I saw Constantino on the main floor with Blackie and Rufus. The trio was having what appeared to be a quiet yet animated discussion, and it didn't look particularly pleasant. I had barely seen Constantino since dinner and I wondered what he could be talking to his minions about. Unfortunately, whether by chance or by design they stood too far away for me to hear what they said. I had some skill at reading conversations and would have tried to decipher their conversation had Blackie and his substantial size not had his back to me, blocking Constantino entirely and Rufus most of the time. All I could see was that the three of them were quite animated and possibly agitated in their discussion.

After a couple of minutes Constantino turned abruptly and walked toward the door, trying to look at ease but stiff and strained to the trained eye. As Blackie and Rufus fell in step with him, Constantino exited the ballroom into the oval atrium to retrieve his coat while telling the attendant that he desired his car and driver.

I moved toward the atrium, trying to glean what little I could from this abrupt departure. As Blackie and Rufus retrieved their coats, it was clear that the trio was leaving. Equally clear was that Constantino's two associates remained vigilant, ensuring that no harm came to The Don. Because of this, I could not move closer and could only watch helplessly as the old Cord stopped outside the door to collect them. With one last look back, Constantino stepped into the car ahead of Blackie while Rufus assumed his place next to the driver. The doors shut behind them, the car pulled away quietly and whisked Constantino away to his warehouse fortress, back to his guarded solitude and the secrets it held.

I returned to my seat, dejected and fretful. I tried to listen to Benjamin's speech, but my worry prevented anything more than superficial comprehension. I raised my head after a moment to find both Iris and Daisy watching me intently. They had seen the frustration and hopelessness in my actions and realized my genuine worry. Instead of expressions of boredom or laughter, I saw concern on both of their faces. All I could do was shake my head. Now her sisters shared in my distress.

A few minutes later, I noticed Malcolm on the side of the stage. Obviously flustered, he fidgeted about as Benjamin Winterhaven spoke at the lectern. Once he stepped away and to the side of the stage, Malcolm urgently took him aside as the band began to play. Something had happened, that much was visible from their body language and I moved quietly to the side of the stage to both find out what was happening and see if I could offer any assistance. When Ben saw me, he ushered me to his side and told me that something had happened to Violet, then urged me to go with him to the garage.

As Malcolm moved off for another purpose, Ben and I took a back door from the stage and ran out and toward the greenhouse. As we entered, I followed Benjamin Winterhaven down the central path and out the back of the building. The garage's doors were fully open, and as we entered, we saw two of the Winterhaven staff in the back of the building. In the darker rear corner near the large hydraulic jack. Where Constantino Gandini's Cord had been parked. Although my legs felt weak, I urged myself to run, run as fast as I could toward the horrible scene that would await me. By now I knew, felt the certainty that Violet had met with a terrible fate. I wanted to close my eyes, wanted to block out what I knew awaited, but I had to witness, had to see for myself.

28

Violet lay on the ground, clothed in dark pants and shirt rather than her deep blue dress. A shop towel, folded, lay under her head, while her blue eyes were closed. She was still, almost serene save for the two gunshot wounds in her chest and a pool of blood underneath her. As the sirens of an ambulance began to sound in the distance, she opened her eyes partway. I kneeled on the concrete and took her paw, weak and shaking as she reached for me. I was barely conscious of Ben as he knelt by her side across from me. He spoke to her softly, speaking low in her ear something that brought a faint smile to her face. Then she turned to me and began to speak, but so softly that I had to lean over her to hear it.

"Max, my Max… Please don't ever forget me… Hold on to me, Max, hold on to me so I can live on in you…" With tears in my eyes, I promised that I could never forget, not even for a day. Violet smiled a slight smile as she faintly squeezed my hand, then pulled me closer and whispered faintly as her strength ebbed. "We will see each other again, my love… I promise you; we will see each other again."

As she fell silent, I sat with her, her delicate paw in mine as she continued to look at me. She squeezed my paw one last time, so softly that I barely felt it, and as her eyes grew fixed and glassy, her arm ceased to function.

I carefully folded her arm across her chest and saw her father gently close her eyes, then lean slowly backward, his head tilted back. I heard a sound come from him, low and quiet at first, but it soon gained volume and presence, caught somewhere between a moan and a wail. It was an awful sound, suffering and pain, a sound only made by someone in absolute grief. As it subsided, wrenching sobs replaced it as Benjamin Winterhaven slumped over the lifeless body of his youngest daughter, his tears flowing into the wounds, only to disappear forever. As for me, I could only kneel silent, stunned into disbelief that someone I had cared for so deeply could be gone in an instant, vanished into a singular moment in time.

A minute or so later, the ambulance rounded the corner to the garage and entered the building, cutting its siren as it came. I stood numbly as two paramedics quickly brought a stretcher to Violet and hurriedly assessed her injuries, only to slow and shake their heads as the finality of her condition became apparent.

As they carefully placed her body onto the stretcher, Ben came to me. "Max, would you go back and tell my wife what has happened? Eleanor doesn't know." As I nodded, he turned and stepped into the ambulance, which barely had room for a family member. I watched in silence as the car drove away, no lights, no siren, no urgency.

The area was quiet, the garage sitting open with some cars left inside, their drivers coming to collect them. None of them spoke to me. Most tried not to look me in the eye. In that moment, I cared nothing for their thoughts or feelings. The loss I had yet to still fully feel rendered me numb, devoid of any caring for the rest of the world.

The rest of the evening turned into a blur inside my grief-addled mind. I walked back to the ballroom, heavy in both feet and heart, and saw Eleanor Winterhaven by the podium next to Claude. Now it was my turn to fidget. As the band played a big band tune I quickly forgot, I motioned to her to get their attention. She greeted me calmly, but nearly collapsed as I told her the awful news. Only Claude's quick reflexes kept her from crumpling to the floor, and she was lowered into a chair. He shot a single gloved hand into the air and made as if to snap, and within moments two staff members rushed to Mrs. Winterhaven's aid. After another hand motion or two that sent the rest of the staff scurrying, Claude ascended the stage. He motioned the conductor to stop the music and stepped to the microphone.

"Ladies and gentlemen, I regret to inform you that an

emergency has arisen and that we must end this function early. Please leave any final donations with staff members by the front doors as you depart. Your drivers have been informed and will be picking you up shortly. Thank you for attending." With this, Claude took charge of the staff while also quickly and politely seeing guests to their waiting limousines. Within thirty minutes, only I was left as I did not have a ride. I sat next to the stage as the musicians packed away their instruments and the staff began to strip the tables of their finery. Eleanor Winterhaven was nowhere to be seen, as she had quickly come to and rushed off to tell her remaining daughters what had become of their sister. My thoughts were turned inward, recoiling in shock from the world around me, a world that had grown so very cold in just a moment.

I did not notice as Claude came and sat down near me. He pushed a bit of fur back in place and turned toward me. "I don't know what to say at this moment, Max. I'm just the head butler, and though I'm very good at my job, all of my experience means nothing in this situation. Violet is- was, a very special lady. From the time she was a young kitten and I was a younger tom, she always treated me with kindness and respect. She was a special lady because of how she made people feel." He smiled sadly, his eyes beginning to fill with tears of his own loss.

"I know the two of you were close. She would come home and talk about you when my day was done. She loved working with you, loved the cases and the way the facts led to a tangible conclusion at the end. It didn't matter to her if it was a small case or a large one, she loved them all. And she loved them because you were with her, Max. I wish you could have seen the look in her eyes when she spoke of you, the joy and the happiness she felt. You were a friend and mentor, but as she got to know you, her feelings changed." Claude's face reflected the sadness in his heart as he continued. "She was afraid to tell you, afraid to change the relationship you had. She would rather stay with you and love you from afar than risk everything. She was afraid to tell you how deeply she loved you. She wanted more than anything to stand by your side and share in your companionship. But she was always too afraid to tell you."

I looked at Claude, looked into his sad eyes and saw someone who also loved Violet, loved her as a close friend, perhaps even as a father loves a daughter. I realized that Claude was someone in whom she confided. With a small shake of my head I said, "She wasn't the only one who was afraid. I think I fell for her in the first month. I was afraid she would laugh and reject me, the poor cat to the rich girl. But I saw that look in her eyes, that crafty clever smile. I feel… felt… so strongly for her, but I believed in my heart that it was never meant to be. I love her so strongly. I likely always will."

I looked Claude in the eyes. "She died in front of me, Claude. She held my paw, spoke to me, and then she was gone. I can't even register that she'll never come back. She said to never forget her, for we would meet again. She told me to keep her memory alive so she would live on in me. As if I could ever forget her! Nothing makes sense now. Nothing. The lady I love is gone and I never got to tell her. I don't know how I'm going to live with that." I sighed. "I just want to go home. I need to be by myself now. I'm sorry, but I can't stay here anymore."

A limousine was quickly arranged to take me back to my apartment. Claude retrieved my belongings from the guest room and before long I was walking up the stairs to my floor and my apartment. As I pulled the key from my pocket, I glanced down the hallway toward my door, but as always it was empty and less than brightly lit. One of the bulbs flickered in its death throes, soon to burn out entirely. I passed it by with barely a thought and arrived at my door. I turned the lock with an audible click, then grasped the worn brass doorknob and went inside, closing and locking the door behind me.

No lights shone inside, but in the glare of the outside signs I saw as well as day and walked to my bedroom with my bag underneath my arm. As I passed by the mirror, I only then noticed that I was still in my tuxedo. I looked as disheveled as I felt; though my bowtie remained knotted at the neck, the shirt was wrinkled, and the jacket now stained. I pulled it off piece by piece and let the whole affair drop to the floor. Even the shoes were not spared, but were removed without thought and abandoned where they fell.

I walked into the living room and turned on the radio, then sat heavily on the sofa. I hoped the music would calm me, help to drown the cacophony inside my weary head, but as the last remnants of music faded away, the opening notes of Moonlight Serenade began to play. In my sorrow I felt an upwelling of grief begin to surge to the surface, already held back and repressed for too long. The grief erupted in sound and tears, with wracking sobs to accompany them. All I could do was collapse my head into my paws and let it flow like lava on scorched earth, to let this immediate misery run its course. Only after several songs did my tears abate, drained of water, leaving me spent both physically and emotionally. Though I knew I should lay down, I remained where I sat, the radio playing on in the background.

29

My night crawled by as a blur of sleeplessness and waking nightmares, one indistinguishable from the next. The rays of a dull morning found me on the sofa, my blanket on the floor and my body shivering. Unable to bring myself into unconsciousness by force of will, my day began to the radio's din, having been left playing the night before.

My best friend was gone.

Today was the first day of my new and sad reality. All I could do was to lie on the sofa, my mind awash in waves of despair as I stared at my clothes on the floor. Though I had failed to close the shades, my view consisted of more heavily clouded skies that ensured that the light was feeble at best. As morning transitioned into afternoon, the skies opened in a violent cacophony of thunder and lightning, a prelude to an afternoon of hard rain. I had always liked rain before, but today it seemed a sign of just how wrong events of the past day had gone. The untouched radio continued to play but I barely registered it. But in the early evening, the music was interrupted with breaking news of a major crime bust.

"This just in," the announcer said. "According to sources, New Amsterdam Police have had a major breakthrough with a raid on the home of businessman and philanthropist Constantino Gandini. Explosive information leaked to the police about the recent tuna shortage has led to the arrest of Gandini and many of his henchmen. Though some of Gandini's officers may have slipped away and may remain at large, sources within the department have not commented as to the validity of what are, for now, just rumors. We will continue to report future news as it breaks." With that, the radio returned to music.

To say that I was stunned would be a gross understatement. The only reasons that I could think of as to how the police had arrived at information that implicated Constantino Gandini in the tuna shortage was either that an independent investigation by the police or other detective agency had uncovered Gandini's involvement. Either that or Violet had found something incriminating in Constantino's Cord and had managed to get it to someone else before she had been shot. If the latter were the case, then Violet had solved the case. And had died solving it. I slumped into the old sofa and shook my head. I no longer cared about the case, no longer cared about Constantino Gandini. At that moment, New Amsterdam and everyone in it could go to hell for all I cared because the one cat I cared about more than anyone else was gone, and nothing I could do could ever bring her back. And the business, the detective agency? Snuffed out like the flame atop the candle, leaving only the ghostly trail behind. Ours was a partnership, a duo, and it couldn't function with one half gone. She was the flame that shined so brightly, and now that she was gone only the candle remained, alone in the dark and growing ever colder. Alone, lost.

My anger grew, my paws clenched into fists, and I hit the sofa on which I sat. Though it was a gesture of complete futility, I pounded the cushions again and again, finding it hard to stop. After a minute or so, my breathing was heavy and ragged as I went into the bathroom and looked into the mirror; the face that stared back at me looked ten years older, with wide, dilated eyes and teeth showing through a jaw hung partially open. I turned away, stepping to the claw-footed bathtub. I turned on the faucet and pulled my undergarments off, leaving them in a heap in the floor. Like most cats, I didn't use a tub often, but at that moment, clouded as I was by fear and pain, nothing seemed more appealing than a dip in a bath of hot water. As I lowered myself into the deepening pool, my head fell into my hands, my body wracked by silent sobs.

30

As I lay in bed two days later, I heard a knock on my door. Hoping it would go away, I made no attempt to move, but it sounded again, then again. I sighed in resignation, quickly put on a pair of pants and moved to open the door. To my surprise, I looked down into the large and concerned eyes of Lizzie Cahill, while her mother Victoria stood behind her. "I've been worried about you, Mr. Max," Lizzie said. "I hadn't seen you at the newsstand in days and I wondered where you were. Then I heard about Miss Violet and I knew that you needed someone to give you a hug."

She walked forward and put her arms around my waist, burying her head into my stomach. "I'm so sorry, Mr. Max, really, I am. She was my friend too." I hesitated for a moment or two, then placed my hand on top of Lizzie's head and gently rubbed her between her ears, which resulted in her squeezing me even tighter. I looked at Victoria, whose gentle smile was betrayed by eyes full of tears. Though my apartment was a bit of a mess, I invited them inside.

As Lizzie walked into the living room, I saw her taking in the sorry state of affairs. As neither she nor Victoria had seen my apartment, I felt myself blush slightly with embarrassment. I imagined that after a few days of this I likely didn't smell quite so nice either. I also realized that I was walking around without a shirt, having neglected to put on one when the knocking started. As I picked my wrinkled shirt from the floor and hastily buttoned it, Victoria walked around me and gave Lizzie a quick rub on her head, then turned back to me.

"I'm so sorry, Max. Violet was one of the kindest, sweetest people we have ever known. She came by every morning as Sean was taking the daily papers, before the shop even opened. She helped us set them out for the customers, then picked your daily standards and would read them with Liz. They would spend an hour or so going through and picking out the important stories so she could discuss them with you if you wished. Even though we gave her the papers, you would always come anyway."

Victoria began to tear up anew. "Violet was so good to us in so many ways. We met her when we started the renovations to the shop. She just showed up in a Packard one day, came up to us and said she was glad that someone was repairing the shop. Then she asked if there was any particular thing we needed for the renovation, and when Sean noted that we needed some lumber and trim to finish the interior but that he would buy it later when the money came in, Violet asked him to write down what he needed and she would see if she could get us a discount. That afternoon a truck came and delivered everything, bought and paid for! Because of her, we had a little extra money left over to get the shop up and running, and it made a huge difference."

Lizzie had sat on the sofa, looking down and sullen. I asked her a question. "Lizzie," I said, "Violet came by and read the news with you?"

Lizzie smiled wanly and replied, "Almost every morning. She would get there before I woke up and ate, and when I went down to help set up, she was always there. We would read together and compare the stories, and she said she needed me to help find the important ones for you. That was always fun, and then later in the morning you would come by and I'd let you know what was in the paper!"

I closed my eyes and chuckled a little. I looked at Lizzie and said, "Violet never told me that she visited with you every morning. I always thought she would read the papers in the office for the first time, but now I know better. My guess is that she wanted to keep that time just for you, so it would be your special time together." Lizzie sadly smiled, remembering the time she spent with Violet, time that had meant more to her than she had realized. I wanted to add how much I missed her, but I needed to remain strong for Lizzie, the black kitten whom I called my friend.

A thought occurred to me, something that would have made Violet happy. I got up from my chair and walked to the bookshelf. After pulling several leather-bound volumes from the shelves, I turned back toward Victoria and Lizzie. "Tell me Lizzie, have you ever heard of Sherlock Holmes?"

Lizzie scrunched her face up in thought, then replied, "I've heard the name, but I don't know anything about him. Why?"

I smiled for the first time in days and said, "Well, your mother told me that you are interested in detectives, and Sherlock Holmes is a master detective, the best that ever lived. He is a brilliant and cunning super sleuth who solved crimes that no one else could solve. He and his partner, Watson, were the greatest detective team ever written! I wasn't much older than you when I read these stories, and they had a big impact on my life. You see, Sherlock Holmes inspired me to become a detective."

I set the books in Lizzie's lap. "Violet bought these books for me a few years ago as a Christmas present. They are a bit old and you'll have to take care of them, but the pages are intact and ready to enjoy. I think if she were here, Violet would be happy for you to have them so you can read them whenever you choose." Lizzie looked up at me with wide eyes. I looked at her, my eyes suddenly filling with tears of their own. "Now you have something from both Violet and me."

Lizzie stood and set the books carefully on the chair, then hugged me again. This time there was no hesitation as I picked her up and held her close in my arms. She rested her chin on my shoulders as she wrapped her arms around my neck, and as I held her, she couldn't see the tears running down my cheeks.

They stayed for a little while longer, then left to return to the newsstand. I placed Lizzie's books in a paper grocery bag to protect them from the now intermittent rain and thanked them both for coming to visit. In my grief, I hadn't thought about the other people in my life, as my sadness over losing Violet becoming all consuming. I began to wonder if this is what Turk Ryder had felt when his beloved Helena, his Lady Messina, had left him behind. The big Turkish Van was obviously affected by the loss in a permanent way, but he had eventually found a way out of his darkness to come to terms with what had happened. I stood in the middle of the living room and closed my eyes, then took in a deep breath. Letting it out slowly, I remembered a conversation about a year and a half prior.

Violet was remembering when her grandmother Margaret's companion John had passed away and the stoic calm with which her grandmother had processed her grief. Violet had found her alone in the garden one morning, walking silently through some of the trees. She asked her how she could be so calm, and her grandmother turned to her and smiled. "I wasn't so calm when your grandfather died. To be honest, the grief nearly wrecked me. I ended up travelling to Greece to get away from it, but it was a part of me and came along for the ride. I finally realized that the grief and the pain of loss is normal, and in time it fades, which is also normal. But carrying this anger and pain after a certain time isn't right. I finally realized that Dom was gone, that nothing I could do would ever change that, and that I had to make the choice to live a happy life again or suffer forever. It's what Dom would have wanted, and what John would have wanted too."

"I love John just as much as your grandfather," Margaret had said. "They were two very different people and my love for one never changed how I felt about the other. John was so understanding. He asked me to tell him about Dom so he could get to know him too as best he could. He said that Dominic was a part of me and that he had played a part in making me the woman he loved today, and because of that, among other things, Dom should be remembered for the good man that he was. Later, when John was near the end, he told me not to mourn for too long, but to grieve only as long as I needed to. Then he said I should get on with life, that I should travel to Greece again, but this time go with a happy heart and enjoy the experience."

Violet told me that Margaret had spent six weeks at the estate after his death, then packed her bags and took the Pan American to Istanbul and then toured the Aegean by boat. She had never come back, instead choosing to remain tucked away in a fishing village on the coast of Crete. Violet had longed to see her but had never been able to make the time to do so. I hung my head. Time was such a fleeting commodity, irreplaceable and relentless. At that journey's end, death comes to us all.

I spent the rest of the day alone in my apartment, the radio playing softly in the background. An evening spent in quiet contemplation and grief. I toyed with the idea of packing my bags and leaving, just walking away, but I knew that wherever I went, my sadness would follow, just as it had with Margaret when Dominic had been killed. Still, my mind wandered, thinking of places to run to, but the realization that I still wanted Violet to join me on a grand adventure put an end to my musings.

I went to the cupboard and took out a tin of sardines, accompanied with some milk I hoped would still be fresh. I realized as I peeled the lid back that this was the first thing I had eaten in several days; in my sorrow I just hadn't felt hungry. I didn't, even now, but I hoped that some snack might ease my troubled mind some. Later, I thought about venturing to Russian Joe's milk bar, but decided I just wasn't ready for that yet. At the end of the day I had not left, preferring the solitude of my small apartment to the company of others. All I did was turn off the radio, pull off my clothes and fall into bed, hoping my dreams would not torment me as they had the night before.

31

Violet's funeral occurred a week later. I received a call a couple of days prior from Claude that a limousine would pick me up at a specified time, then take me to the cemetery for the service. Though I hadn't expected nor requested this kindness from the Winterhavens, the seat of a limo was surely preferable to the questionable stains and smells of a bus. Though I was hoping the service might bring some closure to my grieving, inside, I dreaded the whole affair. There is always a certain finality in a funeral, one that crushes every hope that somehow this has all been some huge cosmic mistake. I also wondered if the Winterhavens secretly blamed me for their youngest daughter's death; if she had never chosen to work for me or come with me on our recent excursions, she would most certainly still be alive today.

That morning, I woke early. I cleaned off under a warm shower, ate a small breakfast, then put on my best suit and hat. The air was damp and chilly, and the threat of December rain necessitated my raincoat and gloves, both set out near the door. With nothing left to do, I sat on the sofa. I leaned my head back on the cushion, listening to the radio and waiting for the limo to appear. I must have nodded off because a knock on the door startled me into wakefulness. I looked around the apartment as I turned off the radio, but everything was in place, more or less. I put on my coat, gloves and hat and walked to the door, then followed the driver as he led me to the waiting car.

I had the back of the vehicle to myself, and though the partition to the driver was down, I rode in silence. I tried not to think of the day ahead and stared out the window as I rode, watching the scenery change from concrete and steel to suburban progress, the new postwar construction of single-family homes and yards. The trees, bare of leaves like wooden skeletons, became more and more prominent as we ventured further from New Amsterdam, for the

Winterhavens had long ago chosen a rural cemetery at a quiet country church as the final resting place for their beloved. My thoughts betrayed my solitude; I had heard it spoken that while a mausoleum existed that housed earlier members of the family, Violet had wanted to be buried nearby with a simple headstone marking her final resting place. I was sure it would be a peaceful setting and a beautiful service, but I could think of no worse way to spend the afternoon. All I could do was stare blankly out the window as the car drove ever onward.

By the time the black Cadillac slowed for the turn into the cemetery, we had been riding for well over two hours. The land rolled in hills and valleys in this part of the state, enough to remind even the most casual viewer that the sea and the city were miles behind. I caught a glimpse of the Hudson out the right-side windows a couple of times, but we soon drifted westward into farm country. Though I was miserable, I was glad to be miserable alone, and the cold, dreary weather, all clouds, dark and christened by an intermittent rain, reflected the way I felt.

My night had passed in an awful way, first, in a fitful state between awake and asleep, lost in thoughts given free rein to morph into the demons of my darkest conceptions. After several hours, I finally fell into true sleep itself, a nightmare scenario of my worst fears colliding into one, a kraken to pull my frail ship of consciousness into the blackest depths of madness.

I awoke panting, my fur matted and my sheets wrapped around me from my unconscious thrashing about. Though the windows behind the blinds shone dark, I knew that any further sleep would prove elusive at best and terrifying at worst. What lingering images remained after the moments where even the worst dreams fade into oblivion were blown apart by the sound of radio as I tuned into my favorite classical channel. While I listened, I was not alone, for my companion Johann Strauss, Jr. stood beside me as we pushed away the worst of my nightmares. I sat in my chair and closed my eyes, letting the notes carry me down his Blue Danube. I even smiled as I thought that Strauss had the right idea; he had lived and died in three-quarter time and his music, so carefree and light, could bring cheer, however fleeting, to the most blighted of souls.

As the big car pulled to a stop, I saw that a substantial number of mourners had already gathered by the gravesite. I didn't know how many knew Violet personally, but some faces in the crowd stood out. As I walked over, I recognized the Cahills, modestly dressed in somber greys and blacks. Lizzie, held close in her father's arms, her head resting on his right shoulder, waved lightly as she saw me though she made no attempt to move. I walked to her and patted her head wordlessly. Sean turned and lowered his head as he whispered a somber 'I'm sorry Max', then shook my paw with his left, his only free arm at the moment. Victoria hugged me without a sound, holding me a moment longer than normally comfortable, though in truth her warm embrace was welcome. I thanked them softly, for they were welcome faces on such a bleak occasion.

As I made my way toward the family to offer my own condolences, I saw Violet's cousin Basil Jones in the crowd. Though we did not get an opportunity to speak, we waved to each other from a distance. Soon after, I saw Joe Antonov engaged in discussion with a gentleman I did not know. A moment later Joe saw me and disengaged from his conversation, then walked a few steps over to me. We spent a couple of minutes engaged in awkward small talk, trying to find some normalcy in the situation, but predictably we could not. We quickly ran out of things to speak of, and after a strong paw on my shoulder and shared condolences, we parted ways.

Though I kept a respectful distance from the center of the ceremony, I was soon found by Silas Winterhaven. We shook paws, as we had never formally met, and then he ushered me to the family, telling me that his brother wished to make me feel as welcome as possible. He then spoke of how fond Violet had been of me, noting that while he had hoped to meet me one day, he was devastated that it had to be under these circumstances.

When he left me with Benjamin, Silas smiled a wan grin, telling me that he hoped to meet me again in better times. As he left, Benjamin approached and put his left arm around my shoulders. His wife Eleanor and daughters Iris and Daisy crowded around me, and as we mourned together Benjamin told me that I was not to blame. With tears in their eyes, each of the three women hugged me in turn, and as they each took their turn in their comfort and reassurance, I finally broke down.

As my knees buckled under the weight of my silent sobs, they gathered around me, holding me tightly and keeping me from falling. As I stood there, hemmed in by bodies and blindly holding on for life, I felt an additional set of arms wrap around my waist. Through blurry eyes, I looked down to find that Lizzie Cahill had threaded her way through and had latched onto me as well. I took a paw and placed it on her shoulder, comforting her as she comforted me. No one spoke, and we mourned as one.

I was asked to sit just behind the family for the service, facing an open tent with both a large wreath and a podium. By then I was cried out, a shell emptied of its contents. I asked if Lizzie could sit by me, and with both Ben and her parents' blessing, she sat quietly by my side. The priest began with a few words of sorrow, then told the story of Violet's short life. As he began to recount her friends and loved ones, Lizzie took my paw and held it in hers, as tears began to well up in her fragile eyes. As she held onto my paw, I enfolded hers in both of mine, both gently squeezing hers. Though Lizzie maintained a brave façade, she was hurting inside, and whatever comfort I could provide might reassure her that in her pain, she was not alone.

Soon, Violet's white casket, draped in a sash of velvet purple with gold rope for trim, was brought to the grave, held by six of her cousins, most of whom I had never met. At this, Lizzie buried her face in my side, her small body broken by sobs, as I placed my arm around her for comfort. Several people spoke, each speech seemingly more personal and poignant than the last, but all ultimately a blur in my grief-stricken mind. Finally, the service ended with the priest giving last words of hope amidst our collective sorrow.

As the guests slowly filed away, Benjamin approached me and asked me to stay with them. Though all I wanted was to climb back into the car and barricade myself in my apartment, I agreed to stay. We watched silently as the beautifully colored casket was slowly lowered into the earth, then stood in the cold a few moments longer as the rain began to fall, as if tears from the heavens themselves.

Our last actions concluded, the Winterhavens and I piled into the waiting limousines. I noticed Benjamin say a few quick words to my driver, though I thought nothing of it. I settled into the seat as the car began to roll, my eyes focused once again out the window and my thoughts wandering in rhythm with the scenery. The patches of rain were giving way to snow, the first of the season. I was tired, both physically and emotionally, and within a few miles I nodded off as the soft ride of the Cadillac lulled me into a fitful sleep.

32

I awoke as the large car came to a stop, its engine shutting off a moment later. I found myself not in front of my apartment, but rather inside a large structure. The only other occupant of this space rested in the middle of the mammoth floor, dwarfed by the enormity of the building in which it sat. A Lockheed Constellation in Pan American colors, sleek and graceful with its four engines and triple rudders, rested on its gear facing the mammoth open doors. Still in a daze, I tried to shake the feeling of sleep from my head, disbelieving what I saw. I couldn't understand quite where I was, why I was here and what exactly was happening.

The driver came and opened the door beside me. As I slowly stepped from the car, two other limousines drove out of the rain and into the hanger. They stopped behind mine, and for a moment I worried that somehow Constantino's remaining men had found me. My apprehension eased somewhat as I watched Iris and Daisy step out of their car; they seemed as confused as I was. As I pondered what was happening, the large hanger doors began to shut. As they drew to a close, Benjamin Winterhaven emerged from the last limousine, followed by his wife Eleanor. They strode over to the plane and a waiting staircase that had been rolled to the airliner's door, and as he neared the steps the aircraft's door opened to reveal a figure at the top.

As Violet stepped out of the fuselage, my knees went weak and I nearly dropped to the floor. I heard a muted thump and realized that Daisy had fainted with shock and surprise. As Benjamin, Eleanor and Iris tended to their middle daughter, I stood by the car, wide-eyed and speechless in complete disbelief. When she reached the bottom of the staircase, Violet spoke. "I'm so sorry I had to lie to all of you, but there was no other way. If I hadn't, I really would be dead now." She walked to a now sobbing and visibly shaking Iris and held her close while looking over at me with her impossibly blue eyes. Daisy began to come to and soon joined her sister in tearful celebration while her parents and I looked on.

After a few minutes, Violet moved to her parents as well, giving them tearful hugs and wishing them goodbye. When she turned to me, she smiled as she moved to hug me, and to my surprise she kissed me intently. As she pulled back slightly, she put a paw on my cheek. "Oh Max, what are we going to do with you? I have to go now, but I want so much to stay with you! You have come to mean so much to me!"

I looked at her and shrugged, then said, "Well, if you're getting on this plane and heading somewhere else, I could always come with you."

I knew I'd been had by the gleam in her eyes and the wily smile on her mouth. "I'm so glad you said that because I'd really hate to have to ship your luggage back to you from abroad. Who knows when it might get here?"

I looked at her in confusion, and before I could say a word, Violet put a finger to my mouth and said, "Yes, I said luggage. I had Claude go to your apartment and pack a few bags for you. When he told Louie that you were taking an extended vacation, he let Claude in! It's on the plane and ready to go. Anything else you need we will purchase as necessary."

Her face became serious. "But Max, we have to leave. Now. I'm in grave danger if I stay here, and I don't mean that as a joke. I'll explain it to you once we're off the ground, but it's safe to say that if I'm in danger, you are too, especially as I'm on the move and someone might see us. That's why we need to get airborne." She looked at me, her eyes beginning to tear up. "I'm sorry this is so abrupt, but there isn't any alternative. I promise that I will explain why."

I turned to Violet's parents, aghast. "You knew this whole time! Both of you! Why didn't you tell me she was alive?" I stared at them blankly, trying to process what had just been revealed.

"Whatever you all have done, I would have happily gone along with it just to know she was alive!"

Ben raised his paw, silencing me with a calm gesture. "Please believe me, Max, letting you think Violet was gone was one of the single, hardest things I've ever done. We didn't tell Iris or Daisy either, and they're her sisters! I know you have been suffering, believe me I know, but once you hear why, I think you will agree with our choices. I beg of you to hear Violet out. If you are still angry, if you want to come back home, I will pay to rent this plane again and bring you back. No questions asked and no hard feelings." He leaned in, his face mere inches from mine. "Please believe that this was never, never to keep you from Violet. Eleanor and I would never willingly put anyone through this, not even someone we hated, but we had little choice."

Eleanor approached me and softly placed a paw on the side of my face. "Please, go with her Max. Our Violet needs you now more than ever. She needs someone to watch over her, someone to care for her. Without you, she has no one. You may stay angry at Benjamin and I as long as you need to, but please, don't take your anger out on someone who loves you."

I looked into the pleading faces of Benjamin and Eleanor Winterhaven, trying to process the last several minutes. They had not only faked their own daughter's death, but for her safety and quite possibly those around her, they had kept her resurrection a secret from those closest to her. It dawned on me the enormous strain they must have been under, the weight of the secret they had kept. And now that it had been revealed, the Winterhavens had called on me to keep their daughter safe in whatever unknown destination awaited her. As I turned to look at Violet, her lovely face wearing an expression of concern, my choice was already made.

I turned to Eleanor Winterhaven and took her paw in both of mine. "I promise you that I will do everything in my power to protect your daughter. I have loved her for a long time and have spent too much time keeping it hidden inside. I lost her once, and I don't want to lose her again. Where she goes, I'll go for as long as she wants me by her side."

I turned to Benjamin, taking a paw and placing it on his shoulder. "I believe you when you say you have your reasons, Ben. I haven't known you for very long, but I can see that you're a good cat and a good father. You must be to have raised such an amazing daughter. I'm not angry at you and Eleanor. I believe you when you say that you had to keep Violet's false death a secret, and I'm sure Violet will tell me soon enough. Someday we'll see each other again."

Benjamin smiled and took my paw, then surprised me by drawing me into a bear hug, with Eleanor joining in an instant later. I turned to look at Violet and saw the smile on her face, mixed with the tears on her cheeks. I knew that whatever my life might hold for me from this moment onward, Violet and I would face it together.

As we had talked, the Constellation was being readied for travel. The few minutes that remained were spent on goodbyes. Although she spent some moments with her parents, her last before the plane powered up, were spent with her sisters. The three of them hugged each other, tears and affirmations flowing in equal amounts. And then the time was up and we walked to the waiting airplane. As we climbed the steps, we turned to look back one last time, then walked into the airliner and took seats next to each other at the front of the cabin. As one of the crew sealed the door, Violet and I looked out the window and saw the steps being moved away from the fuselage, then her family waving one last time as they got into a single limousine for their trip home.

33

As the doors opened and the cars left the hanger, Violet turned to me and said, "There are two last secrets you need to know about, and as soon as the engines start, they will come out of the back of the plane and join us. I know it's been a difficult time Max, but once you know everything it will make a lot more sense."

I smiled weakly and said nothing. Violet could have told me she was from another planet at this point and I doubt I would have batted an eye. I thought there wasn't much left that could surprise me. But when the first engine roared to life, I was in for another shock, for as the mechanical cacophony echoed off the hanger interior, I looked behind me to see two of the last cats I had expected to see.

Blackie Lawler and Rufus Segovia stepped out of the rear lounge and took seats across the aisle from us, almost unrecognizable in casual clothing. Blackie wore khaki pants and a cream shirt, while Rufus wore brown twill pants, scuffed brown shoes, a black sweater and a wool newsboy. I was already so blindsided by the last half-hour that all I could do was stare blankly. Still, I was nothing if not curious as to how exactly this had come to happen.

Once all four engines had started, the airliner left the hanger and I could finally see where we were. Though I had expected the main airfield at La Guardia where Pan American flew in and out from, we instead had been housed in one of the Winterhaven's abandoned hangers on the decommissioned Army Air Corps base. Between my sleep and shock, I had entirely failed to notice. It certainly made sense; save for the local motorhead contingent, the airfield was almost always abandoned. It was on the edge of an industrial area and away from prying eyes, and featured hangers plenty large enough for a modern airliner to hide with extra room for all the equipment necessary to service it between flights. As soon as it landed, the plane could be taxied into the hanger and even turned around inside the giant building with plenty of room to spare. With the doors shut, it all looked like business as usual, and once the plane was serviced it could be easily taxied out of the hanger straight to the runway. Just as it was doing at that moment. Even with such a large plane and commercial markings, it was likely that no one on the ground even knew it was there.

I noticed that Rufus appeared nervous, continuously looking around and out the window, while Blackie had tilted his head back and into the headrest of the seat, staying as still and silent as he possibly could. I thought he was merely resting his eyes, but as the engines roared to full power his paws gripped the armrests so fiercely that I thought the metal underneath would be crushed.

As the airliner gained speed and soon took off, I saw that while Rufus visibly relaxed, Blackie remained in a locked battle with the armrests, his eyes now squeezed as tightly shut as was possible. Only when Rufus looked over at him and nudged him a bit did he let up on his grip. He opened his eyes, then looked over and saw me looking at him. With a surprisingly skittish voice, Blackie informed all three of us that this would be the last flight he ever took. Ever. He then scrambled from his seat and took off running toward the rear of the plane, presumably to empty his stomach contents into the lavatory bowl.

Once the Connie had reached cruising altitude, the engines were throttled back for the sake of long-range fuel economy. When I looked out the window, I saw that we were over open ocean; this meant that if we were flying normal Pan Am routes, we were likely headed for a fuel stop in the Azores, the volcanic archipelago some 850 miles west of Portugal. It seemed like a good place to refuel a chartered plane where no one would be looking, if the goal was to avoid trouble. I had studied Pan American's routes with the idea of taking a trip someday and knew that after the Azores, the flight would likely travel to Lisbon. This was another location where it might be easier to stay disappeared as fewer people would likely speak the same language as those presumably looking to find us. Violet had yet to fill me in as to what our trip entailed, but it was entirely possible that we could disappear along the coast and lay low for a while. Of course, this was all pure speculation, as Violet and our unexpected guests had yet to share with me a single thing at all.

When Blackie returned from his fourth trip aft, looking a bit worse for wear, he nodded to Violet. She stood, urging me to join her, and the two of us filed toward the small lounge near the back of the plane. Blackie and Rufus followed. The lounge contained two small sofas, each facing the other with a low table in between. Though it was still loud, the lounge was somewhat quieter than the main cabin and allowed for easier conversation.

As we took our seats, I sat next to Rufus while Blackie took station next to Violet and closest to the lavatory in the event that he became unsettled again. Violet placed her paw on the back of Blackie's neck, massaging him gently. This seemed to calm Blackie, whose motion sickness had definitely gotten the better of him. Now that we were seated, I would finally learn just what had happened to make Violet Winterhaven fake her own death. I hoped it would be a riveting story.

"I'll keep this short," she said, much to Blackie's obvious relief. "When you found me, Max, what you saw was fake. The blood, the gunshot holes, the way I spoke, everything, obviously. I didn't plan it, but it came about and when it did, I had to play along, because it was no longer just me whose life was on the line.

"After I slapped you, I stormed inside and disappeared into the family quarters, but this was to change into something more suitable for prowling around. You know this. What you don't know is that while I set you up as a decoy, Blackie figured out what I was up to and intercepted me. While you three were in the garden, he told Rufus to stop you before you could leave the garden but to not hurt you if he didn't have to. Meanwhile, Blackie slipped out of the greenhouse and into the garage to catch me. Which he did, in

Constantino's car, with incriminating papers in hand. I thought I was done for, considering where he caught me and what he caught me doing, but instead of shooting me, he put his gun away and offered me his hand. Blackie Lawler, the toughest stooge in Constantino Gandini's private army, had a proposal to make, and it was a real doozy too." She turned to Blackie. "Do you want to tell it?"

At that, Blackie moaned and slowly put his head down into his paws. Violet stopped massaging Blackie's neck and placed her paw lightly on the top of his head. "I'm sorry Blackie. If I had known this would happen, I would have put you guys on a ship instead."

Blackie looked up slightly and replied so softly that we could barely hear him over the din of the engines. "This will only last a day and then it's over. If I were on a ship this could last a week, maybe more. I'd probably throw myself overboard and hope that the sharks ate me. At least this only feels like death for a few hours."

Violet looked at Blackie in obvious sympathy, then turned back to me and continued her story. "Blackie told me that we wanted the same thing, to get rid of Constantino for a long, long time. He had been planning for months on how to make that happen, be it getting him arrested on charges he couldn't dodge or setting him up for a long dirt nap. He already knew we were looking to bring Constantino down from our warehouse excursion, so when he found me snooping around the car, he realized that we could work together and make it happen. I had already found the papers in one of the compartments Sterling told us about, and while Blackie had known they probably existed, he had no idea where they were hiding. When he looked through the papers, he told me that there was enough on Constantino's tuna racket and other schemes to put him away. And when I asked him why he was doing this, he told me it was because he wanted out and wanted to bring one other cat with him. That was when we devised a plan, and even though it was quick and dirty, it was simple and thus easy to execute. We had a good chance of it working."

Violet took a breath, then continued. "The plan was to make it look like Blackie found me, shot me, and made it look real enough that I could pretend to be dead. Blackie handled that himself, mixing a few items he found to make something that looked enough like blood and then staging how the scene would appear. It wasn't perfect, but in the dim light of the garage we figured it would be enough. Then, while Blackie went back to Constantino and told him that he killed an intruder going through his car, I would swap out the papers and then pretend to die. When the ambulance came to get me, the papers would be tucked in the waistband of my pants, up against my back where they wouldn't be visible.

"The trick was to get the ambulance to be staffed with some of our people. That was when I brought Malcolm in. I told him to run and find my father and get him to find an ambulance and man it with his own staff members. Malcolm did us one better; he knew a friend who was repairing an ambulance and convinced him to loan it to us for the evening. Once I was inside the ambulance and we were off the property, I took the papers and gave them to the police.

"I returned to the estate later, I snuck in through a service door and have been holing up in the guest wing ever since. I made sure Daddy knew what would happen and what I needed him to do, but to not tell anyone save for my mom. Blackie and I were both worried that if I let you, my sisters, or anyone else know that someone might find out that I was still alive and would figure out what had happened. And it's not just me, Max, it's Blackie and Rufus too. They have their own reasons and I have no idea what they are. I just know that I need to preserve the illusion to the world that I'm dead. That's why I brought you with me. If word got out that I'm still alive, Constantino might come after you too. He's in jail now and awaiting trial, but even if he is sent to prison, he is still very dangerous. He could find out and send someone after me. So far, he and most everyone else thinks I'm dead, but I'm still leaving for somewhere that my face isn't known. Somewhere small and out of the way. Someplace like I've envisioned for years, my place without a postcard."

Violet sighed and closed her eyes. "I wish it wasn't this way. There are so many people whom I've hurt. Lizzie Cahill for one She and I are friends and I adore her, and now she thinks I'm dead. If I ever get to reconnect with her, I'm worried she'll think I abandoned her. And I've taken you away too! What about her parents? And Joe? I've gotten to know him well over the last few years and now, as far as he's concerned, I'm just gone! These people have become so important to me, such a major part of my life, and now they're gone! It's horrible!" Her blue eyes began to mist over.

"And yet, I chose to do this, and I would choose to do it again! The tuna shortages will be over, the case is solved, and now, lots of desperate people will finally eat their fill again. I'm happy that I could do that for them, but it came at such a great personal cost. I don't want to complain and moan, but I'm hurting so much and I don't know what to do!" She fixed her eyes on me as the tears rolled down her cheeks. "Tell me what to do Max. Tell me how to live with this. I'm more alone now than I've ever been, and I don't know how to reason with it. What do I do now?"

I saw the pain in her eyes and it hit me like a runaway truck. Any lingering frustration melted away in the depths of her eyes. I couldn't be angry with her, nor with anyone else; the plan had been a spur of the moment decision, but it was simple and had a high chance of success. She was also correct in her assessment that she needed to remain safe, and staying dead was a pretty good way to stay alive. The price of her success was high, the road to her victory steep and narrow. I finally began to realize what she had sacrificed for the people of her city, people who would never know the price her generosity had cost. At that moment, Violet Winterhaven was more hero than anyone I had ever known, the embodiment of selfless altruism.

I reached out and took her paws in mine and held them

tightly. Across the table, I looked her in the eyes. I took a deep breath and slowly released it, then said, "You are not alone, not when I'm with you. You have stayed with me for a long time, and it's time I returned the favor. I'm not here because I feel I have to be, I'm here because I want to be. You are the closest friend I've ever known, and I don't want to ever lose that. I don't know where we will go, and I don't know what we will do, but I'll be with you as long as you want me." I took another breath and released it. "Because, I love you. I've known it inside for a long time, but I couldn't bring myself to say it. I thought you were gone and that I would never get to tell you how I really felt. This is a second chance in every sense of the word; this morning I watched your casket as it was lowered into the ground. I won't make that same mistake again. I love you Violet, and I always will."

As Violet looked at me, tears rolling down the fine fur on her cheeks, she lightly squeezed my paws and moved to stand. As I rose, she pulled me to her, placing her arms around my neck. As she looked up at me with her infinitely deep blue eyes, she said softly, just loud enough for me to hear over the din of the engines, "I've wanted to hear you say that for a long time. Longer than you may ever know. I've known that I've loved you for a long time, Max, and I've known you had feelings for me too. I was just happy to be with you, to be your friend, but I've hoped that you could finally say what I thought you felt inside. I was afraid to rush you, to drive you away, and so I've waited.

"And now you're here with me. I know we'll be all right even in exile. We have each other now."

34

A bump shook the airliner slightly, reminding us to return to our seats in the cabin. I looked over and gestured to Rufus, who stood and circled the table to help Blackie back to his seat. The large cat groaned in obvious distress but was soon by the window with his head leaned against the side of the plane. Rufus, seemingly oblivious to any movement, pulled a book from the satchel he had brought and began to read, lost in the pages of the finest in pulp literature. Across the aisle, Violet and I sat in silence, her head resting on my shoulder, our paws intertwined. After a while I noticed that Violet had fallen asleep, a soft snore coming from within that I felt rather than heard.

While the secret of Constantino's demise had been revealed, the day had begun to transition into night. Now, as we flew onward and eastward, the window beside me had turned pitch black. Even if it were daylight, there was nothing to see as the plane flew. Only hundreds of miles of empty ocean lay around us, and then a landing on a small island hundreds of miles from anywhere. As far as we were concerned, the Constellation was an island unto itself, sealed off from the world outside by a metal skin and driven by four engines through the air both cold and thin. I drew a slow breath as I leaned my head back and closed my eyes, letting the drone of the engines lull me into a calm, almost hypnotic state.

At some point I must have fallen asleep. I came to as the fuselage began to angle downward and the pitch of the engines changed slightly. Outside, the sky was still dark, but we had clearly begun our descent. I looked over at Rufus, his nose still buried in a book, and whispered to him. He looked over and I mouthed the word 'time', only to have him shrug. Unlike his companion, Rufus didn't carry a timepiece. Violet still slept against me, though now both of her arms wrapped around mine and a minor stream of drool had formed a small wet spot on my shirt. Soon, she too awoke with a snort and immediately checked her mouth; she wiped the drool away, saw the spot on my shirt and whispered a bashful 'Sorry'. It appeared that Blackie had mercifully fallen asleep as well, and for the moment he rested still and silent.

We descended with the sound of the engines droning, and while I could not read the others' thoughts, I secretly hoped that Juan Trippe's best and brightest would find the island in the darkness and land the plane without incident. As we descended, we began to encounter turbulence, which made us check our belts and woke Blackie from his slumber. Soon enough we heard him moaning in obvious discomfort with every bump we took. After what seemed like ages, we began to see lights out the windows as the plane circled in for its final approach. A few minutes and one uneventful landing later, we were on the ground.

The plane taxied from the runway and came to rest as each of the engines was shut down in turn. One of the crew, presumably the captain, came back to our compartment and told us that the plane would be refueled momentarily and necessary checks would be made to the airliner. We were welcome to leave the aircraft if we wished, and stairs would be provided if we wished to do so, but that we needed to stay close as we would depart within the hour. None of us decided to exit the airplane. Forty-seven minutes later, according to Blackie's dull pocket watch, the Connie was refueled and had been given a quick once over to make sure all was still well. The crew took their places in the cockpit, and within minutes the engines roared back to life and we took to the air once again.

This time, the flight was shorter, though somewhat rougher. We touched down in Lisbon a few hours later, and when we exited the airliner next to the terminal, the sun was in the eastern sky, full and bright. It was the first time I had seen it in more than a week, and combined with everything we'd been through, it looked like the purest beauty as it shone. As the four of us found our footing on solid ground, I felt the cool air of an Iberian fall on my face. For a moment, I closed my eyes, feeling the warmth, little though it was, coursing over my fur. After a few moments, I opened my eyes to find Violet standing beside me, looking up at me with an inquisitive grin. I smiled at her and walked hand in hand toward the terminal.

Because our flight had been chartered, presumably at great expense, we were taken to a more private area of the terminal. A few moments later, our luggage arrived, and after a quick check to ensure all belongings were accounted for, we were politely ushered to a private door where we exited the building. On the road before the terminal, a black coupe, prewar in design but low and sleek for its age, sat quietly, awaiting its owner. Blackie, having quickly recovered from his ordeal once reunited with terra firma, walked to it and opened the trunk to accept his luggage.

As Rufus loaded his bags in back, Blackie smiled and said, "Citroën Traction Avant. Means 'Front wheel drive' in French. Would have annoyed Constantino to know I bought something he didn't yet own." He shut the trunk and walked back to us as Rufus waited by the car. "I owe you both. I've been trying to figure a way out for us for the last year or so, but I haven't been able to find anything that would work. When I found out what you were doing, I did what I could to assist you. When I found you, Miss Violet, by Constantino's Cord, the solution made itself clear.

Blackie closed his eyes and smirked slightly. When he looked back at us, he said, "Because of this, I'll be a marked man for the rest of my days. Constantino will always remember, always be looking for me. I didn't have time to fake my own demise, but I was able to make it look like Rufus was killed. At least I hope so. Maybe Rufus might be able to live his life free and clear. I made a lot of mistakes, a lot of them, so I owe him that much at least." Violet and I both looked confused as to why Blackie would put so much effort into Rufus. After a moment, he smiled and nodded in understanding. "Only one other person in the world knows what I'm about to tell you, but I think I can trust your silence. For you see, Rufus Segovia is my son."

233

Blackie continued with his tale. "When I was a young lieutenant, Constantino sent me to Spain to act as a liaison with some hoods in Barcelona. The deal eventually went south when Constantino double-crossed them, which meant I had to leave the country quickly. But while I was there, I had fallen in love with a pretty lady from a small town near the French border. She was innocent, full of life, and when I was with her, I felt more alive than I'd ever had. I wanted to quit the life, but when the deal went south, I was marked and had to return to New Amsterdam without her."

"I got a letter from her two months later saying that she was pregnant and that she was afraid for the kitten; I told her to go to her relatives, as her father's side was Basque and she could disappear among them. She raised him apart from me, sending me letters as I sent her part of my pay, safe in the Basque country. But as Rufus grew older, he fell in with a bad crowd. His mother worried that the gangsters in Barcelona would find him and kill him, so I offered to take him on here and protect him as best I could. I figured the best way to keep him safe was to keep him close, so I brought him into the life. I taught him how to act and what to do so that would make people think twice about messing with him. It wasn't a great plan, but it worked for a while. When he came to me, I was able to downplay any potential shortcomings, but in time it became harder and harder."

"I know you've both heard rumors that Rufus is afraid of the dark. He's not afraid of it, but he can't see in it like the rest of us can. He learned to compensate for it well before we met, and while we never told Constantino or anyone else this, he began to suspect it for himself. Loud, sharp noises set him off too, like thunder or explosions. Constantino began to doubt his usefulness as an enforcer, fearing that an enemy might exploit any weaknesses. That's why I took on Rufus as my second, to keep Constantino at bay. Ultimately though, I knew I had to get him out. I needed a way to bring down Constantino and make our escape in the chaos. That's why I helped you."

Blackie took a deep breath and exhaled. "This life, the excitement and the power, it means nothing to me. It's just a job and a means to an end. But Rufus is a part of me, my flesh and blood, and I couldn't let Constantino destroy him. He would be dead and I would have butchered Constantino, then I would have died in a hail of gunfire. It would all be meaningless. If I can spend the remainder of my life with my son, at least this life might have meant something."

Blackie turned and walked to the car, then stopped at the driver's door and turned back to us. "This will be our final goodbye. It's time we all disappear." He took something out of his pocket and tossed it to me. When I caught it, I saw that it was his watch. I looked at it, feeling the weight in my hand. I looked up and asked him why he was leaving this behind. "I thought you'd like a cheap souvenir. Plus, it even works!" With that, he and Rufus got in the car. I saw him raise a paw for a last moment before he lowered himself into the car.

As I walked back to Violet, I heard the engine start and the transmission grind slightly into place, and when I turned, I saw Blackie and Rufus drive away into a separate future. As their car disappeared into the distance, I pondered the scope of their secrecy, the conditions in which they had kept it for so long, and the incredulity that they had come out the other side. So much of their lives had been a fabrication, to the point that in all the world, only they knew where reality ended and fiction began. Then I wondered if they themselves could keep it all straight. I shook my head and put the watch in my pocket, leaving such questions for another day. I turned to Violet, seeing the bright light of day reflected in her infinitely blue eyes as if for the first time.

35

The sunlight shone on the beautiful Mediterranean landscape, including the narrow two-lane road we drove on. The windows were down, the air was warm without being uncomfortably hot, and the crisp smell of the ocean blew in from the sea. Once again, Violet was at the wheel. She loved to drive, no matter where we were headed or what we were doing; a drive in the mountains or a trip to the store, it all felt like freedom to her. We had recently purchased the little Simca sedan I generally rode in, and she couldn't get enough of it. The prewar Renault it replaced had served us well, but Violet wanted something newer, and I had learned over the past year or so that on some topics, arguing with her was just a bad idea. Little did I know she planned on taking road trips with it. Europe really had brought out her appreciation for driving.

The past seventeen months had proven interesting. We had left Lisbon on a chartered flight to Marseilles, and from there to Milan. Once in Italy, Violet had been fascinated with the idea of living in Venice, but we both saw that it was too populous and too full of tourists to make an effective hiding place. We took the trains toward Brindisi near the heel of Italy's boot and found a small town an hour's drive north that fit our needs. It was a nice little seaside village, isolated and quiet, but when I saw a face that looked too close to one of Constantino's enforcers, we packed quickly and boarded a ferry to Greece. Once there, we made our way to Crete and found a small town where we could hide for a while.

We heard after the fact, Constantino Gandini had been found guilty on a whole slew of charges and was locked away for a decades-long sentence. Unfortunately for him, he would never live to complete it; trapped in a cage containing allies and enemies alike was difficult enough, but when enemies far outnumbered friends, the situation quickly became untenable. We had heard through the wire that Constantino Gandini's death was both quick and extremely violent, a fitting end to his life of avarice and brutality.

His criminal empire had swiftly fallen apart with both Constantino's death and Blackie Lawler and Rufus Segovia's disappearance and presumed demise. Those cats who were left were either rounded up, joined other operations or destroyed each other in gangland civil war. With that, the Gandini Syndicate disintegrated and collapsed, and few, if any, missed it. A number of goods Constantino had acquired either questionably or outright illegally were recovered and returned to their owners, including one Cord L-29 sedan which was reunited with Sterling Elias.

Though Violet and I both hoped to return to the States after Constantino's death, on some advice we had received, we decided to stay in Europe for a few years until everyone had long forgotten the events which had happened. This was initially difficult for both of us, but we found ways of keeping in touch with the folks we cared about. I wrote a letter each month to Lizzie Cahill and mailed it from a different place each time, and always with no return address. Even so, a trusted source, possibly a former sea captain, would find a way to deliver Lizzie's return correspondence each month. Though for her own safety she didn't yet know that Violet remained alive, I had told her about a special lady whose company I kept.

I sometimes sent a second letter to Joe Antonov at the same time and though he didn't write as often as Lizzie, his letters were a welcome diversion all the same. He informed me that Aurora Kowalski's career as a painter had recently taken off with a one cat show in a prestigious gallery. Though she had given up fishing as a career, she kept the *Inferno* and used it for pleasure cruises or as a floating studio she used on the Hudson. As for Joe, his milk bar was doing about the same, and the friendly Russian Blue couldn't be happier.

Violet wrote letters frequently to her family; her relationships with her sisters had blossomed into genuine care and affection, while her parents remained a source of inspiration and guidance throughout these tough times. Violet had instructed her father to donate her Chevrolet to Warm Blankets as they could either use it or sell it at their leisure, but not before first taking it by my landlord Louie to see if he could indeed tune the engine better. She soon learned that her father had purchased my apartment building outright from Louie and had hired him to maintain the Winterhaven fleet alongside Malcolm. Apparently, the same wily butler who had broken into my apartment to pack me a supply of clothes and other necessities had also overseen a sprucing up of the place but would not tell me what he had done. With my permission, he also retrieved a certain Italian chair from behind my desk and had set it up in his personal office. I was glad someone was enjoying it, as I genuinely missed that chair.

I often wondered about Turk Ryder and how he was getting on out there on the high seas. I would have to look him up when I returned home and see if Violet and I could book a private cruise on the *Lady Messina*. I had a feeling they would hit it off well. As for Blackie Lawler and Rufus Segovia, we never saw or heard from them again. We could only hope that they had found Rufus' mother and had put their lives as a family back together. They had missed so many years, but hopefully they could make up for them with the time they had left. They were interesting characters to be sure, but this lack of contact was likely a good thing for all.

I looked over at Violet as she drove the car, completely relaxed with left arm hanging out the open window. She felt my gaze, looked back at me and smiled. "I still wish we had gotten the Jaguar," she said again teasingly. "It didn't even have a roof! We could have saved some money!" She had seen a picture of a Jaguar roadster somewhere and had fallen in love; I had fought tooth and nail to talk her out of importing one to Greece as it didn't exactly seem like the most inconspicuous form of transportation.

"Do you think we're nearly there yet?" Violet asked. "You would think being able to speak and read Greek would make using kilometers easier." I smiled and laughed to myself. I had never realized when I worked with her that Violet was fluent in three languages, proficient in another three, and could get by in a couple more. She could now add modern Greek to the list of the get by ones, what with a gift of language allowing her to learn quickly. I wasn't sure I'd ever get a real handle on Greek, though my ability to order off a restaurant menu had certainly improved. At least the cat at our destination spoke English, and American English at that.

With that thought, Violet saw the turnoff she sought and slowed the car. The unpaved road didn't have a name, but a hand-drawn map and a very accurate drawing of the scenery had been included. She was so excited she could hardly contain herself: we had wanted to come here sooner, but fears of discovery nagged at us until we were told that it was safe. As we drove down the road, we rounded a small hill and saw a modest home in the distance. The door stood open and as we watched, an aged cat walked into the opening, leaned and waved as the car drew closer.

Violet parked next to a tiny dented Fiat and shut off the engine, opening the car door in such haste that as she exited, she left it wide open. As I climbed out, I saw Violet running toward the house. Her grandmother, Margaret Winterhaven, hurried across the small porch and down the two steps to enfold her granddaughter in the warmest of embraces. I had seen Margaret in pictures but of course had never met her face to face. The older cat looked well, as the warm climate and fresh sea air agreed with her. At that moment, I found that it also agreed well with me. As Violet introduced me, I took her grandmother's paw and smiled a genuine smile. The world around us might be chaotic and strange, but for this moment, outside of a small house overlooking the Aegean Sea, the little world which Violet and I shared was a beautiful place to be.

Max's World

Max Persian is a character I dreamed up when I was about seven years old. I envisioned him as a walking and talking cat detective in the noir vein (though I didn't know the word 'noir' then) and attempted to draw him a few times as a comic character. As an adult some 35 years later, I revisited Max and found that I wanted to create the story for him I couldn't create as a child. Though I expected only ten pages or so, the story became a book. As such, I've had the opportunity to flesh out both Max and the world in which he lives.

Many of the characters in my story are based on cats I know or have known through my life. For example, Violet Winterhaven was based on the lovely cat I had growing up, my Violet. Her in-story appearance is a direct reflection of her appearance in life: blue eyes with white and gray fur, small in stature and the occasional drool when she slept. Her personality also reflects Violet's real-life persona, kind and gentle, though with a streak of mischief from time to time. Some are like their real-life counterparts but with name changes; Lizzie Cahill is based on my parents' cat Betsy, a feisty black feral they adopted as a three-week-old kitten. Constantino Gandini, my mafia-style antagonist, is based on a large cream-colored cat I met in Lubec, Maine. His real name was Simon and according to his neighbors, "Simon runs this street." I ultimately changed his name so as not to upset his owners by implying that their beloved boy had gone bad. Other cats are purely fictional. John "Turk" Ryder, for example, is an homage to nautical painter Albert Pinkham Ryder and is thus given the identity of a Turkish Van, a breed of cat known for their love of water.

The world in which my story is set is very similar to the real world, but not completely so. Probably the most notable departure is that New Amsterdam retains its original Dutch name and no doubt its geography is a mess. This allows me to cover my mistakes as differences in an alternate reality. Honest. Most things, however, remain the same in both worlds. Cars are the same, aircraft are the same, the geography of the world is (largely) the same. It's a very similar world populated with highly evolved cats instead of moderately evolved primates.

I had fun writing this, though I'm sure there remain plenty of errors. I hope you, the reader, can look past the flaws and enjoy the story.

Lastly, but certainly not least, I would like to specifically thank Hailey Marguerite Mariano, without whom my dream of writing, illustrating and publishing a book might never have happened.